# The President's Birthday Ball Affair

## Also by Kelly Durham and Kathryn Smith

*Shirley Temple is Missing*

## Also by Kelly Durham

*The War Widow*
*Berlin Calling*
*Wade's War*
*The Reluctant Copilot*
*The Movie Star and Me*
*Hollywood Starlet*
*Temporary Alliance*
*Unforeseen Complications*

## Also by Kathryn Smith

*The Gatekeeper: Missy LeHand, FDR and the Untold Story of the Partnership that Defined a Presidency*
*A Necessary War: Anderson County Residents Remember World War II*

# The President's Birthday Ball Affair

## A Missy LeHand Mystery

## By Kelly Durham and Kathryn Smith

In honor of the 1.2 million members of Rotary International, who continue to work for a world free of polio.  Learn more at
https://www.rotary.org/

# PROLOGUE

He had gone to Mexico City during his summer break from college. He had wanted to put his Spanish major to good use, sharpen his skills, practice conversation, and immerse himself in the culture.

He had sweltered on the long train ride through the American southwest, sweating his way from Texas down into the humid coastal plain of Veracruz, then up into the mountains, where he had taken two days to become acclimated to the thinner, drier air at seventy-three hundred feet above sea level.

It was on his fourth day in the city that he'd run into her, quite literally. He was chasing a young street urchin who had snatched a two-peso coin from his hand during the purchase of an avocado. The kid owed him plenty of change, but he had to run fast if he expected to collect.

The kid had ducked into the first alley off the plaza. He'd followed, racing around the corner and colliding with her, knocking both of them to the sidewalk, skinning his elbow and tearing the knee out of his trousers.

*Oh my God*! he had thought. He had scrambled to his feet and leaned over the woman. She had a panicked look on her face, uncertain of how she'd come to be sitting on the warm sidewalk, aware only that she couldn't breathe.

"*Discúlpame, por favor! Lo siento mucho*!" he apologized.

The woman stared at him, as though wishing to speak yet unable. Finally, she gasped. Her breath returned in deep, thirsty gulps of air. She rubbed her shoulder. "I speak English," she said, attempting to smile. Once he had helped her to her feet, she had introduced herself. She was petite, the top of her head reaching only about to his chin, and she was stunning in her appearance, curvaceous, with olive skin and long, dark hair. But it was her eyes that snared his attention, the irises a chocolate brown lightening steadily from their outer rims to a mocha shade by the time they reached the pupils.

"I'm so sorry," he repeated, helping her pick up the stack of posters she had been carrying. "Please allow me to make amends."

She had agreed, instantly taken with the chagrinned but handsome young American. She had guided him to a nearby *taqueria* where he had bought tacos and beer for both of them. He had explained his pursuit of the young entrepreneur, causing her to laugh.

"An expensive avocado, wasn't it?" she had asked, her eyes dancing over a brilliant smile. He thought he detected a British accent. He had asked about her posters and she had explained that she had been putting them up all over the university district. They announced a political meeting scheduled for the next evening, a meeting to protest the horrible conditions of the city's poor.

"They have nothing," she explained. "No homes, no jobs, no prospects, no hope. They live from hand to mouth and they do so in the shadow of these fine buildings and spoiled rich students who've never sweated in a field or labored in a factory; whose only worries are making a good grade and getting papa's next check in the mail. We have to unite the people so that they will understand that they are not helpless. There is great power in the masses, as Comrade Lenin and Comrade Stalin demonstrated in the Soviet Union. There they now have a paradise for the people. If Lenin and Stalin can turn that cold, snowy desert into paradise, think what Mexico could be."

The afternoon in the *taqueria* led to dinner and more conversation, until finally, she led him to a narrow alley and up the stairs to a small flat with one open window and a mattress on the floor beside it.

They made love, then lay on the mattress holding each other in the humid night air, sipping warm beer, and staring out the window at the stars in a cycle they repeated throughout the night. He had gone to her room a virgin, and woke the next morning totally besotted.

The next evening, he attended her rally, listening attentively to the speakers, especially to the woman. She combined a passionate plea for justice with a fiery presence. Several thousand men and women, many of them wearing cheap cotton trousers and dresses, most of them barefoot or shod in sandals woven from cane scraps, listened enraptured as she spoke of equality and prosperity for all, of challenging the ancient order. It was apparent to any observer that the crowd responded more vocally and with greater enthusiasm to her appeals than to those of her male colleagues. She spoke Spanish as effortlessly as she spoke English; he was embarrassed by his command of the language in comparison to hers.

At the same time, he found a swelling pride in the woman—*his* woman! He felt as if he were watching a miracle: a crowd of thousands of men and women, young and old, poor and poorer, breathing as one, responding as one, to her. They locked eyes at one point, and she gave him her brilliant smile.

And then he heard the first whistle, then shouts, then shots, then screams.

He had escaped with nothing more serious than a bruised shin, though he knew others were not so lucky. He had sought refuge at her apartment, but after a lonely hour and a half, he had forced himself back down the stairs and out into the night. He had made his way back toward the square where the rally had been held, ducking into a doorway or alley or gutter each time he saw the *Policía*.

The square was illuminated only by the dim, reflected light from the low clouds covering the city, but still he could make out the bodies. Many of them moaned as he passed nearby. *"Ayuadame! Ayuadame por favor."* He would stop, kneel, look, then move on. He was looking for one body, hoping that he would not find it.

After stumbling in the dark for two hours, he turned down yet another alley. Ahead in the gutter, a figure was crumpled against a wall. As he approached, he recognized her. He knelt and looked at the bloody gash below her hairline. He pulled out his handkerchief and blotted at the wound. She stirred. She turned her head toward him, her beautiful dark eyes fighting to focus on his face.

When she finally spoke, her words knifed into his heart like a dagger.

"Why did you leave me?"

His reply came out in a hoarse gasp. "I'll never leave you again."

# SUNDAY, DECEMBER 15, 1935

# CHAPTER 1

**Chicago**

Owen Knox stood in front of a wood-framed mirror in the radio studio green room. He carefully combed his brown hair straight back from his high, pale forehead, and then turned his head from side to side, making sure the thick, vanilla-scented pomade kept every hair in place. He still had five minutes left until air time, and he wanted to look his best.

Not that anyone would be able to see him. Well, no one except the radio technicians and the announcer and the handful of others who worked on his twice-a-week radio program. Still, it was important that he look the part of one of the most popular social commentators in the United States—the one with the fastest growing radio audience.

His looks didn't change the message heard by his devoted listeners—a plea for social justice—but his looks certainly influenced the way his message was delivered. Because when Owen Knox—"Deacon" Knox to his ten million listeners—looked his best and felt his best, he tended to sound his best as well. At those times, his words carried the strength and passion of a true believer, a committed follower of Jesus Christ, a man dedicated to helping realize God's Kingdom here on earth. And what better place than in the United States of America, the great experiment in democracy, that had survived now for nearly a hundred sixty years despite rebellion and war, treachery and greed, six years of the worst Depression in world history, and Franklin Delano Roosevelt on top of that?

Knox set down his black plastic comb and, still peering into the mirror, fastened his spotless white shirt collar and cinched up his dark tie. Shrugging on his brown suit jacket and fastidiously flicking dandruff from the shoulders, he began to hum "The Battle Hymn of the Republic." Its soul-lifting refrain always helped warm up his vocal chords, always made him mindful of the importance of his message and the thirst of his listeners for the righteous Word of the Almighty.

And tonight, Deacon Owen Knox planned to call on his listeners to rally to the cause of social justice, to repudiate the capitalistic greed and corruption of the Roosevelt administration, to prepare to send new leadership to Washington as the next election year struggled to take hold, and to move forward in the midst of a cold and dark winter. Yes, tonight would be Knox's opening salvo in a struggle for the very soul of America, a struggle that would determine whether the levers of capitalism would remain in the grasp of a handful of the wealthiest citizens of the land, including a president practically choking on the silver spoon in his mouth, or whether the people would rise up and claim their birthright as natives of the richest nation on the face of the globe.

A light tap came on the door and Henry Bowman, Knox's private secretary, stuck his smiling, bespectacled face into the small green room. "Ready, Deacon," he said.

Knox relied on Henry to handle the administrative details of his growing ministry. Knox would craft the spiritual, public message, while Henry would keep the whole enterprise running from behind the scenes. Henry had first come to the Deacon's attention as the young leader of an effort to organize the city's meatpackers. With his passion for the "forgotten man" and his organizational skills, Henry had made a significant impact on the ministry's organization. Behind steel-rimmed glasses, his pale green eyes never missed a number on a ledger, and he had an almost photographic memory for names and faces. As they walked down the dim corridor, their highly polished shoes clicking on the dingy green linoleum, Henry said, "I added a few lines at the end of the script." He handed Knox a crisp manila folder.

Knox flipped the folder open and tugged out the last page of his script. He always worked with the script in front of him, even when speaking before a live audience. But the script wasn't there for him to read. No, he always memorized his message, practicing out loud the cadence and timing with which he would deliver it. During these solitary rehearsals, Knox would experiment with different phrasing and varying emphasis. Of course, when he spoke to a live audience, he drew energy from the crowd, taking his cues from the almost telepathic connection he developed with the mass of sweating, smiling, encouraging people before him.

But he had no audience tonight. No, tonight he'd have to rely on his instincts, instincts honed over four years of his radio broadcasts; four years in which he'd gone from an enthusiastic supporter of Franklin Roosevelt to the president's most caustic critic. His had become one of the most popular radio broadcasts in the country; he aimed to make it the *most* popular.

Knox's eyes swept down to the bottom of the page as Henry opened the door to the recording studio. Knox paused, bathed in the studio's brighter light. His brown eyes flicked back up to Henry's expectant face. "Is this really necessary?"

"Well, Deacon, it's either that or you let me sell advertising, but one way or another, we've got to keep the money coming in. Between the broadcasts, the magazine, and our mailing campaign—well, we're not exactly running on a shoestring, you know. We received ten thousand letters last week! I had to add two new corresponding secretaries and that also meant two new typewriters. But the problem is that only five hundred of those letters contained donations. To pay the staff, we need at least a thousand of our listeners to send money every week."

"Thirty seconds, gentlemen," said the sound engineer, who was seated behind a console of gauges and large black knobs. In front of Knox stood a sturdy wooden lectern with a wide top. He placed the script there, next to the built-in red light bulb and the Mutual Broadcasting System microphone.

"Of course, I understand, Henry, it's just that tonight's message—"

"I know, Deacon, I know. But trust me on this: it is vital to your message, to your ministry, to all the good things that you are doing. We have to keep money coming in. And we're not asking for large donations from the rich. All we're asking is for a nickel or a dime or a quarter. We're asking the regular people of America to believe in what we're doing."

"Ten seconds!"

Owen Knox stepped up to the lectern, cleared his throat, and looked toward Henry. "I know, and I appreciate that we have a staff to take care of. It's just that my talk tonight—"

"Five seconds!" The engineer held up his hand, his fingers extended. As the second hand on the clock swept up toward the top of the hour, his fingers ticked off the seconds. The red bulb illuminated and the engineer pointed to Knox.

"Good evening to my friends all across America, from the great cities to our fertile heartland, from the coastal plains to our mighty mountain ranges. Good evening, and God bless you on this cold winter evening. This is Deacon Owen Knox speaking to you from Chicago over the Mutual Broadcasting System.

"Those of you who have made a habit of allowing me into your homes over these past months remember that I was an early and enthusiastic advocate for policies of the

New Deal. I believed that these policies would help lift our great country from the morass of this awful Depression, a calamity brought about by the greed, corruption, and unstinting selfishness of the cynical manipulators of our economy. You know about whom I am speaking!

"These are the rich who inherited their wealth and have never had to work a day in their lives, but also the railroad barons, the oil magnates, the bankers from Wall Street to Main Street, the mine owners and insurance executives. So many among us live from hand-to-mouth, never secure in the knowledge that our children will tomorrow have their daily bread, uncertain from whence will come the dollars to pay the rent or to heat the home. But these most affluent Americans go about business as usual, lining their pockets at the expense of their fellow citizens, their focus ever on the bottom line and never on the human costs."

He paused, then deepened his voice and injected some venom in the tone.

"You know them, they've been around for the ages. 'Captains of industry' we call them. 'Titans of business.' Our good Lord Jesus Christ knew these people two thousand years ago. He recognized the money-changers in the temple. And, like Jesus, we must now rise up and throw these evil men out of the temple of self-government! We must wrest their hands from the reins of business and industry which they have demonstrated only too well they are not fit to lead. And the chief money-changer himself? We must rise up; rise up and overthrow Franklin Delano Roosevelt! We must remove this arch-capitalist, this panderer, this friend of international banking. We must force him from the powerful office in which he sits, not with bullets—no!—but with ballots!"

Now freely perspiring as he reached the halfway point of his speech, Knox, without the cues from an audience, had to rely on experience to match the timbre of his voice with the emotions of his listeners, to sound just the right note of alarm without inspiring anarchy—a most un-Christian condition. He silently pulled a crisp white handkerchief from his jacket pocket and dabbed his forehead as he spoke.

"We've been promised so much, so often by this so-called friend of the 'forgotten man,' and yet one in five of us is still without a job. Family farms dating back to the founding of our country continue to be foreclosed upon, the farmers thrown out into the rural lanes. The laborer sees his wages cut and his hours reduced even as his employers build great mansions, monuments to their own self-importance. The President's own Public Works Administration, rather than investing in the people, subsidizes private business, enabling these robber barons to make massive profits at the public's expense.

"It is time to demand change! It is time for the people, through our duly-elected government, to seize control of the machinery of capitalism, to regulate it, to turn it to the public rather than the private good." Knox paused and again mopped his forehead with his handkerchief. "It is time to drive the chief money-changer from office and to set America on a Christian path. It is time that the forgotten man rise up and demand that 'love thy neighbor' become the impetus of our government instead of a phrase confined to Sunday School."

Knox glanced to the bottom of the page now, to the unfamiliar lines Henry had added to the script.

"It is time, friends. I know you are with me in spirit. I know you feel the pain of our neighbors who haven't the ability to feed and shelter their children. Maybe you suffer from this pain as well. I pray that you will allow the Holy Spirit to move you tonight. I pray that in the morning you will send us your spare coins so that we may continue our ministry to bring an end to the sufferings and misery of unenlightened capitalism. March with us as we work to make America a beacon of hope to the rest of the world, a place where the love of neighbor is more powerful than the lure of the bottom line.  Send your contributions, no matter how small—remember the widow's mite?  Send them here to the station, WGN, Chicago, Illinois.

"Good night, my friends.  God bless you."

# CHAPTER 2

**Washington, D.C.**

"Crackpot," said Marguerite "Missy" LeHand as she and her boss, President Franklin Delano Roosevelt, listened to Deacon Knox's broadcast. "That man doesn't have any idea what the New Deal has done for the working man. Why, the Social Security Act we got through Congress last summer will give millions of working people a pension—including my poor sister, who stands on her feet all day as a department store clerk."

"Yes, my dear," said the President. "In fact, even that pious rascal Knox will probably benefit." There was a twinkle in the blue eyes behind his gold pince-nez glasses.

The pretty woman laughed. As Roosevelt's private secretary for almost fifteen years, Missy adored his keen wit and sharp mind. "You see the humor in everything, don't you, F.D.?" she said fondly. Her throaty voice carried the distinctive accent of Boston, where she had been brought up, the youngest daughter of second-generation Irish immigrants. She had the classic "black Irish" looks, dark hair and eyebrows, pale skin, blue eyes. Although she was not yet forty years old, her hair, worn in a neat roll at the back of her head, was heavily streaked with silver. "That's probably what keeps you sane in this crazy town." She gave him a mischievous grin through slightly crooked teeth. "Are you sure you want to run for a second term?"

"I am straining in the traces!" the President proclaimed. "Ready for whatever the Republicans throw at me. And any pugilistic Democrats who might want to get in the ring."

"Well, if you can stand another term, I guess I can too," she said.

"Missy, I couldn't do it without you."

"I know."

# CHAPTER 3

**New York**

"Crackpot," Wallace DeWitt muttered as he switched off the radio and turned to a colleague in his office in New York's Empire State Building. "If the poor working man is so down-trodden, how come we're the ones at the office working at eight-thirty on a Sunday night?"

"'For unto whomsoever much is given, of him shall much be required,'" replied James Eustace with a chuckle. "The Gospel of Luke, chapter 12."

"What verse?" DeWitt asked, crossing to the sideboard to refill his Scotch.

"How should I know? I'm your attorney, not your priest." Eustace held up his glass. "Since you're up…" DeWitt splashed a portion of the amber liquid into his lawyer's glass. He returned to his desk, set the bottle on the dark green blotter, then swiveled in his heavy oak chair and stared out into the black night.

"How the hell anyone can think Roosevelt is pro-business is beyond me," DeWitt said with a shake of his head. "The first thing he did was shut down the banks!"

"C'mon, Wally, that worked out all right. At least for us. DeWitt Southern bought up a lot of those so-called 'underperforming financial assets' for pennies on the dollar during the banking crisis. We're stronger now than ever. Your old man would be proud."

DeWitt ran a hand through his wavy blond hair. The old man. He'd been gone three years, dropped by a heart attack a month after turning over the reins of the company to his namesake and only son. Following his father's death, Wallace DeWitt had embarked on a campaign of modernization, updating equipment and hiring arborists and economists to help manage the tens of thousands of acres of timberland owned by the company and stretching from the Carolinas and Georgia all the way to Arkansas. Despite the decrease in demand for building materials, DeWitt Southern had managed modest profits each year since the old man's death, a feat of note in the difficult business climate of the Depression.

Wallace sipped his drink. "Hope he would be," he said softly. He turned back to his general counsel. "But that crackpot holy-roller on the radio is right about one thing: Roosevelt's got to go. He's practically a socialist! He's cozied up to the unions. He's cut our defense spending. He's got the government into everybody's business. Hell, he's even paying farmers not to grow stuff! Where's the sense in that?"

"Maybe he'd pay us not to grow trees?"

"Go ahead, make jokes. He's spending money the government doesn't have. He's dumped the gold standard. We're going to end up not only with twenty percent unemployment, but inflation to match. If we're not careful, Jimmy, the whole economy will really and truly collapse, and the government will step in and run everything. He's setting himself up to be a dictator, a modern-day Julius Caesar. We could end up with fascism or communism. Take your pick, one's as bad as the other to my way of thinking."

Wallace leaned forward and loosened his striped tie. "I was down at the dock yesterday, talking with Guy Muldowny about our next shipment. When I left, I noticed there was this huge stack of apple crates just sitting there. I said, 'Won't that stuff freeze if it's not hauled off to the market?' Guy says, 'Yeah, but the dock workers are refusing to move it.' He said they weren't getting paid enough. Roosevelt's giving labor the 'fruit' all right, but without any of the risk. Pretty soon we'll have the inmates running the asylum."

The natural ruddiness of Wallace's complexion had darkened as he spoke, and his face looked as sour as if he had just bitten into a green apple.

"What do you have in mind?"

"I don't know." Wallace turned back toward the window, looking down twenty-two stories to the lights of the taxis heading east on West 34th Street. The theaters would be out by now, their wealthy patrons heading home to their mansions, their warm fires, their trust funds. Wallace had money, sure, but it wasn't "old money" and he still had to work at earning it every day—and many nights. "Maybe I'll go upstairs and see Al Smith."

Smith, FDR's predecessor in the governor's mansion in Albany and his erstwhile political mentor, was the president of the company that owned the Empire State Building, sometimes snidely referred to as the "Empty State Building" because of the many unleased office suites it contained. He had battled his former protégé for the 1932 Democratic nomination, had lost, and had never forgiven him. Roosevelt's ascendency had pushed Smith, a man of the humblest beginnings, into the arms of some of New York's wealthiest citizens, while FDR, the son of privilege and fortune, had styled himself as the working man's friend. The wealthy, in fact, called the President a "traitor to his class."

"Al Smith's a has-been, Wally."

"Maybe. But he's well-connected and he hates Roosevelt as much as I do. This American Liberty League he started may be something we can rally around for next year's election."

"So, in addition to running DeWitt Southern, one of the five largest lumber and banking concerns in the country, in addition to serving on the board of the New York Chamber of Commerce, in addition to being the national commander of the Legion of the Air, now you're going to take on a campaign to defeat the most popular president since Calvin Coolidge?"

Wally laughed and leaned back in his chair, lacing his hands behind his head. "You forgot about the University of Georgia Alumni Association. I'm president-elect."

James Eustace stood and set his Scotch glass on the sideboard. "In that case, I better get home and get my beauty rest. Just in case you decide to start working late hours."

# MONDAY, DECEMBER 16, 1935

# CHAPTER 4

## New York

"Thirty-two, please," Wallace said to the elevator operator the next day. One of the advantages of working in the world's most modern and tallest office building was that it was less than half full. That meant the elevators were rarely crowded and that sometimes, as on this morning, Wallace was the only passenger.

Wallace adjusted his red-and-blue-striped tie. He'd worn his favorite charcoal gray suit and had stopped at the shoe shine stand in the lobby that morning to have his black wing-tips polished and buffed. He wanted to look his best. His trousers were a little snug in the waist; he'd have to get the tailor to let them out.

At five feet, eight inches, Wallace was the same height as when he'd joined the Air Service in 1917, but at one hundred seventy-five pounds, he weighed about twenty-five pounds more. Of course, his meals these days were on a grander scale than the mess of the 94th Aero Squadron—though the company wasn't nearly as fraternal.

The elevator slowed, then stopped. Wallace swallowed hard to pop his ears. He'd had to get used to the changes in air pressure experienced as the 102-story building's elevators ascended—another reminder of his flying days.

"Thirty-two, sir," the operator said, as the brass-paneled door slid open.

Wallace stepped out of the car and turned to the right. In front of him was a glass wall, behind which sat the office of Alfred E. Smith, four-time governor of the State of New York, former Democratic nominee for president of the United States, and president of Empire State, Inc.

Wallace brushed his fingers through his blond hair, glanced at the shine of his shoes, and then headed toward the door.

"Good morning," he said, smiling at the attractive, young receptionist, her brunette hair arranged in elaborate marcelled waves. "Wallace DeWitt to see Governor Smith."

She smiled and said, "Please have a seat, Mr. DeWitt, and I'll let the Governor know you're here." Wallace sat in a comfortable leather arm chair and picked up that day's issue of the *Times* from the low table in front of him. His eyes skimmed the headlines, something about the French Assembly cracking down on its citizens attempting to volunteer to fight in Spain. Wallace smelled Smith's cigar even before his host appeared.

"Mr. DeWitt!" Smith's homely oblong face broke into its famous tobacco-stained grin as the sixty-two-year-old former Governor offered his hand. "I'm Al Smith." Smith had a noticeable paunch—*What true Irishman doesn't?* DeWitt thought—though Smith's expensive-looking three-piece suit was immaculate and perfectly fitted.

Wallace sprang to his feet, grasping Smith's strong hand. "Wallace DeWitt, Governor. It's a pleasure to meet you."

"Call me Al, and the pleasure is all mine. C'mon, let's go back to my office." Smith's thick Brooklyn brogue tended to roll his vowels, one of the traits that native New Yorkers had always found appealing in the man they called "the Happy Warrior."

Wallace followed along behind his host, who seemed full of energy for a man of his age. When Smith reached his office, he stepped aside to let his guest enter first. On the walls were framed photographs of Smith with luminaries from the past thirty years, including one with then-Governor Roosevelt. Stacks of papers, some held together with thick rubber bands, were piled on the credenzas beside and behind Smith's desk. On the desk, beside a telephone, was a framed picture of his wife, Catherine, and a handsome pen set, a souvenir from the former Governor's years in Albany.

"Have a seat and tell me how I can be of assistance, Mr. DeWitt. My secretary told me you wanted to speak on a private matter."

Wallace settled into an oversized, bottle-green leather chair in front of Smith's desk. It was even more comfortable than its cousin in the waiting area. Smith took his seat behind the huge, highly polished desk and picked up a cigar from a massive glass ashtray. "Care for one?" he asked.

"No, sir, thank you very much," his guest said. "First, please call me Wallace. When I hear people say, 'Mr. DeWitt,' I always think they're speaking to my father. And second, thanks for working me into your schedule. I know you're busy running this place," Wallace gestured to their surroundings, "and tending to all of your other commitments as well."

Smith, his friendly smile still in place, nodded.

"I'll get right to the point, Governor."

"Al."

"I'll get right to the point, Al. I'm concerned about the direction our country is going. I'm afraid the current administration, in its understandable ardor to beat back this Depression, is throwing the baby out with the bath water."

"How do you mean, Wallace?" Smith asked as his smile faded.

"The President seems intent on spending us into the poorhouse. I don't think he has a very firm grasp on economics. And this National Labor Relations Act that was passed over the summer is a threat to free enterprise. It gives the government too much power over what should be private contracts between capital and labor. I don't trust big labor, but the President seems to be taking his marching orders from those hooligans."

Smith held up his hands, his eyebrows arching upward. "I've got to interrupt you there, Wallace. I've known plenty of financiers in my time, some good, some bad, and I've known lots of labor bosses. Same thing: some good, some bad. What I know about free enterprise—and mind you, I've had to work my whole life—is that it takes both capital and labor to be successful."

"Yes sir. I couldn't agree with you more. My business is a case in point. Without our loggers and machinery operators, drivers and shop foremen, we wouldn't be able to cut the first tree or produce a single piece of paper. But the President is saying that the government, which has no standing in our labor contracts, is in a better position to judge the fairness and validity of those contracts than the actual parties which negotiated the agreements. That seems wrong-headed to me, sir."

A twinkle played at the corner of Smith's eyes as his grin reestablished itself. "Well, the problem with Frank is that he's never actually worked a day in his life. He's never run a business—well, except for that asylum for polios down there in Georgia. He's never had to sweat for a living or meet a payroll. Now he's in Washington surrounded by all these college-boy advisors who have plenty of book-learning but no real business sense and they're playing God with the most dynamic economy the world has ever seen." Smith puckered his lips and nodded. "It's a little scary, I grant you."

"Yes sir, exactly."

"Now, me, for example: I went to work when my father died. I was fourteen. Got a job at the Fulton Fish Market down on the Lower East Side. Never finished high school, never went to college, but I learned all about people, yes sir. You can learn an awful lot about people just by watching. Who thinks he's better than you just because he wears a nicer coat or has a little coin in his pocket. Who respects a man for his labor. Whether a man judges you by your character or your pedigree. I come from poor Irish Catholics, Wallace. I know the worth of a man is in what he's done in life, the decisions he makes, the way he treats other people. And I know the worth of the man in the White House."

"So I've heard."

"And I know a little about you too, son. You fought in the Great War when a lot of boys your age were hiding in classrooms and Franklin Roosevelt was sitting behind a desk at the Navy Department, out of harm's way. You took over your father's business and grew it into one of the country's top companies. You're a mover and shaker with the chamber of commerce, a real go-getter, from what I hear. So, tell me, Wallace: what can I do for you?"

"I was thinking maybe I could do something for you, Al."

# CHAPTER 5

Al Smith reached into his vest pocket and extracted a large gold watch. "How about lunch?" he said. "There's a good place just a couple of blocks away."

"Sounds great," DeWitt said, eager to continue the conversation.

Smith jumped to his feet, smiling, and deftly grabbed his overcoat and derby from the coat rack in the corner. By the time they reached the elevator, Smith's secretary had pressed the call button and the operator was holding open the door.

Smith and DeWitt rode down together, the former Governor talking the whole time, telling stories from his winning campaigns for governor and recalling some of the colorful characters he'd met. "I was campaigning down in the Fourth Ward, my old stomping grounds on the Lower East Side, out shaking hands and kissing babies, you know. This fellow, big burly Italian guy, shouts, 'Hey, Al!'" Smith put his hand up beside his mouth to imitate a shout. "He's wearing a stained white apron like he's been working, and he's come outside just to see me. He wraps me up in this big bear hug and I'm thinking, Who the hell is this guy? I never seen him before in my whole life and the next thing I know he's lifting my feet off the ground. He finally puts me down and I'm straightening my coat 'cause he's got it all bunched up and he's still beaming and just standing there looking at me like some palooka. Finally, his smile starts to droop a little and he says, 'What? You don't remember me?'" Smith chuckled.

"So, I says, 'Of course I remember you, Tony! How are things at the restaurant?'"

"What happened?" Wallace asked.

"I'd guessed right. I went with the most common Italian name I could think of. The guy's smile got even bigger and he slapped his arm around my shoulder and practically dragged me inside his little restaurant, practically forced me to eat some cannoli. It was good too."

The elevator came to a halt and the operator opened the door. "Thanks, Ricky!" Smith said, slapping the young man on the shoulder. "See you after lunch."

"Yes sir, Governor!" Ricky replied with a smile.

Smith and DeWitt walked briskly through the lobby and out onto West 34<sup>th</sup> Street. "You know what that experience taught me, Wallace?" Smith said as they turned east.

"What's that?" Wallace asked. The cold wind made him wish that they'd stopped at his office and picked up his overcoat.

"It taught me the power of a name. When you can call a man by his name—a woman too for that matter—you can count on their votes. Of course, a governor's never going to remember every name, but boy, what a difference it makes when you do!"

"Hello, Governor!" a man called out as he passed by walking in the opposite direction.

Smith smiled and waved. "How ya doin'?" He winked at Wallace. "People remember. They remember how you treat them, especially when they think you're important."

The men stood in the cold breeze until the light changed and then crossed Fifth Avenue. Wallace watched the faces of passersby as they recognized Smith. Many called out a greeting, others smiled and nodded. A few frowned. *Republicans*, Wallace thought.

Just before the corner of Madison Avenue, Smith pulled Wallace's arm and led him beneath a green, white, and red striped awning into Giuseppi's Ristorante Italiano. "You like Italian food, Wallace? This place is the best.

My grandfather was Italian. Bet you didn't know that! You thought I was a hundred percent mick, huh?" Smith laughed again.

*No wonder they call this guy the Happy Warrior,* Wallace thought.

Giuseppi himself led them to a booth at the back of the restaurant. "Chianti, yes?" he asked.

"Yes!" Smith replied, shucking off his overcoat and hanging it on a hook on the side of the booth. He slid onto the padded seat, facing the restaurant's front door. "I like to sit close to the kitchen—unless I'm campaigning. Then I want to sit as close to the front door as possible where everybody can see me."

"But you don't want to be seen today?" Wallace asked, smiling at him across the red-and-white checked tablecloth.

"Not while we're eating." Smith removed his red cotton napkin from the table, unfolded it and tucked it neatly into his collar. A heavy-set waiter, wearing a white jacket, black bowtie, and white apron over his black pants, set a basket containing a bottle of chianti on the table and placed a small wine glass in front of each man. He poured the red liquid and then struck a match and lit the candle stuck in the mouth of an old wine bottle.

"Thank you, Emilio," Smith said. "How's Maria and the kids?" Once Emilio had taken their orders and withdrawn to the kitchen, Wallace felt Smith's eyes focus on his. "So," the older man said, leaning against the booth back, a sly grin on his face, "how is it that you think you can help me?"

Wallace cleared his throat. "I'd like to see a more pro-business president, one with a little more respect for the Constitution and a better..." He hesitated. "A better-regulated moral compass. I know several other business leaders who feel the same way. I suspect you also know a few. Anyway, I thought maybe we could combine efforts and show the public how dangerous Roosevelt's administration is. We do that and maybe we can nominate a more reasonable candidate at the convention in Philadelphia."

Smith stared at him without speaking for several seconds—which, given his non-stop flow of conversation on their walk to lunch, seemed like a long time to Wallace.

"Who do you have in mind?"

"I'm looking right at him," Wallace said, a smile creeping onto his face. He chuckled. "But I'm not a politician, Al. I'm a good organizer and a good leader, but I don't know how to run a campaign."

"I got people that can do all that stuff," Smith replied, leaning forward like a thoroughbred ready to break from the starting gate. "People been with me for years. All we got to do is call them," he snapped his fingers, "and they'll respond like they was shot out of a cannon. I already got a skeleton organization in place. It's called the American Liberty League. Maybe you heard of it?"

"I have."

"I started the Liberty League last year with a few associates to rally the businessmen of the country against this socialist dictator we've got in Washington. We've got thousands of members, and our newsletters and position papers are filling mailboxes across the country. But we want to do something that will make a big splash right in the lion's den, so to speak. We're planning a big dinner in Washington in January at the Mayflower Hotel when we'll lay all of our cards on the table. I'll be making a major speech that will be carried by radio stations nation-wide." With his Brooklyn accent, Smith pronounced the word "raddio."

"What we really need," Smith continued, warming to the challenge, "is somebody inside Frank's organization; someone who can feed us intelligence on what that rascal is up to. Who's he listening to? What promises is he making behind closed doors? Got anybody who can fill that bill?"

"You're looking right at him," Wallace said with a smile.

# SATURDAY, JANUARY 25, 1936

# CHAPTER 6

## Washington, D.C.

After a quiet dinner in the family quarters of the White House, President Franklin Delano Roosevelt and Missy LeHand retired to his private study to listen to the American Liberty League dinner speeches being carried on the radio. Eleanor Roosevelt was entertaining out-of-town guests down the hall.

The President and Missy spent many evenings in the oval study, a large, comfortable room that adjoined the President's bedroom on the second floor. Like most of the rooms in the private portion of the White House, it was homey and cluttered, furnished with the dark, heavy old furniture the Roosevelts had brought with them from the family home in Hyde Park, New York or colonial reproductions made at Val-Kill Industries, the enterprise owned by Mrs. Roosevelt and her friends Marion Dickerman and Nancy Cook. The exception was the President's desk, which had been made from timbers of a wrecked British ship called the *Resolute*. Massive and ornately carved, it had been a gift to President Rutherford B. Hayes from Queen Victoria in 1879.

FDR loved ships and sailing. He had been assistant secretary of the Navy under Woodrow Wilson and owned a large collection of naval prints, many of which were displayed on the walls of his study. The Revolutionary War Captain John Paul Jones was one of his heroes. Sometimes he teased his secretary about her short and ignominious career at the Department of the Navy during the Great War. Bored by her job in the secretarial pool, Missy had played hooky from work with a friend to go sight-seeing at Mount

Vernon, was caught, and washed out after just three weeks on the job.

It was a rare instance of irresponsible behavior on her part. Since coming to work for FDR during his ill-fated campaign for the vice presidency in 1920, Missy had set the standard for an efficient, hard-working, and devoted private secretary. That she chose to spend a Saturday night with her boss when she might have been out to dinner or the theater with friends was one of the many ways she demonstrated her loyalty.

The evening had started out light-heartedly, with the two enjoying some liquid refreshment and joking about how ridiculous Al Smith must look in a white tie and tails, but as Smith's attacks on FDR and the New Deal blared from the radio's speaker, Missy and the President fell silent. FDR's mouth formed a grim line as he listened to his one-time friend's final salvo.

"Now, in conclusion, let me give this solemn warning," Smith said. "There can be only one Capital—Washington or Moscow. There can be only one atmosphere of government, the clear, fresh air of free America or the foul breath of Communistic Russia. There can be only one flag, the Stars and Stripes, or the red flag of the godless union of the Soviet. There can be only one national anthem, 'The Star-Spangled Banner' or 'The Internationale.' There can be only one victor. If the Constitution wins, we win, but if the Constitution—Stop! Stop there! The Constitution can't lose. The fact is, it has already won, but the news has not reached certain ears."

His words were met with thunderous applause from the two thousand guests crowding the ballroom at the Mayflower Hotel. The reception in the oval study was decidedly cooler as FDR turned off the radio with a snap of its Bakelite knob.

"Did he just call me a communist?" he asked rhetorically. "Damn the man! And to think I invited him to spend the night here at the White House while he was in town."

"My goodness," Missy responded mildly. "Did you hear that soft thud at the end of his speech? I think it was the sound of his derby being thrown into the ring. You would think he learned his lesson after his sorry showing against Herbert Hoover in 1928."

"Not to mention 1932," the President said. After losing the nomination to Roosevelt, Smith had left the Democratic National Convention in a huff, despite the fact that it had been announced that FDR was enroute by plane, the first candidate to ever accept the nomination in person. Roosevelt's landing at the Chicago airfield had been met by twenty-five thousand people—but not by Smith, who left town on the train, a decidedly *unhappy* warrior.

Missy stood up, stretched, and walked around behind her boss's chair. She placed a hand on each of his shoulders. "Don't worry, F.D.," she said soothingly. "I have a feeling this may be the high point of Al's political comeback. He said some pretty awful things in that speech, and it just may backfire on him."

"Missy," the President said, putting a big freckled hand over one of hers, "What would I do without you?"

"I don't know," she chuckled. "But you're about to find out. I'm going to bed. Good night!"

# CHAPTER 7

**Washington, D.C.**

Wallace DeWitt drank the last of his Scotch and watched from his seat as a crowd of well-wishers gathered around Al Smith. White-haired men, many of them thick around the middle, were pumping Smith's hand and slapping the former Governor on the back.

*Is that what I'm to become? An old, rich, fat man warming in the glow of someone else's celebrity?*

Smith had really hammered the President, giving voice to the many on Wall Street and in the executive suites of the country's largest corporations. He'd painted the President with a bright red brush, depicting the New Deal as a domestic brand of communism. Wallace's finger traced the rim of his glass as Smith smiled and laughed with his admirers.

*Well, you had to give it to the old man, he didn't leave anybody wondering about where he stood.* Wallace hoped the virulence of Smith's remarks hadn't alienated those in the middle of the political spectrum, those whose votes would be essential to a successful campaign to unseat Roosevelt. He also hoped it wouldn't backfire on the sponsors of tonight's dinner, among whom he was prominently listed.

In the back corner of the ballroom, among the gentlemen of the press, Henry Bowman scribbled in his pocket notebook: *Here, in stark relief, is the opposite end of the political spectrum, the lunatic faction that feels that*

*Roosevelt, instead of not having moved far enough to the left, has gone too far!*

Bowman had worn his best suit, gotten his shoes shined and purchased a new gray fedora to wear to the dinner. He had, of course, attended under an alias, purporting to be a stringer from a small weekly newspaper in Kansas. He doubted that any of the dinner-goers or members of the press would recognize him, even if they bothered to look. Deacon Knox would have been immediately identified, given his public profile and the way the press covered his speeches. Henry, on the other hand, made it a point to work behind the scenes, pulling the strings, stacking the deck, but keeping out of the spotlight.

Henry stood to leave. He'd identified a couple of the DuPont brothers and some of the other big shots bankrolling the Liberty League. He picked up the dinner program from his table and stuck it into the pocket of his coat. The evening's sponsors were listed on the back. *It's so important to know your enemy*, he thought, as he made his way to the exit.

# THURSDAY, JANUARY 30, 1936

# CHAPTER 8

The following Thursday night, Missy LeHand and Grace Tully were changing clothes in Missy's third-floor suite at the White House, where she had lived since FDR took office in March 1933. Grace, Missy's assistant, shared an apartment in Washington with her elderly mother. Given the tight schedule of events surrounding the President's birthday that day, she had brought her evening gown from home that morning, storing it in Missy's bedroom closet.

Anyone seeing the women when they entered the suite would have sworn they had just time-traveled in from ancient Rome. They were dressed in flowing white robes, their hair held back in gilded headbands, costumes from the private staff, friends and family birthday party for FDR they had just attended. Their next stop of the evening was a formal ball at the grand and glittering Shoreham Hotel, one of thousands of parties being held across the country to raise funds for polio treatment and research. They were collectively known as the President's Birthday Balls.

"I don't know how the Vestal Virgins managed without safety pins," Grace said. "Here, can you reach this one without sticking yourself—or me?"

Missy laughed. "One of the greatest inventions of mankind," she said, deftly removing the pin at Grace's waist. "Gosh, that was fun! Mrs. Roosevelt comes up with the best themes for F.D.'s birthday parties. All the men looked very convincing as Roman centurions and F.D. looked every inch a Caesar in that crown of laurel leaves."

"And that cake!" Grace said. "It was so nice of the Willard Hotel to send it over, so we didn't have to eat one of those horrid dried-up cakes with runny icing that comes out of Mrs. Nesbitt's kitchen." The food at the White

House, produced under the proudly incompetent director of housekeeping, Henrietta Nesbitt, was a frequent source of both complaints and jokes among the staff.

"I can't wait to see Ginger Rogers dance!" Missy said. "She's supposed to be arriving any minute now and Mrs. Roosevelt is going to take her in to see F.D. before we leave him to his poker game."

It was FDR's fifty-fourth birthday, and for the third year in a row he had given it over to fund-raising for the polio patients of America. The first President's Birthday Balls in 1934 had been staged to shore up the finances of the Georgia Warm Springs Foundation, the polio rehabilitation center which Franklin Roosevelt had started in 1926. He had found the mineral-rich warm waters in the little town in rural Georgia helpful as he struggled to walk again after his devastating attack of polio in 1921.

The President's popularity, less than a year into his first administration, had been at a high point in 1934, and enthusiastic supporters around the country had staged six thousand balls and similar events, ranging from a society shindig at the Waldorf Astoria in New York to a square dance for the polio patients in Warm Springs. More than a million dollars had been raised.

But prior to the balls, FDR had gathered his closest friends and associates around him for his private celebration, a reunion of the Cuff-Links Gang. Following his defeat in the race for vice president in 1920, he had given all the men who worked on his campaign a set of gold cuff-links from Tiffany's, with FDR engraved on one side and their initials on the other. Although Missy and Eleanor Roosevelt had been part of the campaign, they didn't get a gift of cuff-links— which would have been a waste for women, anyway—but they were included in the reunions. Over the years, Grace Tully and many others who had joined the Roosevelts' orbit had been inducted into the gang.

"That picture of us crowded around 'Caesar' better not ever leak out," Grace said. "Can you imagine the uproar it would cause?"

"Yes, indeed," Missy said ruefully. "Can you help me unpin this headband? Ouch! Thanks…There are plenty of people who believe F.D. wants to become a Caesar. Goodness gracious, that speech Al Smith gave last Saturday night made it sound like our man in the Oval Office was trying to out-Stalin Stalin."

Missy pinched her nose and imitated Smith's harsh Brooklyn brogue. "Alfred E. Smith, coming to you live over the *raddio*, coast to coast! My friends, there can be only one Capital—Washington or Moscow. There can be only one atmosphere of government, the clear, fresh air of free America or the foul breath of Communistic Russia. Remember, we don't want any autocrats, in or out of office; we wouldn't even take a good one!"

Grace began giggling, showing the deep dimples in her cheeks. "Oh, Missy, you are such a good mimic! But, boy, that speech must have made steam come out of the Boss's ears." Her face grew more serious. "I don't know what's happened to Al. Gee, I used to admire him so much when he was governor of New York. I even worked on his presidential campaign in '28. But once the Boss succeeded him in Albany and showed he wasn't going to be Al's puppet, he turned sour as a lemon."

"I'm sure Steve Early will keep the 'Hail, Caesar' pictures under lock and key and make certain only members of the gang get one," Missy reassured her. "If Steve can prevent every photographer and newsreel camera man in America from getting a shot of the President in a wheelchair, this should be easy."

Grace agreed. "Steve's the best press secretary the Boss could ask for."

"Yeah, but he still owes me a bottle of Scotch for that bet we had about the winner of the Kentucky Derby last year," Missy said. "I keep reminding him to pay up and he keeps saying, 'How about waiting until the next Derby? Double or nothing.' Cheapskate!"

Missy sighed. "Still, I wish he could come to the ball tonight, because I've gotten stuck handling one member of the press I could do without."

"Oh? Who's that?"

Missy made a face. "Our friend Joan Roswell."

"Oh no!" Grace said, looking concerned. "What's she doing in Washington again? I thought you had satisfied her when you let her eavesdrop on one of the President's press conferences last month."

"Apparently the Los Angeles *Standard* and Associated Press have pooled their resources to send her to cover the Birthday Ball," Missy said. "She called a couple of days ago and asked to have an exclusive on the counting of the money at the Shoreham. I felt like I had to say yes."

The two women exchanged meaningful glances but said no more. The previous October, Missy and Grace had been involved in recovering child star Shirley Temple from kidnappers during a trip to California. Joan Roswell, a failed actress trying to prove herself as a newspaper reporter, had stumbled into the case, and Missy had been forced to share a hotel room with her—at the request of the FBI, no less—in order to keep Roswell under control. In a soap dish in the bathroom, Joan had found Missy's signet pinky ring, a gift from the President, and made much of the fact that it was engraved "To MALeH from FDR, with love." Although both Missy and Grace had tried to convince Joan that the President used such language with many gifts he gave to his female staff, Joan had responded that most members of the public probably wouldn't appreciate the nuance. She had held her knowledge over Missy's head ever since, promising not to write a story about the ring as long as Missy granted her special favors.

With their white robes removed, Missy and Grace began donning their evening wear. Missy slipped into a light seafoam green silk jersey dress, bias cut to flatter her trim figure, with diamante clips at the shoulders. Grace, who was more curvaceous, donned a full-skirted gown in deep coral taffeta with a black lace overlay. The two women, fast friends for almost eight years, assisted each other with zippers, hooks and eyes, hair pins, and jewelry clasps, while chattering about the night ahead.

Grace helped Missy fasten her gold charm bracelet, fingering the tiny charm shaped like a mousetrap with a heart as bait. "Hear anything from Corey Wainwright lately?" she asked innocently. Wainwright, the FBI special agent in charge in San Francisco, had led the effort to recover Shirley Temple from kidnappers. Saving Shirley had been a thrilling experience for the two secretaries, but they were sworn to secrecy about it. The charm was a gift from Wainwright, who had taken a particular shine to Missy.

Missy smiled, coloring slightly. "Yes, he's arriving here tomorrow for a meeting of senior agents from all the regional offices," she said. Then she sighed. "It could get complicated with Bill home from the Soviet Union for a few weeks." Bill was William Christian Bullitt, the American ambassador to Moscow, who had been romancing Missy for several years, mostly from a distance. She was quite fond of him, but always had a nagging feeling he was less interested in her personally than the access she provided to the President.

"I wish I had the problem of juggling two men," Grace said teasingly.

Missy insisted that Grace borrow her ermine cape, while she donned her prized mink coat. The furs had been her one big splurge when she came to work at the White House and realized how often she would be required to wear formal dress in the winter social season. Her old wool coat with the flea-bitten fox collar had gone into a Salvation Army barrel.

Standing side-by-side in front of the mirror in Missy's sitting room, the women critiqued their appearances.

"Well," Grace said doubtfully, "I guess I'm ready to meet Ginger Rogers. Are you?"

Missy squeezed her friend's hand. "The press won't be able to tell you apart," she said. "Until you start to dance, that is."

"Oh, you!" Grace said. "C'mon, before I lose my nerve."

Ginger Rogers had been invited by the Birthday Ball Committee to be the signature Hollywood celebrity at the ball in Washington. Just twenty-five years old but a veteran of years in vaudeville and more than thirty feature films, she had leaped into super-stardom two years before as dance man Fred Astaire's leading lady in the film *The Gay Divorcee*. They had continued to wow audiences in *Roberta* and *Top Hat*, with their latest film, *Follow the Fleet*, due for release in February.

"Oh, my, she's just gorgeous," Grace whispered to Missy as they walked down the stairs to meet the petite blond film star, who was standing in the entry hall with First Lady Eleanor Roosevelt and an attractive middle-aged woman who they assumed was Ginger's ever-present mother, Lela Rogers.

Also standing in the hall were three women Missy and Grace knew well: Malvina "Tommy" Thompson, Mrs. Roosevelt's private secretary, and her close friends Nancy Cook and Marion Dickerman, who shared a home in Hyde Park, New York that the President had built for them some years before. It was called Val-Kill Cottage. Eleanor Roosevelt much preferred to bunk with them when she was in Hyde Park, rather than stay at the home of her domineering mother-in-law, Sara Delano Roosevelt.

Mrs. Roosevelt looked quite elegant in an evening gown of shrimp-pink satin accented by a cape of filmy lace. A sumptuous white fox fur stole hugged her shoulders. She was explaining the origin of her unusual necklace to Ginger Rogers.

"My father hunted tigers in India and had these eight claws mounted in gold as an engagement present to my mother," she said. "I treasure it as a memento of my father, who died when I was a little girl. He was my hero."

Miss Rogers couldn't keep her eyes off the stunning necklace with the huge, sharp claws. "He must have been very brave," she said, her voice faltering a bit.

"Oh, he was indeed," Mrs. Roosevelt said. "The bravest man I ever knew."

After making brief introductions and exchanging pleasantries and compliments on their attire, the women departed for the ball: Mrs. Roosevelt, the two Rogers women, Tommy, Nancy, and Marion in White House limousines, Missy and Grace in Missy's blue Buick coupe.

# CHAPTER 9

The idea behind the birthday balls was as radical as the New Deal itself. Rather than depend on the usual wealthy contributors, who were triple-knotting their purse strings due to the Depression and their distaste for Roosevelt, tens of thousands of small donations were sought from FDR's "forgotten men" and the middle-class citizens who had put him in office. Even small gifts, if there were enough of them, could help a child walk again. Who wouldn't want to chip in?

However egalitarian were the polio events elsewhere in the country, in Washington, the ball at the Shoreham was one for the upper crust, the movers and shakers of government, the wealthy and the well-connected. Located off Connecticut Avenue overlooking Rock Creek Park, the huge building of yellow-and-caramel-colored brick had become the premier site for Washington social and political events since it opened in 1930. FDR's inaugural ball had been held there in 1933.

In the hotel's grand ballroom, Wallace DeWitt sipped his Scotch as he watched photographers snapping pictures of Ginger Rogers, who was wearing a form-fitting gown, its bodice supported by two thin straps, one of which was straining under the weight of a tremendous orchid corsage. The gown had long slits on either side, showing off the actress's spectacular legs. She was standing beneath a large banner proclaiming "We Dance So Others Might Walk."

*All very nice,* Wallace thought, glancing around as portly Postmaster General James Farley, who was so proud of his Irish heritage that he always signed his name in green ink, stepped up next to the pretty, blonde-haired actress and posed for his own picture.

And there it was in a nutshell, another example of how Roosevelt and his cronies were using the federal government for their own ends, Wallace thought sourly. Tonight, while the big-wigs danced in the capital, seven thousand other balls, dances, and assemblies were taking place all over the country. And how had such an unwieldy collection of related events been coordinated? Through the auspices of the balls' honorary chairmen, America's local postmasters—all appointed by the President, all beholden to the man in the White House for their jobs and livelihoods, all working on the government payroll for what was—despite its laudable nature—essentially a private enterprise.

"Mr. DeWitt?" Wallace turned to his left to face an eager, round-faced young man in a dark suit holding a clipboard in his hand. "I'm Casey Malloy with the President's Birthday Ball Committee." Wallace shook the man's hand. "I wanted to personally thank you on behalf of the President and the committee for your most generous donation."

"Good cause," Wallace replied, nodding his head and lifting his glass. Casey wasn't finished.

"I also wanted to let you know that we've reserved a spot for you on Miss Rogers's dance card. It's just a small token of our gratitude." Casey beamed.

"A nice token," Wallace said, smiling and glancing from the young man to the photographers' popping bulbs. "I fancy a dance with Miss Rogers."

Casey laughed. "I'll find you when it's your turn." He glanced at his clipboard. "You'll be at Table 22?"

"Or at the bar."

"Very well, sir." Casey extended his hand again. "Thank you so much, Mr. DeWitt. Your generosity and your support mean a great deal to our efforts to care for polio patients in Warm Springs and elsewhere, and to find a cure for polio."

"Glad to be able to help."

Casey scurried away to find his next donor.

*A dance with Ginger Rogers. Maybe the night wouldn't be all work after all.*

# CHAPTER 10

A very different sort of party was taking place in the President's second-floor study. Facing each other around a wooden card table for the traditional Cuff Links Gang late-night game of poker were the President; White House physician Ross McIntire; Harry Hopkins, a versatile aide whose latest assignment was running the massive Works Progress Administration work relief program; and the American ambassador to the Soviet Union, William Bullitt. The air was heavy with cigarette smoke, and the men were well into the President's stash of select liquor, which he usually kept under lock and key. They were all seasoned drinkers, however, and held their liquor well.

"That 'Hail, Caesar' party was as fine a celebration as I've been to in many a year," said Harry, a wraith-thin man whose shirt collar always seemed too big for his skinny neck. "I'm just sorry poor old Louie is so laid up at the naval hospital that he couldn't come."

"Yes," the President said, his smile fading a bit at the mention of his ailing long-time political strategist Louis McHenry Howe. "I made a trip over there today to see him. Do you know, as sick as he is, his mind is churning with ideas for the campaign? He's got this notion about something he calls the Good Neighbor League to get out the Negro vote. Barney Baruch has written a big check to pay for it." Baruch, a wealthy Wall Street financier from South Carolina, was a generous contributor to FDR's election fund, as well as the First Lady's many causes.

"Don't let Deacon Knox hear about that," warned Harry. "You know how he feels about those Wall Street fellows."

The others around the table nodded in agreement, muttering a few disparaging remarks about the radio preacher. Then Dr. McIntire turned the discussion back to the absent Louis Howe, who had been FDR's political strategist since he was elected to the New York Senate in 1910. "Good ol' Louie," he said. "I don't know how the man has survived this long. Remember when he fell into a coma last year, while he was still living here in the White House?"

"Do I!" laughed the President. "Eleanor and I were keeping vigil next to his oxygen tent, thinking he was going to kick the bucket at any moment, and he rouses himself and says, 'Somebody give me a damn cigarette!'"

The men had all heard the story before, but they nevertheless joined the President in laughter.

"Speaking of parties," Harry said, "I'd like to hear some more about that fancy ball you gave in Moscow last spring, Ambassador. Did you have to kiss General Stalin again?"

"Thankfully, no," said Bullitt, grimacing. "Once was more than enough." Bullitt, who had been appointed the first American ambassador when the United States recognized the government of the Soviet Union in 1933, was a suave, patrician Philadelphian with long-lashed blue eyes, a dazzling smile, and a silver tongue. Only a bald head detracted from his good looks, but most women didn't notice it when he was paying them attention. He had certainly been able to charm Missy LeHand, whom he began squiring about as soon as he reached Washington in 1933. They kept up a lively correspondence with letters slipped into the diplomatic pouches.

Bullitt was an engaging story teller, and he proceeded to entertain the table for the next fifteen minutes with tales from the ball. "It was the best party since the Romanovs left town," he laughed. "The wife of one of my staff members had the idea of turning the dining room into a collective farm, complete with animals, and she insisted on the real thing. That's where we got into trouble."

The animals, borrowed from the Moscow zoo, had behaved like, well, animals. A rooster had escaped its cage and landed in a platter of foie gras and someone had fed a baby bear champagne, which it had promptly vomited on the uniform of Stalin's chief of staff. "Still, I think everyone had a grand time. It was ten o'clock the next morning before the last of the guests left and we could round up the livestock," Bullitt said.

"Did Stalin come?" asked Hopkins.

"No, he didn't," Bullitt replied, the smile disappearing from his face. "And that was a signal of what was to come. In the last hour of the ball, the Soviet commissar of defense was performing an energetic Georgian peasant dance with a ballerina from the Bolshoi Ballet. We never saw him again. He disappeared during Stalin's next round of purges."

"Hmmm," grunted FDR, who disliked having his social occasions dampened with bad news. "Anyone need another little sippy?"

Bullitt, demonstrating his skills in diplomacy, quickly changed the subject. "You can freshen up my glass, Mr. President. But first let's have a toast to the birthday boy!"

The men clinked glasses and began a spontaneous chorus of "For He's a Jolly Good Fellow." Just then, press secretary Steve Early entered the room. "Mr. President, we've got your broadcast set up in the studio downstairs," he said in his rich Virginia-accented baritone. "We'll come call for you in about half an hour."

# CHAPTER 11

Wallace scanned the room over his glass, deciding that most of the women were too old for his attentions. Those who might have attracted his notice were all on the arms of other men. When he'd agreed with Al Smith that he should contribute to and attend the Shoreham's ball, it had been with the understanding that Wallace would attempt to gain access to that ever-evolving group of advisors surrounding a chief executive already notorious for duplication of effort, for pitting one counselor against another, none aware that he wasn't the only minion assigned to his task.

The first step in the process, Wallace and Al had agreed, was to flash some cash. So far, it seemed to be working: Casey, as pleasant as he had seemed, wasn't experienced enough to be calling the shots. Wallace's guess was that he had earned some higher-up's attention on the basis of his five hundred dollar donation. He calculated that he'd not only made the donor list of the President's Birthday Ball Committee, but that his name would soon find its way onto the list of potential donors for the President's upcoming reelection bid. If Wallace could infiltrate the campaign, he might be able to provide Smith and his allies with actionable intelligence.

In the meantime, he'd have another drink. The dishes from the evening's meal had been cleared. Most of the attendees had left the tables to dance or mingle, smoke or drink, and await the President's radio speech at 11:45. Portable bars had been set up in three corners of the ornate ballroom. An orchestra was playing *Stardust* and the parquet dance floor was filled with couples swirling in their gowns and tuxedoes. Wallace walked among the round tables which surrounded the dance floor and caught the eye of one of the bartenders.

"What can I get you, sir?"

"Scotch, rocks." Wallace glanced to his right. An attractive woman in an emerald gown, her blonde hair swept up into a chignon and showing off her graceful neck, was digging through a black sequined purse, the strap of which was looped about her wrist.

"I know I've got change in here somewhere," she muttered, flashing an apologetic smile to a second bartender.

"Allow me," Wallace said, laying a two-dollar bill on the bar. He glanced to the server and pointed back-and-forth from the blonde's glass to his own. "I've got both of these."

"Oh, how gallant of you!" the woman said with a smile, her green eyes widening with delight.

"Wallace DeWitt," he said, offering his hand. "Would you care to join me at my table?"

"That would be lovely, dear." She accepted his hand with her gloved one. "My name is Joan Roswell."

Wallace led the woman back through the tables and held a chair for her. Taking the seat next to her at the now empty table, Wallace leaned forward to be heard over the music and the general hum of the ballroom. He inhaled the woman's pleasant orange and jasmine scent and smiled. "Where are you from, Mrs. Roswell?"

"It's Miss, and I'm from Hollywood."

Wallace was pleased. "You're an actress, then? You certainly have the looks for it." He grinned.

"Aren't you the flatterer—and the flirt!" Joan cocked her head and smiled. She reached back into her purse and pulled out a Chesterfield, which she inserted into a long ebony holder. Wallace reached into his pocket and retrieved a book of matches he'd picked up earlier in the Shoreham's men's room. He didn't smoke, but he'd long ago discovered that a lot of women—beautiful women—did, and that carrying matches had its advantages. He lit Miss Roswell's cigarette.

Roswell inhaled deeply, then blew smoke toward the ballroom's high ceiling. "No, I'm not an actress, not anymore." She leveled her emerald-eyed gaze at Wallace. "These days I'm just a humble working girl," she paused and watched Wallace's eyebrows shoot upward. "I'm a reporter," she said with a laugh. "Perhaps you've read some of my stories? I work for the Los Angeles *Standard*, but some of my work has been picked up by AP."

"I mostly read the *Wall Street Journal*," Wallace replied, enjoying the company of the pretty woman. "I don't have a lot of time for leisure activity."

"And yet here you are." Roswell gave him a sideways look. "What brings a handsome, well-dressed man like you," her eyes traveled up and down his body, "an obviously successful man, judging from your tailored tuxedo and expensive shoes—one who doesn't have time for 'leisure activities,' to this ball? You're clearly not one of the locals. Why are you here, Mr. DeWitt? Are you motivated by the illness of a family member to help find a cure for polio, or is there some hidden, more interesting reason for your presence?"

"You're very observant."

"I'm a reporter."

Wallace chuckled. "Who doesn't want to see polio cured?"

The reporter stared at him, a skeptical smirk on her face, the cigarette's smoke curling upward in a blue ribbon. "No other...aspirations?" she asked.

"Like what?"

"Like the seduction and the glamor of politics?" Her cat's eyes never wavered from his.

Wallace laughed. "I'm in the lumber business, Miss Roswell. I work out of New York and I know a lot about trees, a good bit about paper, and even a little economics, but politics is not my game."

"Mmmmm." Roswell tapped her cigarette against the clear glass ash tray on the table. "Guided by altruism?"

A smiling Casey Malloy rescued Wallace from the inquisition, approaching the table from behind the reporter. "Ah, Mr. DeWitt, your number is up."

Wallace stood and shot his cuffs. "Please excuse me for a few minutes, Miss Roswell. I'd love to continue our conversation."

Roswell smiled up at him. She laid a slender finger on the lip of her glass. "I'll be right here, dear."

"Right this way, Mr. DeWitt," Casey said, leading Wallace toward the orchestra. "I have to confess I'm extremely envious."

"Why's that?"

"Well," Casey glanced over his shoulder, "I'm pulling you away from one beautiful woman so you can dance with another one!"

Wallace looked ahead of his guide. Standing beside the orchestra, taking a sip from a tall glass of what appeared to be ice water, was Ginger Rogers. Wallace felt his palms begin to sweat. It was true, he didn't have much time for leisure. He hadn't been to the pictures in several months, but even he recognized his dance partner. She was already one of Hollywood's most popular female stars—maybe not as big as Shirley Temple, but then, who was? And he didn't particularly want to dance with a child actress anyway.

"Miss Rogers? This is Wallace DeWitt," Casey was saying as Wallace came up behind him.

"How do you do, Mr. DeWitt?" Ginger Rogers said, holding out her hand.

"Enchanted, Miss Rogers," Wallace said, lifting her hand and kissing it lightly.

"How charming! Please call me Ginger."

"Only if you'll call me Wallace."

"It's a deal!" Ginger laughed.

"Look this way!" called a voice. When Wallace turned, he was momentarily blinded by a flash of white light. "Great!" said a figure emerging from Wallace's flash-blindness. "Now, put your arm around Miss Rogers and say, 'New Deal.'" The flash again.

As his eyes cleared, Wallace led the actress to the dance floor. Ginger nodded toward the orchestra leader, who lifted his baton and led the musicians as they began to play *I Only Have Eyes for You.*

Wallace stepped off into a simple box step, then he twirled Ginger and pulled her back into the step with gentle pressure on her waist.

"What number am I?" Wallace asked, as they stepped around the dance floor.

"Number?"

"I know you're dancing with big donors."

"Oh, I guess you're about my fifth so far."

"How many more to go?"

"However many Casey brings me."

"How're your feet holding up?"

Ginger laughed. "Not too bad. Although the fellow I danced with to *Stompin' at the Savoy* was taking the title literally. I was glad when that number ended!"

"How did you get roped into this shindig?"

"It seems like a good cause, doesn't it? Plus, I got to meet the President and Mrs. R." Ginger leaned forward and whispered, "To tell the truth, I'm a Republican."

Wallace laughed, and Ginger joined in. "To tell the truth," Wallace said, "I'm not the President's biggest fan either. Still, I have to admire his courage and his efforts on behalf of polio research."

"You sound like a PR man, Wallace."

"Just a businessman trying to make a small contribution in my own modest way."

Ginger giggled again. "Part of the joy of dancing is conversation, but most men can't talk and dance at the same time. You're a welcome exception to the rule, Wallace."

"As good as that Astaire fellow?" The music faded away and the dancers began to clap.

"Almost," Ginger replied with a smile. "But remember, I have to do everything Fred does, only backward and in high heels." She shook Wallace's hand, thanked him for his generosity, and then it was over.

Wallace headed toward the nearest bar. It had been a nice dance. Ginger Rogers was as pleasant in person as she had seemed to be on screen. He ordered another Scotch. He didn't know what Joan Roswell was drinking. *I'll just have to make another trip.* But when he got back to Table 22, the pretty reporter was gone.

Wallace stood beside his seat and scanned the tables. Except for the dance floor, where Miss Rogers was now waltzing with Number Six, the ballroom was in semi-darkness. That made it hard to pick out peoples' faces if they were more than a few tables away. After a few moments, Wallace gave up his search. He was about to sit down when he saw someone he wanted to speak to. He set his half-finished drink on the table and made his way back to the edge of the dance floor where the photographer was popping a fresh bulb into his camera's flash.

"Hey, pal, how can I get a copy of that picture?"

The photographer, a whippet of a man with a tiny moustache, laughed as he mopped his brow with a handkerchief. "Which picture? I've taken about a hundred already."

"The one with me and Ginger Rogers. I think it'd be a nice memento of the evening."

The photographer reached into his vest pocket and pulled out a business card. "Come by my office about ten o'clock tomorrow.  Use the west entrance.  I'll see what I can do."

Wallace looked at the card:


Mike Wanner
Office of the Press Secretary
The White House
1600 Pennsylvania Avenue
Washington, D. C.


"Thanks," he said. "My name is Wallace DeWitt."

Mike Wanner looked at him carefully, cocking his head. "I remember seeing you at the Liberty League dinner last week. You get around Washington, don't you?"

Wallace gave him a quizzical look. "Why on earth did the White House send a photographer to the Liberty League dinner?"

"Oh, I freelance a good bit," Wanner said. "We working men have to figure out all sorts of ways to make ends meet. Keep that to yourself, if you don't mind. I don't know how my boss, Mr. Early, would feel about it."

"Sure," Wallace said, dropping the card in his jacket pocket and headed back toward his waiting drink. He looked at his watch.  Eleven-twenty. *I think I've stayed long enough*, he thought.  He picked up his drink and took a long sip.

"I thought you'd forgotten about me," Joan Roswell said from behind his shoulder.

Wallace turned, smiling broadly.  "I thought you'd gone."

"No such luck, darling."  She smiled at him and he realized again how lovely she was, and how good she smelled.  "I hate to see you drinking alone—even if you did just dance with another woman." He held her chair out as she sat down.

"What can I get you?"

"How about your room number?"

# CHAPTER 12

Joan Roswell eyed her scarlet lips in the small mirror. Satisfied with her lipstick, she snapped the compact closed and tucked it back inside her purse. She was looking forward to a more relaxed visit with Wallace DeWitt, but first she had some work to do.

"Here you go," Wallace said, setting a fresh gin and tonic on the table in front of her, a slice of lime gleaming in the clear liquid.

"Thank you, dear." Joan took a sip, leaving a film of her carefully applied lipstick on the rim of the glass. "I just have a few little errands to attend to and then I'll meet you upstairs."

"You're still working? It's nearly eleven-thirty."

"No rest for the wicked, darling," Joan purred, laying her hand on Wallace's arm. "You should know that by now. The President is due to address all the balls through a nationwide radio hook-up at eleven-forty-five. It'll be piped into the ballroom. He'll also announce a preliminary total for the evening's contributions. It's rather like election night, everyone sitting around waiting for the returns to roll in. It's kind of exciting, isn't it?"

"Sure, but I can think of even more exciting things," Wallace said with a wink.

"Oh, you! You're going to make me blush."

"There you are, Joan," said a tall, silver-haired woman, approaching the table from behind Wallace. "I promised I'd give you an exclusive on the counting. Are you ready?"

Wallace stood up. "I'm Wallace DeWitt from New York. I don't believe we've met."

"Forgive me, Mr. DeWitt. Sometimes I get so focused on my work that I forget my manners. I'm Marguerite LeHand, the President's private secretary. I promised Miss Roswell that she could have a behind-the-scenes look at how much money's been raised tonight." Missy's cool demeanor said volumes about her feelings for the reporter. "Come along, Joan. We've got to complete the count quickly and phone the results in to the President, so he can include the totals in his radio address." Missy smiled at Wallace and said, "Nice to have met you." She pivoted toward one of the ballroom's side doors without waiting for Joan to stand up, calling over her shoulder, "We've set up a counting room down the corridor."

Joan rose, placed a hand on Wallace's shoulder and leaned toward his ear. "I'll meet you upstairs after the President's broadcast." She hurried after Missy.

Grace Tully and two women from the White House secretarial staff were standing behind a pair of long work tables placed end-to-end in a small conference room just down the corridor from the Shoreham ballroom. There was a telephone on one corner of the tables, an adding machine next to it. On the floor behind the tables, Joan saw several small canvas bags. As Joan followed Missy into the room, she noticed a photographer standing by with his Speed Graphic camera—and Ginger Rogers. Missy stepped aside to let Joan enter the room, then pulled the door closed, drowning out the orchestra music floating down the hallway.

"Well, if it isn't the star of tonight's dance," Joan purred as she glided over and air-kissed Ginger on the cheek.

"Hello, Joan. I haven't seen you since RKO. You're still as pretty as ever."

"Oh, you're one to talk! How lovely you look, dear. And how successful you've become!"

"Joan," Missy interrupted the reunion, "I'm sure you remember Grace Tully. That's Antoinette Bachelder – she goes by Toi—and Lela Stiles, and this," she pointed toward the photographer, "is Mike Wanner. Everybody, this is Joan Roswell of the LA *Standard*. She's covering the ball tonight for AP."

The others, already into their work, looked up and offered greetings. Grace just nodded. She remembered Joan from her and Missy's trip to San Francisco the previous autumn—and not with any great fondness.

"You all look as busy as little beavers," Joan said, smiling. "Explain to me what you're doing."

Missy swept her hand across the table. "What you see before you are the donations brought here tonight by our guests. We've already separated them into piles. Toi and Lela are working on coins, Grace is counting bills, and I'm sorting checks. As soon as we sort, we'll count. As soon as we get a total, we'll report to the White House." Missy glanced at her watch. "We've got about ten minutes, ladies."

"So, the President will announce tonight's take on the radio?"

"Right. He's got some prepared remarks and we've left a blank for Steve Early to pencil in the total. Everybody's figures have to be in by eleven-thirty eastern time. Of course, we won't actually get all the figures in by then, but we'll have the totals from the major events, like the ones here in town, New York, and some of the other big cities."

"And what's your role, dear?" Joan asked Ginger.

"Oh, I'm just here as a visiting Hollywood celebrity. For some reason, the Birthday Ball Committee thought more people would attend if I showed up."

"I'm sorted," Grace announced.

Toi sat down in front of an electronic adding machine. "Tell me what you've got."

"I've got fifty one-dollar bills; twelve two-dollar bills…" Grace continued to call out the number of each denomination as Toi's dexterous fingers tapped the data into the adding machine. "…and four one hundred-dollar bills."

Mike clicked a picture of Missy leaning over Toi's shoulder as she read the total displayed on the tape. "One thousand, one hundred seventy-nine dollars."

"And five minutes to go!" Missy added.

The coins, from pennies and nickels to silver dollars, added up to $326.65. But it was the checks that brought in the largest donations.

Missy called out the amount of each check as Toi punched the keys. "That's it. Lela, get Steve Early on the phone while we total everything up."

Missy referred to the adding machine tapes for each category of donations, calling out the totals to Toi and watching the numbers add up on the tape. As soon as Toi hit the total button, Missy announced with a broad grin, "Twenty thousand, two hundred fifty-five dollars and sixty-five cents!" Mike popped a flashbulb in her face, capturing her genuine smile as Toi, Lela, and Grace clapped.

"Here, Missy," Lela said handing her the phone. "It's Steve."

Missy reported the Shoreham total. "What's that bring us up to?" She paused while Early did some quick addition. "Grand! Even better than last year! Make sure you fill in the blank on the Boss's speech before he gets in front of the microphone. I'd hate for him to get there and not have the number!" Missy chuckled, but behind her good humor was a woman committed to making sure her boss came off looking good—and in this case, sounding good.

Missy hung up the phone, looked at Grace and the others, and said, "One point one million! And that's before we get the results from the West Coast and all the little celebrations. This will be F.D.'s best birthday ever!"

"Very impressive that you can raise that kind of money in this kind of economy," Joan said from the other side of the tables. "What's the key?"

Missy hesitated. Joan had removed her gloves and her reporter's pad and pencil were in her manicured hands. Normally, she would have referred Joan to Steve. He dealt with the press every day and he was good at it—but he was tied up right now with the President, getting him ready to go on the air. *I can handle this*, Missy thought, then added, *but I've got to be careful with this snake*.

"It's for a wonderful cause," she began. "So many families all across the country have been afflicted by this terrible disease or know someone who has. Toi, who works with my staff at the White House, is one of them. We met her at Warm Springs years ago, right, Toi?"

For the first time, Joan noticed the crutch leaning against the young staffer's chair, and realized her long evening gown probably covered braces on her legs.

Missy continued, "People just want to help, and the President's Birthday Balls have given us a fun way to do so. Why, just think how many patients can be given the best medical care possible at Warm Springs and what modern science will be able to accomplish with hundreds of thousands of dollars for research. If not for the treatment she got there, Toi might never have been able to come to Washington, and she always volunteers to work at the ball. Of course, we wouldn't have been nearly as successful here at the Shoreham without the selfless support of Miss Ginger Rogers." She smiled at the actress. "How many dances did you give away?"

"Eight hundred and ten," Ginger said, causing the others, even Joan, to laugh. "Actually, I think it was about ten or twelve. A couple of the fellows were pretty good dancers and they were all good sports."

"Very nice, dear," Joan said as she scribbled. "And what happens to the money now?"

"It will be taken to Riggs National Bank on Pennsylvania Avenue and left in the night drop," Missy said. "Tomorrow, it'll be deposited into the Birthday Ball Committee account. Some of it will go to help patients in Warm Springs, some to polio patients being treated at other hospitals, and some will be granted to the best medical researchers in the country."

"Let me get a shot with Miss Rogers and you girls standing behind those piles of dough," Mike said. "Say 'mucho moola!'" Mike clicked off a shot. "All right, hold still while I change the bulb." Mike took one more photo and then turned to Missy. "Can I hitch a ride back to the White House with you tonight? I'm going to spend a couple of hours in the dark room, because I know there will be a clamor to get these photos done for the big donors. You came in one of the White House cars, didn't you?"

"Oh, sorry, Mike," Missy said. "I drove my little Buick since I'm a volunteer tonight and not, strictly speaking, working for the White House. I have to stay until the bitter end. In fact, I'm even delivering the money to the bank, with a Pinkerton man handling security, of course."

"Oh, OK," Mike said. "I'll just grab a cab, I guess." Mike gathered up his gear and left the room as Grace, Toi, and Lela began rubber-banding like bills together and placing the bundles into the canvas bags. Ginger, ever the good sport, sat down at the table and began to roll the coins and put them into color-coded paper sleeves. Missy banded together the last of the checks. When all the currency and coins had been dropped into the bags and the table tops were clear of any remaining money, Missy watched as her colleagues tied the bags closed.

"I guess that's that," she said. "Do you want to ride to the bank with us?" she asked Joan.

"I'll go," Ginger volunteered. "I've never actually carried that much cash before. The studio always pays me by check."

"You girls go right ahead," Joan said. "I've got another assignment. A long night ahead."

In the White House radio studio, the President settled in behind a bank of microphones, carefully inserting a false tooth in a gap in his lower jaw so he wouldn't whistle when he spoke. He adjusted his pince-nez glasses. His script was lying on the top of the desk, a glass of water next to the red "on air" light.

"Thirty seconds, Mr. President," the radio technician said, glancing from the sweeping second hand of a large wall clock to the man behind the microphones. "Let me get a quick sound check."

Roosevelt cleared his throat and said, "Happy birthday to me, happy birthday to me. How's that?" He looked up with a twinkle in his eye.

"Just fine, sir. Stand by. Now, ten seconds." The technician watched the clock. As the second hand stepped its way up the face of the clock, he held up his hand and began silently counting off the seconds, dropping one finger for each tick until the clock reached eleven-forty-five. He flipped a switch on his control panel activating the "on air" light and pointed to the President.

"My friends," President Roosevelt began, "tonight, on my fifty-fourth anniversary, I am very happy because reports indicate that this year's celebration, in the interest of continued efforts against infantile paralysis, will exceed our fondest hopes of success. We are on target to bring in more than a million dollars from every state and in every outlying territory of our nation, where many millions of people are enjoying themselves at all kinds of local parties. They have resolutely aligned themselves to carry on the fight against infantile paralysis until this dread and costly disease is brought under definite and final control.

"Ten years ago, it was made possible for me, with the support of many personal friends, to start the work of the Warm Springs Foundation in Georgia and I dedicated it to one purpose—to apply itself to the task and to keep everlastingly on the job, not by itself alone but with the cooperation of the doctors, the orthopedic hospitals, and those thousands of individuals on whose shoulders falls the brunt of caring for several hundred thousands of the afflicted. This cause has now been joined by the National Birthday Ball Committee.

"Without your local committees, the National Committee could not function. You tonight who are attending these celebrations, and you who are in your homes, have greatly helped to make a reality of what was once only a hope. In nearly seven thousand communities, you are helping to produce concrete results by making it possible for large numbers of those who suffer from physical handicap caused by infantile paralysis to receive aid and assistance. The lives of these people, young and old, will be made easier. Through rehabilitation, by far the greater part of them will become more mobile and will take their places in active life once again with their heads lifted high and their courage unabated."

The President paused and injected some emotion into his voice.

"I wish I could look into your faces tonight. You have made me very happy, more happy than I can express in words. Though I cannot be with you, I want each and every one of you to know and feel that I deeply and sincerely appreciate all that you have done for the cause, all of the inspiration which you have applied to it. To several hundred thousand victims of infantile paralysis, I send very personal greetings, especially to the youngsters among them whose lives lie ahead of them. It is on their behalf that I thank you once more."

# FRIDAY, JANUARY 31, 1936

# CHAPTER 13

Midnight had come and gone. After a brief, fruitless search for the Pinkerton security guard who was supposed to escort the money to the bank, Missy took matters into her own hands. "Here," she said, handing a bag to Grace and another to Ginger. "It looks like we'll have to do the men's work again! Our security man must have gotten into the champagne and fallen asleep somewhere." Missy took the remaining bag, the heaviest of the three.

"Do you need me to come along, Missy?" Grace asked as the three women, now wearing warm furs over their evening gowns, carried the money bags through the cluttered ballroom. The wait staff was busy cleaning up, collecting the remaining glasses, emptying and wiping out the ash trays, picking up streamers and sweeping up confetti.

Missy looked up at the large banner hanging above the orchestra stand. "No, Ginger and I can handle things once we get this cash to the car. But do make a note for the hotel to store that banner. We can use it again next year."

The three women made their way through the Shoreham's motor lobby and out into the cold night air. As Missy emerged from the door, she saw Mike Wanner again, headed into the building. "I thought you'd left," she said.

"I thought I had too," Mike laughed. "I forgot my movie camera. See you later!"

*I love making home movies*, Missy thought. *Maybe Mike can give me some tips; mine always look so jumpy!*

"My Buick's just over here," Missy said to Ginger with a nod of her head. Her arm was getting tired. *Why did I pick up the bag with the coins?* Missy opened the passenger side door and set her bag on the floor board. Grace and Ginger followed suit.

"Sure you don't need me?" Grace asked again.

Missy could read the relief on her assistant's tired face when she said, "We'll be fine. Go home and get some rest. I'll see you tomorrow."

"Miss Rogers, Ginger, it was a real pleasure."

"Nice to meet you too, Grace. Next time you're out in Hollywood, ring me up."

"Will do," Grace said with a giggle and then headed back toward the front of the hotel and its taxi stand.

Missy pulled her Buick coupe onto Connecticut Avenue and headed toward the main office of Riggs National Bank, just a block over from the White House.

"How long will you be in town?" she asked her famous passenger.

"Mother and I head back tomorrow. We take the afternoon train to Chicago and catch the *Chief* from there back to L. A."

"Well, thanks again for helping us. I've no doubt that your presence greatly increased our attendance and our donations." Missy down-shifted as she guided the car into Dupont Circle.

"Here's something you don't see in L. A.," Ginger said.

"You don't have 'roundabouts,' as our British friends call them?"

"Nope. How do you keep a guy like that," Ginger pointed out the window toward a Chevrolet sedan rapidly gaining on them, "from cutting you off?"

Missy laughed. "Oh, there have been times when I've had to go around the circle twice to get out, but most of the time—hey!" The Chevrolet bumped Missy's left rear fender. "Hey! What are you doing?" she cried out, struggling to maintain control of the car. The Chevy continued to shove against her door, guiding her steadily toward the curb in a screech of grinding metal and sparks. Missy slammed on her brakes and at the same time pounded on the horn. Then she and Ginger bounced out of their seats, their heads smacking the roof of the car as the Buick hit the curb. Her car came to a shuddering halt on the sidewalk, one of its front tires blown and ripped off the rim by the force of its collision with the curb.

Missy was dazed, her head throbbing. Ginger was twisted sideways, her legs on top of the money bags, her back turned toward the passenger door. Neither woman moved for a moment, their minds racing to catch up with the violent action they'd just experienced.

Suddenly, both their doors were yanked open. "Get out! Get out! Get out!" multiple voices barked. Missy felt herself being lifted by the collar of her mink coat, her feet barely touching the pavement as she was half-carried and half-hurled into the back of the menacing Chevrolet. *The side is all dented*, she thought just as a burlap bag was brought down over her face. The world had gone gray. What was happening? She felt the car bounce as someone plopped down beside her on the back seat.

"Ginger?"

"Quiet!" one of the frightening voices commanded. Another body pressed into her from the left. The back doors slammed shut.

Missy began to breathe rapidly, her heart pounding in her chest. She wondered if she was about to pass out. That's when she felt a hand grab hers. She gave it a gentle squeeze. It squeezed back. Ginger!

Missy felt the car rock and then heard its front doors slam. The car lurched forward, its tires squealing for purchase on the asphalt. She forced herself to concentrate, to follow the route of the car even though she couldn't see. She was fairly certain they'd turned southwest on New Hampshire Avenue. *This is the wrong direction! We want to go downtown!*

"Where are you taking us?"

"Shut up!" An answering shout.

The car accelerated rapidly, then slowed. Missy felt herself being pushed toward her right, toward Ginger. The car continued to circle for what seemed like several minutes but could have only been seconds. Then it slowed and continued in a straight line.

That must have been Washington Circle. *But how many times did we go around and where did we exit?* The circling had thrown off Missy's sense of direction. All she could do now was wait—and hold on to Ginger's hand.

Within minutes, Missy felt the rhythmic thumping as the car crossed a bridge—a long bridge. It bumped back onto a surfaced road and accelerated. It got darker and Missy guessed they were leaving the city—but in which direction were they heading? She decided to speak up.

"You are making a big mistake. I am Marguerite LeHand, President Roosevelt's private secretary, and I demand to know where you are taking us!"

The answer she got back sent a chilled dagger right into her stomach. "We know just who you are, lady. If you want real trouble, keep asking questions."

Ginger squeezed her hand as if to reassure her.

They drove for another ten minutes or so, the car now traveling at a pace that felt more normal. *Of course, how can I really tell with a musty old bag over my head*, Missy thought. Then, she felt the car slowing, heard the crackle of gravel as it pulled off onto a side road. The driver shifted into a lower gear and continued. Again, the car began to slow and this time it came to a halt. Missy heard the doors opening and felt the car rocking as bodies climbed out of the front seats.

The back door opened. The body that had been pressed against Missy was suddenly gone, causing her to tilt toward the left.

"Out!" a deep voice commanded and again Missy felt herself being dragged by the collar of her coat. She was slung to the ground, her breath knocked from her body. *Am I going to die?* For a moment, she was sure of it, but her diaphragm slowly relaxed and she drew in a tentative breath. She could smell the exhaust from the car. Its motor was still running.

"Now, you ladies sit right there," the voice said. "Keep those nice gunny sack hats on and count to fifty—slowly. Once you get to fifty, you can take 'em off. Understand?"

Silence.

"Understand!"

"Yes." It was Ginger. "We understand."

Missy heard footsteps crunching in the gravel. The car doors slammed. The car was dropped into gear and she heard its tires spinning, throwing gravel against her scratched legs. The crunching of its tires faded away.

And then there was darkness and starlight and cold, fresh air. The bag was off her face and Ginger was staring into her eyes. "Oh, my God! Missy are you OK?"

"What just happened?"

"We were kidnapped!"

Missy's head was clearing, helped by lungfuls of cold night air. "Yes, but why would they kidnap us and then let us go? Where are we, anyhow?"

"You're asking me? I'm not from around here." Ginger helped Missy to her feet.

"As best I can figure, we came from that direction." Missy pointed to the right. "We weren't on this gravel road very long, so I suggest we go that way and see if we can find a highway. Maybe then we can figure out where we are."

Ginger laughed.

"What could possibly be funny at a time like this?"

"You know, I just realized that's the second time I've been kidnapped."

"Really?" Missy asked, surprised. "When was the first time?"

"When I was a little girl," Ginger said. "Just a baby, really. We were living in Independence, Missouri. My parents had separated, and my father snatched me. My mother was simply beside herself."

"I'm sure she was," Missy said, thinking of the state of Shirley Temple's mother, Gertrude, when her famous daughter had been kidnapped off the train enroute to San Francisco. "What happened?"

"Lelee—that's what I call my mother—tracked me down in Texas," Ginger said, "and snatched me back. You know, it's funny, there was a rumor last fall that Shirley Temple had been kidnapped on a trip to San Francisco, but the studio denied it and eventually it just died down. Such a darling child. She had a cameo in a film I made a few years ago, *Change of Heart.* How do these wacky rumors get started?"

"I can't imagine," Missy said. She was glad it was so dark, so Ginger wouldn't see her blush.

The card game in President Roosevelt's study resumed after the radio chat, Dr. McIntire, Harry Hopkins, and Ambassador Bullitt congratulating him on his speech and marveling over the success of the balls. The liquor flowed again as they settled in for another hour or two of play.

Shortly after one o'clock, Steve Early burst into the room. "Excuse me, gentlemen, but something's happened to Missy and Ginger Rogers!" he said. "I just got a call from the D.C. Police Department. Missy's car was found wrecked and abandoned at Dupont Circle. Her purse was found on the floor. The police believe she and Miss Rogers may have been abducted, along with the money."

Bullitt jumped to his feet. "How long ago was the car found?" he asked.

"About ten minutes," Steve said. "They've got an all-points-bulletin out in the district, Virginia, and Maryland."

"Was there any sign of struggle?" asked Harry. Like all of the staff, he was very fond of Missy.

"No bloodshed," Steve said, making Bullitt and Harry both wince. "But there's no doubt they were forced off the road by another car."

"Thank you, Steve," President Roosevelt said calmly. "Gentlemen, I think it best that we fold our cards and await word from the authorities. Steve, you and I will need to talk over a statement for the press...however this turns out."

# CHAPTER 14

Within a few minutes of walking on the gravel road—quite a feat in their delicate high heeled dancing slippers—Missy and Ginger had reached the main highway.

"Any idea where we are?" Ginger asked, pulling the collar of her fur coat tight about her neck.

"No, and my toes are freezing," Missy replied. "Pray that it's not too late for somebody to be out traveling."

"It's not," Ginger said with a smile. "Look!" she pointed toward two small yellow lights in the distance. They appeared to be headlights and they were clearly getting closer.

"Thank goodness!" Missy said.

Ginger removed the white silk scarf covering her blonde hair and began to wave it in the air like a banner. The headlights grew larger, brighter. The noise of the car's engine gradually registered in the women's ears, growing louder until Ginger's scarf was caught in its headlights. The car downshifted and slowed to a halt. Only then did Missy and Ginger discern that the car was really a pick-up truck.

With the engine still running, the driver's door opened, and a man wearing a denim jacket and battered brown hat stepped out. "You ought not be walking this road in the dark. It ain't safe!"

"We were kidnapped!" Ginger replied.

"Kidnapped? If you was kidnapped, what are you doing out here?"

"Where are we exactly?" Missy said.

"Why, you're exactly just west of Alexandria. Where do you want to be?"

"We want to go back to the White House," Missy said.

"The White House?"

Missy approached the truck, shielding her eyes against the bright lights. "I'm Marguerite LeHand, President Roosevelt's private secretary, and this is Ginger Rogers."

The driver hesitated, then he laughed and tugged the brim of his hat. "Clark Gable at your service, ma'ams."

"I really do work at the White House and this really is Ginger Rogers," Missy tried again.

"Tell you what, ladies, how about I take you into town and you can explain it all to the boys at the police station?"

"Oh, would you?" Ginger said, coming up behind Missy. "That would be wonderful!"

"All right, then," the man said. "One of you climb in the front and t'other'll have to ride in the back."

"I'm sure we can both fit in the front. We'll sit close together," Missy said.

"Nope, that'd never do. My shifter is on the floor and your lady legs would get in the way. Wouldn't be fittin'."

Missy sighed and looked at Ginger. "You sit up front. You're still our guest." Missy looked back at the shadowy figure still standing with his hand on the top of the door. "I'll get in the back."

"What's your real name?" Ginger asked as she climbed into the truck's passenger seat. The slamming of her door drowned out the driver's reply.

Missy hiked up the hem of her gown, stepped up on the running board and swung her leg over the side of the bed, wincing when she heard the delicate silk tear.

*Baaaaaaaaaa*! The bleating of a goat startled Missy, causing her to lose her balance and tumble into the back of the truck. She screamed, "Jesus, Mary, and Joseph! What is this thing?"

"That's just Eleanor," the driver said with a laugh. "She won't hurt you." He closed his door and shifted into gear. The truck began to roll, slowly at first, then picking up speed.

The cold air whipped around the cab of the truck and knifed around Missy's legs. Eleanor apparently felt the chill as well, for she snuggled as close to Missy as physics would allow. Missy sighed, thinking yet again, *the things I do for FDR.*

"Thank you for your kindness, Denny," Ginger said, opening the door and climbing out of the cab. Missy stood unsteadily in the back, her feet numbed by the cold. Ginger leaned her head inside the cab and said, "I'll be sure to mail you that picture, so you'll have some evidence to show Marge." She turned and helped Missy down, then the truck drove off.

"How was your trip?" Ginger asked, picking pieces of straw off Missy's mink coat.

"Fr-freezing." Missy's lips were blue, and she was shivering.

"Well," Ginger laughed and linked her arm through Missy's, "at least you smell nice."

"If I had any feeling in my hands, I'd punch you," Missy muttered between clenched teeth.

The two women pushed their way through the front doors of the Alexandria police station and entered a dimly lit lobby. To their right was a pair of wooden benches upon which sat an obviously inebriated man in a dirty, rumpled suit, and a woman with a blackened eye.

The night desk sergeant looked up from his log book at the approach of the two well-dressed but disheveled woman. "How can I help you, ladies?" he asked glancing at the large clock on the wall and noting the time in his ledger.

"We'd like to report a kidnapping," Ginger said.

"I need to call the White House!" Missy exclaimed.

"Not so fast," the sergeant said, throwing up both hands as though to stop whatever was coming next. "Who's been abducted?"

"Us!"

"I need a telephone. I need to call the President."

The sergeant eyed the two strange-acting women. He was about to have them run out of the station, but one of them looked familiar. "There's a pay phone on the wall over there," he pointed to his left with his pen.

"I'll need some change. My purse got left behind when we were abducted."

The sergeant stared into the blue eyes of the older of the two women. She had an air of authority about her that he didn't like—but working just across the river from the nation's capital, he'd had enough experience with political people to know that he didn't want to mess with them—even when they dragged into the station in the middle of the night looking like hell, telling weird tales, and smelling like goats.

"This isn't Riggs National Bank, you know," the sergeant grumbled, digging in his pocket for some loose change. "Here. Call whoever you got to call and then come back over here and tell me what you ladies have been up to."

By the time the White House Packard arrived bearing a relieved Steve Early and Bill Bullitt, Missy and Ginger had given their statements to the night-shift detective and answered his questions as best they could. Ginger had recollected that three of the car's doors had slammed after she and Missy had been thrown inside the

Chevrolet, although neither victim had gotten a look at the faces of their abductors.

When they finally reached the White House, it was after 3 a.m., but the President and First Lady, along with Mrs. Rogers, Harry Hopkins, and Dr. McIntire, were waiting anxiously in the oval study.

Bill Bullitt had his arm protectively around Missy's shoulders, though his nostrils were a bit pinched, as if he was remembering the less pleasant aspects of his Moscow ball with the renegade animals. Ginger Rogers fell into her sobbing mother's arms, and Mrs. Roosevelt telephoned to the White House usher's office for decaffeinated coffee and leftover birthday cake.

It was almost 4 a.m. by the time the women had shared their stories, and one by one the members of their audience left, Dr. McIntire after offering full medical examinations for both women. (He seemed somewhat disappointed when Ginger declined.) Ginger and her mother departed for the Mayflower Hotel, taking with them a special memento of the night: a signed and inscribed master copy of the President's Birthday Ball radio address.

"Take the morning off, Steve," the President told his press secretary. "Mac can cover for you at the morning press conference." Marvin McIntyre, like Early a former journalist, often handled press when the President traveled. But Early was particular about the twice-weekly press conferences he orchestrated in the Oval Office. There was no doubt what the chief topic of Friday's conference would be.

"No sir, I'll just grab a few hours' sleep and be back as usual," Steve said.

Bullitt kissed Missy's hand as he departed. "I was devastated to think something had happened to my dear Lady," he whispered. "Let me take you out to dinner tomorrow night?"

"Thanks, Bill," Missy said. "We'll see how I feel."

Finally, it was just the President and Missy. "Night cap, Missy?" he asked, wheeling himself to his well-stocked cocktail tray.

"Is there any of your good Scotch left?" she asked, dropping into a leather arm chair.

"For you? Of course!"

"Good. I could use a little sippy."

He lifted the lid of the ice bucket and plunked a few cubes in a glass. "Missy," he said over his shoulder. "I believe that's the first time you were ever gotten by a goat."

But when he turned around to hand her the drink, he saw that Missy had fallen asleep in her chair.

# CHAPTER 15

"Why are you in Washington?" Billy Bryce asked through the popping static on the long-distance line.

"I'm here to cover the birthday balls and, in particular, Ginger Rogers's role in the main event at the Shoreham," Joan Roswell replied. She had been dreading this call ever since she'd left Wallace DeWitt's room and seen the headlines in a special edition of the Washington *Herald*: **POLIO PURSE PILFERED! POLICE PUZZLED!** Joan had been planning to go back to her own room and catch up on her sleep, but had made a hasty detour to D.C. police headquarters to find out what she could—which hadn't been much more than she had read in the paper.

Now Billy, the city editor of the Los Angeles *Standard,* was on the phone wanting to know why his "ace" entertainment reporter had been scooped—again! "We didn't send you there so you could see the monuments or visit the Smithsonian. Your long-suffering editor—at considerable expense, I might add—put you in an ideal place at an ideal time to cover a big story. How is it that the United Press reporter had the story overnight and you didn't?"

"I know, Billy, this looks like I wasn't on the ball, but that's not the case," Joan said, trying to come up with a plausible excuse. "And the cost of my trip is being partly offset by AP, don't forget that, dear."

"Don't try to divert my attention from the fact that you don't have the story I sent you there to cover."

"That's not fair, Billy! I filed two stories about the ball Thursday night. You—and AP—got a complete play-by-play of who attended the ball, who they were with, what they were wearing and who they danced with. I even got you the donation total from the counting room."

There was a long silence on the line during which Joan could hear only the fuzzy noises stretching along the phone lines to Los Angeles. Then Billy spoke. "You mean to tell me that you were in the counting room? That you were with all that money until right before it was stolen? That if you'd stuck with the story for ten more minutes— no—five more minutes, that you would have been an eye-witness to history?"

This time it was Joan who paused. "Yes," she said in a small voice.

"Listen to me, Joan, and listen well. You better crack this story and do it fast. If you don't, start looking for a cheap apartment in D.C. because I won't pay your return fare. You understand me?"

"Now, dear, I can tell you're a little upset, but I want you to know you can count on me. I'm on this story and I'll make you proud of your investment in me."

"The only thing I am right now is skeptical. You've got forty-eight hours before I pull the plug on your journalism career. That's two days. Now get to work!"

The line went dead and Joan was left staring at a silent handset, but Billy's ultimatum had jump-started her imagination.

# CHAPTER 16

Mike Wanner hadn't made it home to his Georgetown apartment until nearly one o'clock in the morning. He'd allowed himself to sleep in, grabbing an extra hour of shut-eye before reporting to work in the White House press office on Friday. He would have liked to stay in bed all day, but he had lots of pictures to develop, print, and dry. In addition to his official duties as White House photographer, he also had all the pictures from the big Birthday Ball at the Shoreham. He'd have to work with that Malloy guy from the Birthday Ball Committee to match up donor pictures with names, have the pictures signed by the President, First Lady, or whoever Steve Early decided, and get them to the right addressee.

He'd made steady progress since his arrival in the relatively quiet West Wing at nine-thirty. Things seemed more subdued than usual this morning. *Too many hangovers from last night*, Mike guessed. By eleven o'clock, Mike had developed all the negatives from the previous evening. He'd printed a small stack of pictures of the President dressed in some kind of toga, looking like Julius Caesar, and surrounded by his staff in similar Roman get-up. *Rich people!*

The telephone in the dark room buzzed. "It's Mike."

"Mike, this is Terry at the west gate. There's a Mr. DeWitt here. Says you told him to come by this morning to get a picture you took last night."

"Ask him what's in the picture." Mike heard Terry cover the mouthpiece and relay the question.

"Him and Ginger Rogers."

"Yeah, yeah, I remember him. Send him in. Tell him to come to my office." Mike hung up the phone. He carefully stored his photographic paper, then checked the dark room carefully. Satisfied that no unexposed film or paper was uncovered, he switched on the lights.

He picked up the twenty toga pictures, shuffled them into a neat stack, and opened the door connecting the dark room to his tiny office. He set the stack of photographs on the corner of his desk. *Let's see if this guy is a true Liberty Leaguer*, he thought. A knock on the frame of his office door caused him to look up.

"Mr. DeWitt?" Mike asked with a smile.

"Mr. Wanner," DeWitt nodded.

"Come in. I would offer you a seat," Mike laughed, "but the powers that be think that the photographer's place is behind the lens or in the dark room, not behind the desk. I'm afraid they don't expect me to entertain guests."

"I understand," DeWitt said, looking around the cramped quarters. "I don't mean to come between you and the important work you're doing for the President. I'm sure you're pretty busy around here this morning, after all the excitement last night. I just wanted to get a copy of the picture you took of me and Miss Rogers."

"Of course. I would have gotten pretty excited to dance with Ginger Rogers myself."

"I meant the kidnapping and the theft of the money," Wallace explained.

Mike stopped. "What did I miss?"

"You haven't seen the morning papers?" Wallace asked.

"No, I jumped right into the developing lab. You could say I've been 'in the dark' all morning. Literally and apparently figuratively too."

"The money from the ball last night was stolen. Miss Rogers and one of the President's secretaries, Miss LeHand, were kidnapped briefly."

"Oh my God!" Mike's shoulders sagged and his mind raced. "Are they all right?"

"According to the papers, they were a little shaken up but not hurt. The money's gone, though."

"How much did they get?"

"All of it. All of it from the Shoreham at least. I figured things would be hopping around here this morning after a night like that."

"Well, I'm sure Mr. Early is on top of things," Mike said. "Do the police have any leads?"

"I don't know. I saw an early edition of the *Herald* before I left the hotel. There wasn't much about any investigation, just the usual 'We Hate Roosevelt' stuff." Wallace looked at his watch. "Listen, I know you've got important work to do. I don't want to get in the way, but I was hoping I could get a copy of the picture of me and Miss Rogers. Impress my friends back home, you know?"

"Right, right. I've actually been working on some items for the President," Mike nodded toward the stack of photos on the corner of his desk. "I've already developed the negatives of the photos with you and Miss Rogers. Do you have time to wait for me to print a couple of copies for you? Shouldn't take more than ten minutes or so."

Wallace checked his watch. "Sure, I guess so. Thanks for making me a priority."

"Happy to help out. Appreciate your support of the polio cause." With that, Mike stepped back through the door into the dark room.

Wallace heard the bolt slide to lock the dark room door from the inside. He was ticketed for the two o'clock train from Union Station back to New York, so he had plenty of time to get the picture and grab a bite of lunch before he needed to be at the station.

He stretched. He hadn't gotten more than three hours of sleep, he remembered with a satisfied sigh. He'd nap on the train. He looked around the tight confines of the office, but the only chair was the one behind Wanner's desk and to get to it he'd have to climb over the wastebasket and wedge himself between the corner of the desk and a filing cabinet. Rather than expend the energy, he perched himself on the corner of the desk.

Joan had been a revelation. She had seemed to like sex as much as he did. He had hardly had the energy to order a room service breakfast, but when it had arrived, they had both eaten ravenously. He'd given her his number in New York and invited her to call when she was in the city, but he doubted she would. She didn't seem the needy type.

Wallace's eyes wandered about the room, coming to rest on the stack of photographs beside him. He strained to figure out what he was looking at, then decided to simply pick up one of the prints and turn it toward him. His eyes widened, and his mouth fell open: There in the middle of a bunch of women and men wearing flowing white gowns and what looked like the uniforms of Roman centurions sat the President. He was holding what looked like a scepter and was wearing a garland of leaves around his head. *He looks like Julius Caesar in Rome. Not a very flattering picture. Not flattering at all. Boy, what Al Smith could do with this!* Glancing about, Wallace gingerly opened his coat and slid the photograph against his back, tucking the edge beneath his belt. Then he let his coat fall back into place, covering the evidence of his petty larceny.

After a few more minutes spent recalling the previous night's exertions and pondering what would entice the President to pose for such a ridiculous picture, Wallace heard the bolt slide back. The door opened and Wanner emerged holding several prints by their corners.

"I actually had two of you with Miss Rogers," he said. "I made a couple of copies of each one. Let me get an envelope for these." The skinny man easily edged his way around the desk and reached into one of its drawers.

He withdrew a large white envelope and laid it on his desk. From his center drawer, he removed a tin ink pad and a stamp. Opening the lid of the pad, he inked the stamp and brought it down quickly on each corner of the envelope. PHOTOS: DO NOT BEND!

He slipped the pictures inside and held it out to Wallace.

"How much do I owe you?" Wallace asked.

"Not a thing, Mr. DeWitt. Just keep paying your taxes." Wanner laughed at his joke.

Wallace shook his hand and exited into the hallway. As soon as he turned the corner, he stopped, pulled the photo from behind his back, and put it into the envelope with the other prints.

Mike Wanner waited until DeWitt rounded the corner, then he closed his office door. He picked up the stack of toga pictures and counted them out. *One less than before.* Mike smiled and stroked his tiny moustache.

Steve Early was as good as his word. He reported to the White House at his usual time and joined Marvin McIntyre for a quick conference in the President's bedroom while the Boss finished his breakfast in bed, an old beige sweater pulled over his pajamas to keep his shoulders warm. Missy, who was usually part of this daily ritual, had elected to sleep in.

"The early editions of the papers have big headlines without much detail about the heist and kidnapping," Steve said, "but you can expect a barrage of questions at the press conference this morning."

"I can imagine," FDR said, inserting a cigarette into his ivory holder. "What about Miss Rogers? Will she get out of town in time to avoid the rabble?"

"Yessir," Steve said. "We sent a White House car to pick up her and her mother, and the railroad has arranged for a private waiting room for them at the station. That way they can get on the train unmolested."

"What about Missy?" Marvin asked. "Does she wish to make a statement?"

"I don't wish for her to," FDR said quickly. "The poor girl has been through enough. Let's just say she is resting and hopes the police will soon solve the crime and recover the money."

"What about the FBI?" Steve asked.

"Well, let's see what Hoover's boys do before we start praising them," the President said, dragging on his Camel. "John Edgar's got a big head already. No need to blow it up any bigger before we have to."

# CHAPTER 17

By the time Corey Wainwright arrived early Friday afternoon, J. Edgar Hoover had been pacing the floor of his office for more than two hours. Located on the fifth floor of the Justice Department building, Hoover's office was roughly midway between the Capitol and the White House. The director routinely started his day by reviewing reports from the numerous FBI field offices spanning the United States. When Wainwright, the special-agent-in-charge of the San Francisco office, walked into this office, Hoover turned and smiled.

"Agent Wainwright," the Director said, crossing the room with his hand extended to the tall, neatly dressed agent. "Good to see you. Welcome to Washington." He quickly appraised Wainwright, who exemplified the sort of man Hoover hired for the FBI. He was clean-cut, athletic, smart, and held a law degree. A veteran of the Great War, he was also an excellent shot.

"Thank you, sir," Corey said, matching the Director's firm handshake. "I would have gotten here sooner, but I'd gone out for a walk. The schedule I had said the conference wouldn't begin until later this afternoon. I came over as soon as I got your message."

Hoover waved his subordinate into a black, leather chair and perched on the front of his desk, which sat on a raised platform to give the five-foot-seven Director an appearance of greater height. "I didn't call you in to talk about the conference. Something else has come up, something big. And this time, it's already in the public's eye. There won't be any press blackout!" Hoover smiled. He was energetic, innovative, and enthusiastic, particularly where the reputation of his agency was concerned. He was also fastidiously dressed, with highly polished shoes and a perfectly tailored suit with matching pocket square, tie, and socks.

"Did you read the papers this morning?" he demanded, his dark eyes boring into Wainwright's blue ones.

"No sir. When I got your message, I came over as fast as I could."

Hoover twisted, reaching behind him on the desk top and picking up a copy of the *Washington Star*. In bold, black letters splashed across the front page, the headline proclaimed:

## CHARITY MONEY STOLEN FROM BIRTHDAY BALL; Starlet, Secretary Kidnapped, Released Unharmed

"Yesterday was the President's birthday. These balls and parties to raise money for polio treatments were held all over the country; I'm sure you had several in San Francisco. The idiots in charge of the big ball at the Shoreham Hotel neglected to arrange for any security and the two women taking the money to the bank got waylaid. And get this," Hoover said, standing and straightening his jacket, "your friend Miss LeHand and Miss Ginger Rogers were the two who got kidnapped!"

Corey started. "But the paper says they're OK, right?" he said looking to his boss for confirmation.

Hoover waved his concern away. "Yes, they're both fine."

"Are we getting involved?"

"Is the sky blue? Don't you see what a great opportunity this is for the Bureau? We come in and clean up this mess, find the kidnappers who abducted one of the most popular actresses in the country, not to mention Miss LeHand, and return the stolen money to kids suffering from polio. I'm telling you, Wainwright, this could make our reputation for the next ten years!"

"Yes sir."

"That's why I'm putting you in charge of the case."

"Me, sir? This is pretty far outside of the San Francisco area, sir." Wainwright attempted a chuckle.

Hoover was pacing again now, and Wainwright had to turn in his chair to follow the stocky Director as he stopped in front of the large map of the United States covering the wall of his office. "Sure, it is," Hoover said, glancing back over his shoulder. "But you've already got experience with kidnappings and you've already got a friendly working relationship with Miss LeHand. That could be key, don't you understand? If we solve the case—and keep the White House happy while we're doing it—well, let's just say that all sorts of benefits might accrue."

Wainwright knew better than to argue with Hoover, who had created the most effective, efficient, and modern crime-fighting organization in the world. It was said, not without good cause, that "the FBI always gets its man."

"Where do you want me to start?"

# CHAPTER 18

Joan Roswell's heels clicked along the marble floor of the massive Union Station railway terminal four blocks from the Capitol. Billy's scolding still rang in her ears, still caused her throat to tighten. She'd made good progress in building a network of sources back in Los Angeles, but none of them were on expense accounts and they couldn't very well travel to Washington with her and stake out every conceivable place where something *might* happen.

No, Joan would have to really hustle for the next couple of days to feed Billy stories, even if she had to make them up. She reached the gate leading to the departure tracks.

"Which one is the Chicago train?" she asked the blue-jacketed agent checking tickets.

"Track Two, ma'am, but only ticketed passengers beyond this point."

Joan reached in her purse and flashed her press credentials. "Associated Press," she snapped and strode past the checkpoint. The agent stared after her with a frown.

Billy wanted a story, she'd give him one.

Joan marched directly to the train, its locomotive emitting creaking, cracking noises, gray smoke, and white steam. She stepped up on the wooden stool positioned just below the stairway of the first-class coach and swung herself aboard, ignoring the conductor's request for her ticket. She stalked along the narrow corridor to the left of the staterooms, intimidating approaching passengers and causing them to step aside.

Joan didn't know exactly where she would find Ginger Rogers, only that she was riding in a first-class stateroom with her mother. She stopped at the first compartment door and knocked. A fat man in slacks and a maroon smoking jacket answered the door, a puzzled look on his face. Joan glanced inside, smiled, and said, "Sorry, wrong cabin."

She moved down the corridor, the fat man peering after her. She knocked again, but got no response, so she opened the door herself and looked in: empty.

As she approached the third door, it swung open and an attractive middle-aged woman stepped out. She turned and spoke over her shoulder to someone inside the compartment, pulled the door closed behind her, and headed off toward the front of the train without noticing Joan. The reporter paused, giving the woman time to exit into the adjoining car, then knocked on the door and pushed it open.

Ginger Rogers looked up from a magazine. "Joan? I thought you were Lelee. I thought she'd forgotten something."

"Your mother?"

"Yes, she wanted a cup of coffee before we get rolling. It's a long way to Chicago."

"And you've already had such an exciting trip!"

"You can say that again!"

Without waiting to be asked, Joan sat down on the upholstered couch opposite the movie star. "I need a quick favor, dear, for old time's sake."

Ginger cocked her head and asked, "What kind of favor?"

"I need your story from last night. My editor is angry with me for not getting myself kidnapped with you and Miss LeHand. He's threatening to fire me if I don't get the inside scoop on your adventure."

"I'd love to help, Joan," Ginger replied looking at the slender diamond-and-platinum watch on her wrist, "but we're due to pull out in eight minutes."

"Talk fast. I really need this story."

Ginger laughed. "We took the money to the car, headed toward the bank, got run off the road. Then they put burlap bags on our heads and drove us out of town. We got a little way out in the country and they kicked us out and drove off."

"How many of them were there?"

"I didn't really see, but the car doors kept slamming so I think there were three."

"But you didn't see them?"

"No, no faces."

"Did they call each other by name?"

"Larry, Curley and Mo," Ginger laughed. "No, they didn't use names, not that I heard."

"Did they have guns?"

"Like I said, Joan, they put bags on our heads right after the crash. I really didn't see much."

"How did you get away?"

"They stopped the car and put us out on a gravel road. Missy and I walked back to the highway and after a couple of minutes a farmer drove up in his pick-up truck. He's the one you ought to talk to. Imagine going about your business and coming across me and the President's secretary standing on the side of the road in the middle of nowhere in the middle of the night." Ginger chuckled at the memory.

Outside, a whistle blew, and someone shouted, "All aboard!"

"Were you frightened?"

"Everything happened so fast, I didn't have time to get scared. They barked at us a couple of times but that was as bad as it got—except that it was cold."

The train car jerked as the slack was pulled out of the couplings.

Joan stood, smiled and said, "Thanks, dear. I owe you one."

Ginger said, "You're welcome," but by then Joan had bolted from the compartment. In seconds, Joan had hopped from the staircase of the slowly moving coach and was headed for the station concourse as fast as her high heels would carry her.

## NIGHT OF TERROR ENDS IN DRAMATIC RESCUE; STAR, SECRETARY STARE DEATH IN THE FACE; HERO APPEARS, SCATTERS VILLAINS

WASHINGTON, D.C., January 31 (AP)—by Joan Roswell, Los Angeles *Standard*—

Motion picture star Ginger Rogers and presidential secretary Marguerite LeHand escaped certain death at the hands of nefarious felons Thursday night thanks to the quick-thinking and heroic actions of a northern Virginia plantation owner.

"I was paralyzed with fear," Miss Rogers, the beautiful, blonde star of such movies as *Top Hat* told this reporter during an exclusive interview shortly before departing Washington.

She and Miss LeHand were forced from the road and kidnapped at gunpoint while delivering more than $20,000 raised for polio victims at the Shoreham Hotel's Birthday Ball to Riggs National Bank on Pennsylvania Avenue.

The gentleman-farmer, who asked not to be identified, noticed an automobile driving erratically on Route 1 sometime after midnight. Seeing its badly dented front fender and fearing the worst, the farmer herded the car to the side of the road where, despite the popping of gun fire and being outnumbered five to one, he was able to free the two women from their captors while suffering only minor injuries.

"Thank God for that brave and selfless man," Miss Rogers said fervently. "I am sure Miss LeHand and I would both be dead by now if not for his courage. America needs more people like him."

Both Miss Rogers and Miss LeHand were taken unharmed to the Alexandria police station and later returned to the White House. Unfortunately, the abductors were able to escape with the funds.
State and federal authorities are continuing their investigation of the crime.

Joan's article continued on in similar vein for another two column-inches. Sure, she'd taken a few liberties with Ginger's account, but by the time the actress's train reached Chicago, the story would be old news. And besides, a working girl had to do what she had to do.

# CHAPTER 19

### Chicago

"My initial reaction was one of outrage," Deacon Owen Knox told his listeners Friday night in his regular radio broadcast from Chicago. "How could men sink so low as to steal money intended for the noble task of searching for a cure for a dread disease? These reprobates were stealing not only money, they were stealing hope! And what is life without that most precious commodity?"

Knox was standing before his microphone, his hands gripping the sides of the lectern upon which rested his speech for the evening's broadcast. Henry Bowman sat silently to his left following along on his own copy of the script, his pale green eyes moving side to side behind his glasses. "But, my friends, the longer I thought about this wretched crime, the more I pondered its sinister motives, the more convinced I became that I, that you, that all of the God-fearing people of this rich nation have been hoodwinked once again!"

Knox was hitting his stride now, the pace of his delivery quickening, his voice rising and falling as though he were back behind the pulpit preaching the Good Word.

"Of course, the money is missing! Of course, we've been told it was stolen, that these poor women—" at Knox's insistence, Henry had deleted from the script references to the loose moral character of the two woman involved—a movie star and a "professional" woman— "were kidnapped, held at gun point, and threatened with the forfeiture of their lives! Of course, we were told these lies. And why? Because the ruthless, soulless cynic who sits on his White House throne wanted the money to fund his own selfish, egotistical campaign to 'lead' our country for four more years of broken promises, of catering to the wealthiest Americans at the expense of the hardest-working.

"It is time to rise up! It is time to shout 'no more!' It is time for all true Christians to put the love of their neighbors ahead of the love of affluence, the love of influence, the love of Mammon! Shout with me! Shout 'no more!' until America is restored to holiness by its righteous treatment of its people. Say it with me, friends. Right now, as you hear my voice in Elmira, New York, in Kingsport, Tennessee, in Sheboygan, Wisconsin, on the plains in Abilene, Texas, the mountains of Laramie, Wyoming and the shores of Coos Bay, Oregon. No more!

"Let your voices be heard: No more! No more! No more!"

Knox stepped away from the microphones as the sound engineer switched the live feed to the microphone in his control booth. "You've been listening to Deacon Owen Knox coming to you live from the studios of the Mutual Broadcasting System in Chicago. Your support of our radio ministry is essential for us to continue to spread the Gospel of Jesus Christ throughout this great nation," the announcer continued.

Henry had decided, and Knox had quickly concurred, that the solicitation of donations was beneath the dignity of Deacon Knox. That task had been delegated to the nameless, faceless voice now wrapping up the broadcast.

"How did it go?" Knox asked his associate, once the "on air" light flickered off.

"Wonderful!" Henry replied. "I could almost hear people chanting along with you. 'No more, no more!' I think we're on to something."

# SATURDAY, FEBRUARY 1, 1936

# CHAPTER 20

**New York**

"Can you believe this picture?" Wallace said with a laugh, pointing at the eight-by-ten print sitting on the top of Al Smith's desk. "They look like a bunch of rich goof-balls. What were they thinking?"

Smith leaned forward, adjusting his reading glasses. "They were thinking that they're bigger than everybody else. That they're above accountability." He shook his head and looked up at his young friend. "I tell you, this leaves a sour taste in my mouth. Frank thinking he's an American Caesar. My heavens! It all fits the pattern, doesn't it?"

"How do you mean?"

"They're loose, that bunch," Smith nodded toward the photograph. "They disregard public opinion. They play their little dress-up games while a fifth of the country is out of work. They go to their fancy balls and hob-knob with the movie stars and we've got lines three blocks long of men looking for jobs—or just trying to get a bowl of potato soup. And then, when they finally do something halfway noteworthy, they treat this charity money just like the U.S. Treasury! They don't take care of it. No fiduciary responsibility. Hell, it's just somebody else's money so it doesn't matter if we protect it or not, if we use it wisely or we don't. Makes my stomach turn just to look at Frank. This is disgraceful!"

"I was thinking along the same lines," Wallace said, reaching over and picking up the photo. He looked from the image to Smith. "What do you think would happen if this picture got into the wrong hands?"

"If Cissy Patterson or Colonel McCormick got hold of that picture it would be on the front pages of newspapers all over the country—and with very unflattering headlines. I can tell you that," Smith said, naming the cousins who were among the most anti-Roosevelt newspaper publishers in the country. He shook his head again, then stopped, looked up at Wallace, and began to smile.

# CHAPTER 21

## Washington, D.C.

"Miss LeHand," Corey Wainwright smiled, extending his hand, "what a pleasure to see you." They were in the West Wing on Saturday morning, standing outside Missy's office. She had taken the day off on Friday—in part to avoid the press—and felt almost as good as new.

Wainwright and the President's secretary had worked closely together on the Shirley Temple kidnapping case. In the course of a hectic weekend, Corey and Missy had spent enough time together to feel a mutual attraction. Missy's hasty departure from San Francisco after the little actress was returned to her mother had nipped the budding romance, though they had stayed in touch by letter. Corey had been looking forward to his trip to Washington for the special agents' conference and hoped that it would include a chance to see Missy. Naturally he hadn't expected to see her on official business.

"Special Agent Wainwright," Missy said with a smile, her head cocked to the side and her blue eyes shining. "You're a little outside your jurisdiction, aren't you?"

"I'm an FBI agent, Miss LeHand. My jurisdiction stretches all the way across the country—but most importantly, wherever you're involved." The tips of his ears reddened, and Missy's cheeks turned pink in response. Both looked down at the floor for a moment. "Harrumph!" Corey coughed. "Now tell me about this trouble you got into Thursday night. I've called the D.C. Police Department and the Virginia State Police. Both have detectives working on the case, but they haven't turned up any promising leads yet."

"Come this way," Missy said, leading him into her office. Once they were inside with the door closed, Missy gave the agent an affectionate squeeze on the arm. "I'm so glad Mr. Hoover assigned you to the case. It's comforting to know that the lead investigator isn't out to score political points with the press or the Republicans. Plus," Missy continued, looking into the tall, handsome G-man's blue eyes, and taking in his cleft chin and the endearing little space between his front teeth, "I'm so glad to see you again."

*So*, Corey thought, *here we are*. He felt almost dizzy from inhaling Missy's perfume, which he recalled was her favorite, Guerlain's L'heure Bleue. He cleared his throat. "I expect we'll need to spend quite a bit of time together. I hope you won't mind."

"Not at all. Have a seat," Missy said, gesturing to a plain wooden chair. She settled behind her small desk, which was decorated with a bust of President Roosevelt and an odd assortment of figurines, including an aluminum donkey. The walls of the room were painted pale pink, and the office had large windows overlooking the White House Rose Garden. "Mind if I smoke?" she asked. "I'm afraid we're all hopelessly addicted here."

"No, go ahead," Corey said, pulling a small note pad and pencil from his inside coat pocket. "I understand that Miss Rogers has already left the city."

"That's right. She and her mother left on the Chicago train yesterday. She gave a lengthy statement to the Alexandria police on Thursday night—or was it Friday morning? We both did."

"And she's all right?"

"Yes. No harm done."

"And you? You're all right?"

Missy smiled. "I thought you'd never ask." Corey chuckled. "I got a little cold and ruined my evening gown, but I made friends with a very affectionate goat, so the evening wasn't a total loss."

Corey laughed. "Yes, I read your statements about the white knight in the pickup truck—as well as the highly colored version of the rescue Joan Roswell wrote for AP. I take it she was in town covering the ball for her newspaper."

Missy made a face. "I'm sure Ginger didn't tell her any of that stuff, but I'm glad she left the goat out of her fictionalized version. You would not believe the ribbing I'm getting around here. Marvin McIntyre asked me if I wanted a tin can for lunch today!"

Corey laughed again, enjoying Missy's sense of humor, but got serious with his next words. "I've spoken with Inspector Trent at the D.C. Police Department and Major Bishop with the Virginia State Police. They've each got people working on the case. I know you must be busy, but I wanted to hear the story directly from you, if you've got the time."

"Well," Missy began, leaning back in her chair and taking a drag on her Lucky Strike, "I guess I should start with the counting of the money. We collected it all in a small meeting room near the ballroom and sorted it and totaled it all up."

"Who's 'we?'"

"Grace Tully, whom you know from our little adventure in San Francisco; Ginger Rogers, of course; Toi Bachelder and Lela Stiles, who are on the secretarial staff here at the White House; Mike Wanner, a photographer from the press office; and Joan Roswell."

"So, you knew everyone there in the counting room?"

"That's right."

"Would you suspect anyone of them might be in on the theft?"

Missy laughed, "Oh, no, no."

"Not even Miss Roswell?"

Missy flicked some ash into the large glass ash tray on her desk and narrowed her eyes. She thought for a moment before responding. "No, I don't think so. I only brought her back to the counting room at the last minute. She stayed there in the room until we were ready to go, then she said she had another assignment and left."

"Another assignment? What time was this?"

"Not long after midnight, I guess."

"Seems kind of late for 'another assignment.'"

"Well, remember this is Joan Roswell we're talking about. She gets around a lot, if you get what I mean."

Corey chuckled. "Did you see her with anyone else that evening?"

"No. Well, that's not right. When I went to get her—I had promised her exclusive access to the counting of the money—she was sitting at a table having a drink with a man I didn't know."

"Did you get his name?"

"I'm embarrassed to say that I did."

"Why embarrassed?"

"Because I ignored him at first. I was so focused on getting the money counted in time."

"What was his name?"

"Oh, Corey, I don't remember," Missy put a hand to either side of her head and massaged her temples as though trying to coax her memory to deliver the name. "I think it started with a 'D.' The Birthday Ball Committee will have a guest list somewhere. He's sure to be listed: he'd given enough of a donation to earn a dance with Ginger Rogers."

"What about Miss Roswell, would she remember the guy?"

Missy raised her eyebrows and shrugged. "You'll have to ask her. He was a nice-looking fellow. Had on a tailored tuxedo. When you go to as many formal events as I do, you get a nose for money. He had it."

"Careful," Corey said, smiling. "I may get jealous." Missy giggled. "So, what happened next?"

"Well, Mike left. His job was to take pictures, which he'd been doing all night, so I turned him loose. I let Toi and Lela go too. They're both working today if you want to talk to them later. Then Ginger, Grace, and I carried the money to my car. My poor beat-up car." Missy sighed.

"You know, it seems kind of strange to me that you wouldn't have had some kind of security detail to handle that much money."

"We were supposed to, but we couldn't find the guy. Grace and I looked all over. We went back into the ballroom and the kitchen, but nobody had seen him since earlier. I didn't want to sit around hoping he'd show up, so I made the decision to take the money to Riggs myself. Ginger said she wanted to come along so she did. Grace was ready to go home, so she left. In hindsight, it's not the smartest thing I ever did."

"Who was the security guard? Did you know him?"

"I met him a few days before the ball at a planning session. He was a Pinkerton, hired by the Birthday Ball Committee through the Washington office."

"Remember his name?"

"Mitch something. After that first meeting, I didn't see him anymore."

"Who else was in that meeting?"

"Grace and me. Casey Malloy from the committee. The orchestra leader who doubled as the emcee, the banquet captain, and the hotel's director of social events."

"Anybody else from the White House?"

Missy shook her head.

"Miss Rogers?"

"No, she hadn't arrived yet."

Corey tapped the pencil's eraser against his note pad. "I'd be interested in speaking to this Mr. Malloy. Maybe he can help me run down the fellow from the ball, Miss Roswell's friend. I also want to talk to Mitch, the Pinkerton. He's involved in this one way or another."

"You think so?"

"I'll bet you lunch on it."

Missy smiled. "That would be nice."

He got up to go. As Missy rose to escort him out, she said, "Let's say hello to Grace on your way out. She'd love to see you."

# CHAPTER 22

A small office down the fifth-floor corridor from J. Edgar Hoover's had been made available to Corey Wainwright for the duration of his stay in Washington. It had a wooden desk with a chair on either side, a dark green metal filing cabinet, a black Bakelite telephone and a dirty window. While the office wasn't much, Corey would have the support of the entire FBI behind him—and that wasn't nothing.

When he returned from the White House, two telephone message slips were waiting for him. He picked up the phone and dialed.

"Pinkerton Detectives."

"May I speak with Mr. Harvey, please?" Corey asked.

"He's very busy today," the female voice replied. "May I ask who's calling?"

"Agent Wainwright, Federal Bureau of Investigation, on official business." Within seconds, a new voice was on the line.

"Harvey speaking."

"Mr. Harvey, good afternoon. This is Special Agent Corey Wainwright calling from the Federal Bureau of Investigation. I'm working on the theft of a fairly large sum of money from the President's Birthday Ball at the Shoreham Hotel on Thursday night. I believe your office was contracted to provide security."

There was a silence on the line, then Harvey sighed. "I'm afraid that's correct, Agent Wainwright. Of course, we'll be refunding our fee to the Birthday Ball Committee along with a generous donation and our sincere apology. I've been in this business for eight years and have never had anything like that happen. It's all pretty embarrassing. Not to mention bad for business. As you might suspect, the press has been all over this thing since yesterday morning."

"I can imagine," Wainwright said. "I need to talk to the employee you assigned to this contract. I understand his first name is Mitch?"

"Mitch Novak. Former employee. Inspector Trent from the D.C. Police and a couple of his detectives have already paid us a visit. I'll tell you the same thing I told him. We haven't heard from Novak since Thursday. We've got a man watching his apartment, but no signs of him so far."

*Just as I figured*, Corey thought. "How long had he worked for you?"

"About six months."

"That doesn't seem like a very long time for him to be placed in charge of a detail like the ball."

"Well," Harvey drawled, "hindsight is twenty-twenty, as they say. It seemed like a pretty simple assignment. Meet the client at eleven-thirty and take the money to the bank. Mitch had been reliable up till Thursday night."

"Any personal problems?"

"Not that we're aware of. Believe me, Agent Wainwright, we take this kind of thing as seriously as I know the FBI does. I mean, this is how we make a living, you understand? We foul up a very public job like this and we feel the consequences. We've had two new clients cancel their contracts and I've spent most of Friday and today calling our old customers and reassuring them."

Corey asked a few more questions, got Novak's address and a promise from Mr. Harvey that he'd contact the Bureau if Novak resurfaced.

Corey's next return call was to Major Bishop at the state police barracks in Alexandria.

"We found a car we think you might be interested in, Agent Wainwright," Bishop said when he came on the line. "It's a gray Chevrolet with a bashed-in front right fender and a lot of scratches and dents. There's a good bit of blue paint on the Chevy that doesn't belong to it. Plus, the car has stolen plates on it. We're running the serial number now, but I'd bet my badge it's stolen. Assuming I'm right, the Dyer Act gives you jurisdiction on the theft to go along with your federal jurisdiction on the kidnapping charge."

The Dyer Act made it a federal crime to transport stolen motor vehicles across state lines. It was the same law that had given the Bureau jurisdiction to track down a range of notorious gangsters in 1933 and 1934, including bank robber John Dillinger.

"Where's the car now?"

"Here at the Alexandria barracks."

"I'm on my way. If I can get a paint sample off the Chevrolet to match the paint on Miss LeHand's car, we can make a positive connection. Our lab here can do the work pretty quickly."

"Head on over. Maybe by the time you get here we'll have the name of the car's owner."

Corey checked a black Plymouth sedan out of the Bureau's motor pool and drove out of Washington, crossing the Potomac River. He pulled into the state police barracks at Alexandria twenty minutes later.

Major Bishop greeted him with a paper cup of lukewarm coffee and together they walked to the impound lot. "That's her," Bishop said, pointing toward the gray car.

Corey walked slowly around the vehicle, making notes on his pad. "Did your boys find anything on the inside?"

"No, but since we figured this might be the car you're looking for, we didn't do more than look through the windows. Your methods are more sophisticated than ours and we didn't want to run the risk of messing up any evidence."

"Very thoughtful of you," Corey said with a smile. "I'll send an evidence collection team over from headquarters. Any luck tracking down the owner of the car?"

Bishop unbuttoned the flap of his tunic pocket and pulled out a typewritten piece of paper. "Yep. Belongs to a Mabel Anniston in Chevy Chase. That's just over the D.C. line in Maryland. Assuming that paint matches," Bishop pointed toward the scratched and dented side of the Chevrolet, "you've got yourself a case."

Corey knelt beside the Chevrolet's scarred passenger-side door, and using a pair of tweezers, tugged at a large flake of blue paint. He dropped it and a second sample from the front fender into a small paper evidence envelope.

"I'll get the boys back at the lab to compare this sample to the paint on Miss LeHand's Buick. Assuming they match, all we have to do is find the driver."

# CHAPTER 23

"Say it ain't so, Al. Say it ain't so!" Franklin Roosevelt muttered as he sat at the *Resolute* desk in his study Saturday afternoon scanning the *New York Times*. "Listen to this," he said to Missy. "'Smith, the four-term former Governor'—he was only Governor four times because he couldn't win a national election even with us helping him—'said the theft was "just another example of the profligacy of the Roosevelt administration."' Al Smith never used a four-syllable word in his life until he started schmoozing with DuPont and those other millionaires pumping money into the Liberty League."

"He seems to have drifted away from his roots, doesn't he?" Missy said, shaking her head.

"He certainly seems rootless, not to mention ruthless. So now we're getting fired upon from both the left and the right. Good thing Huey Long's dead or he'd be on his high and mighty horse too, the crook."

"Now, F.D., we mustn't speak ill of the dead," Missy scolded. Long, the populist senator from Louisiana, had been assassinated the year before. To his fans, he was a hero who fought for the little man. His foes said he was a corrupt dictator who lined his own pockets at the public trough.

"We've got real problems in this country and mischief-makers like Al Smith and Deacon Knox and all the other fools out there are a distraction. They're stirring up doubt in our leadership and fear of our objectives. It's unhealthy and it's bad for the country. I've got a mind to get Homer Cummings over here and see what we can do to shut these people down."

"I doubt the Attorney General would look favorably on you trying to 'shut down' freedom of speech."

Roosevelt looked up and snapped his fingers, a smile chasing the scowl from his face. "I've got an even better idea. Get Secretary Morgenthau on the line. He can open tax investigations against ol' Al and Empire State, Incorporated, and Knox and that pseudo-ministry of his."

"I'll get him to come over, F.D.," Missy said, "but if he doesn't tell you that's a bad idea, I will. Al Smith and Deacon Knox are nothing compared to the trouble you'd get if Congress ever found out you were using the machinery of the Department of the Treasury to silence your critics."

"Damn it, Missy!" the President exploded, staring darts at his secretary. "How'd you get to be so wise?" Then he grinned. Missy grinned back.

"The best thing to do, F.D., is let Hoover and his men work the case. You remember Corey Wainwright, the special-agent-in-charge of the San Francisco field office?"

Roosevelt grinned again. "The one who sent you the charm for your bracelet?"

Missy felt her cheeks warm as she nodded. "He's in town for a conference and Hoover assigned him to this. He's already interviewed me and he's working on some other leads. I say we put our trust in the FBI. They always get their man—and I bet they get the money back too."

Suddenly, she smiled at her boss. "Did you get to swim today?"

"Yes, I did have a swim," said the President. Shortly after he took office, the Chicago newspaper published by Colonel Robert McCormick had mounted a drive to raise money to install an indoor pool at the White House. McCormick had soon soured on the New Deal, but the pool continued to provide the hydrotherapy Roosevelt had begun for his paralysis in Warm Springs in 1924. "Unfortunately, your friend Ambassador Bullitt was with me, and I couldn't get him to stop talking about the Russians."

"Yes, he's quite upset at the direction things are going there," Missy said seriously. "I've been reading his cables too. He's certain they're actively involved in abetting the communist movement in the United States." She sighed. "Bill was a bit of a hopeless romantic about the Russians. I think two years in Moscow have shattered those rose-colored glasses of his."

"Well, why don't you and Marvin get him in for an appointment in my office before he leaves again for that 'workers' paradise,'" FDR said grouchily. "I'll listen to what he has to say. I just don't want to listen to him while I'm swimming. Or playing cards!" He looked out the window. "I wish it wasn't so cold on the river, I'd love to get out of this fancy prison and do some fishing on the Potomac. Eleanor's escaped for a week, lucky lady. She's gone out to Seattle to visit Anna and the grandchildren."

"Yes, I know. She's asked me to cover a few events at the White House for her as hostess while she's gone." Missy grinned slyly. "We could watch a movie tonight, if you like. We've got a pre-release copy of the new Myrna Loy movie, *Wife vs. Secretary.* I know she's your favorite actress."

"That would be grand!" he said. Then he gave Missy a severe look. "No date with Ambassador Bullitt or Corey Wainwright tonight? I don't want to keep you from your social life. You work so hard, you deserve a Saturday night to yourself sometimes."

"No," Missy said. "Bill took me out to dinner last night, and I'm spending tomorrow afternoon with Agent Wainwright. Just so I can get a complete briefing on the case, you understand," she said, winking. "But tonight, I just feel like relaxing and watching a movie. And this movie doesn't just star Myrna Loy. It also stars Clark Gable!"

"Let's see if we can rustle up some decent snacks from the kitchen," the President said. "If Mrs. Nesbitt is off, we might even be able to get popcorn that isn't burned to a crisp."

# MONDAY, FEBRUARY 3, 1936

# CHAPTER 24

Wallace DeWitt had taken the train back to Washington on Sunday, an unmarked envelope riding along in his briefcase. He'd booked a room at the Willard, a block east of the White House, and planned to remain in the capital for a couple of days. He had an appointment Monday morning and he wanted to attend a political dinner the following evening. What was the old saying? "Politics makes for strange bedfellows." Well, he'd see about that. After this morning's meeting, he'd contact Joan if she was still in town and take her out for a nice dinner. After that, who knew?

Wallace's appointment was on H Street at the office of Cissy Patterson, the editor and publisher of the *Washington Herald.* The *Herald*, the largest morning circulation daily in the city, covered Washington life, politics, sports, and local affairs with a decidedly conservative bent. And no wonder, it was one of William Randolph Hearst's thirty major newspapers and reflected the views of its owner—as well as its eccentric publisher.

Eleanor Medill "Cissy" Patterson, born into a Chicago publishing family, had married a Polish count, borne him a daughter, escaped from his abuse, and spent the next thirteen years pursuing a divorce. She had remarried, been widowed, and, casting around for something to do, had convinced Hearst to hire her as editor of his money-losing Washington newspaper. She had re-taken her maiden name but was called Mrs. Patterson. Under her direction, the paper had been revitalized, gaining readers along with notoriety for its acidic front-page editorials and the vicious gossip items and shocking stories that appeared on its widely read Page 3. Hearst had rewarded her by naming her publisher.

After all he'd heard about the notorious Cissy Patterson, Wallace couldn't wait to meet her.

It was a chilly day in Washington, but as it wasn't raining, and the distance was short, Wallace put on his overcoat and hat, grabbed the envelope, and set out from the hotel walking north on 14$^{th}$ Street. He crossed New York Avenue and continued for another block until he came to the newspaper's four-story building near the corner of H Street.

"I'm Wallace DeWitt," he said, approaching the receptionist in the lobby of the building. "I'm here to see Mrs. Patterson. I'm a little bit early."

The receptionist, a young woman with an unfortunate overbite similar to Mrs. Roosevelt's, stifled a toothy grin. "She's not in yet, Mr. DeWitt. Would you care to have a seat?"

Wallace settled onto an upholstered sofa sitting against the wall of the lobby. Its arms were scarred by cigarette burns and other stains the origins of which he didn't care to guess. A knee-high table in front of the sofa held several copies of the morning edition of the *Herald*. A large clock on the wall displayed the time as eleven-fifteen. Beneath the clock in gold lettering was a replica of the *Herald's* masthead, including its motto: America First.

Wallace picked up the newspaper and began to scan the headlines. There had been a coup in Japan. Apparently, the militarists had cast a ballistic ballot canceling out the political career—and life—of the premier. In Germany, a group of pro-Nazi clergymen were busy rewriting the Bible. According to a Bishop Weidemann, the new translation was not concerned with the "Luther of yesterday, but with the Christ of today." The German bishop was quoted as saying that "Christ was not, after all, Jewish." *Go figure*. Wallace shook his head.

Wallace's eyes bounced from headline-to-headline, page-to-page, as the clock ticked off the minutes. His appointment had been set for 11:30. Finally, at eleven fifty-five, a sixteen-cylinder Cadillac limousine pulled up to the curb outside. A chauffeur in a blue uniform trotted around to the passenger-side rear door and pulled it open. Two poodles, restrained by bright red leashes, jumped down onto the sidewalk. Wallace's gaze followed the leashes up to the hand that held them. It was gloved and attached to a slender, middle-aged woman wearing sunglasses and a sumptuous sable coat, her auburn hair peeking out from under a matching sable hat.

The chauffeur moved quickly from the car door to the building's entrance and held open the door there as the dogs, zigging and zagging and sniffing, led their mistress into the lobby. Wallace watched over the top of the newspaper as the receptionist stood, smiled, and greeted the publisher, handing her a stack of telephone messages and nodding toward Wallace.

"Molley, where did you get that lovely suit?" Mrs. Patterson asked the receptionist.

"Why, Mrs. Patterson, you gave it to me yourself," Molley replied. "You said you had gotten tired of it."

"Hmmm. Well, I want it back. Have it cleaned first, though."

"Yes ma'am," Molley said quietly.

Cissy Patterson turned toward Wallace, nodded briskly, and motioned for him to follow her. She strode to the elevator, which was now being held for her, and stepped on, the dogs bunching up by her feet. Wallace hopped on just as the doors closed.

Cissy Patterson peered at Wallace over the tops of her dark glasses. "I'm busy today," she said in a rich contralto voice. "We'll have to make this quick. Al Smith said I should make time to see you. Are you a newsmaker, Mr. DeWitt?"

Startled by her brusqueness, Wallace recovered quickly. "I'm just a courier, Mrs. Patterson. You're a better arbiter of what is newsworthy, but I believe what I have to show you is worth five minutes." He paused. "Even if you're busy."

The elevator's doors opened, and Patterson stepped off into the city-room—a huge open loft—with the purposeful stride of a general about to inspect the troops. The dogs, tails wagging, strained on their leashes, charting a direct course down a long aisle on either side of which stood rows of desks, behind which sat men—and an occasional woman—typing away on news stories. The clacking of typewriters was punctuated frequently by the ding of bells as their carriages reached their limits. Smoke from two dozen cigarettes, cigars, and pipes drifted up from the desks to merge into a head-high yellowish gray cloud.

At the far end of the floor, Patterson pushed open the door to a small office with large windows giving her a full view of the city room. She dropped the leashes and the dogs curled up in baskets beside the heavy wooden desk, on the top of which were the two latest editions of the newspaper and a vase of white violets. A portrait of her publisher grandfather, Joseph Medill, frowned down from one wall. Patterson shrugged off her fur coat and took off her hat, carelessly slinging them onto a chair in the corner. An unnatural silence filled the office as Wallace's host crossed behind her desk and flopped into her leather chair.

"Show me," Patterson said, pulling off her sunglasses to reveal clear, intelligent—but impatient—blue eyes. Wallace held up the envelope. He pulled an eight-by-ten print out and placed it on the desk. Patterson stared at the picture for several seconds, then yanked open the center drawer of her desk and withdrew a heavy, old-fashioned magnifying glass. She bent over the photograph, studying the faces arranged around the center figure.

"Where'd you get this?"

"It's authentic, if that's what you're asking."

"That's not what I'm asking, Mr. DeWitt." Patterson looked up. "I'm asking where you got this picture. I have to know if I run this, this ridiculous photograph, that it won't blow up in my face."

Wallace swallowed his annoyance at the rudeness of the publisher. "I picked it up over at the White House. I was there on some other business and I happened to see it lying around in the press office. Do you want it or not?"

Patterson looked back at the picture. "How much?"

"Why, Mrs. Patterson, you mistake me. My motives here are patriotic, not financial. You agree to run the picture with an appropriate story, you agree to share it with Colonel McCormick and with your brother, Joe, and I'll be happy to walk out of this office with nothing save your good wishes."

Wallace knew that Patterson's cousin, Robert McCormick, who published the rabidly anti-Roosevelt *Tribune* in Chicago, and her brother, Joseph Patterson, who was the publisher of the *Daily News* in New York, would jump at the chance to embarrass the President.

Patterson continued to study the picture. "Deal," she said finally. She stood then and offered her hand, still wearing her long leather gloves, and shook. "I always say, I'd rather raise hell than vegetables any day. Nice to have met you, Mr. DeWitt." Suddenly, a brilliant smile appeared on her face, and she wrinkled her pug nose.

"Likewise," Wallace said, suddenly realizing why so many people were charmed by Cissy Patterson. He turned and headed for the door. The two dogs looked up. "I leave the story in your capable hands."

# CHAPTER 25

The FBI crime lab in the basement of the Justice Department building featured extensive files on everything from tire treads and ballistics to fingerprints. It also contained the world's largest repository of automobile paint samples. Working each model year with the big car manufacturers from Detroit, the Bureau updated its samples to include the newest colors available on the newest cars.

Not that Missy LeHand's blue Buick was that new. On Monday morning, Corey Wainwright had returned to headquarters and trooped down to the basement. He'd signed over the paint sample, now being handled as an official piece of evidence under a certified chain of custody, to lab technicians. They would compare the sample from the Chevrolet impounded by the Virginia State Police to a sample taken directly from Missy's wrecked coupe.

During his Sunday afternoon with Missy, they had gone to the Smithsonian's New National Museum—still called that despite the fact that it had been dedicated in 1910—and taken in as much of the collection of natural history specimens as their feet could stand. Over a late lunch, he had filled her in on the stolen Chevrolet and his other efforts on the case. He assured her that her beloved Buick would be released soon so it could get the repairs needed to put it back on the road. Missy said she had already contacted her niece, Barbara, who worked for the agency that insured her car. She didn't mention that the agency was owned by the President's son, James, who had given Barbara the job. Favors ran both ways in the extended White House "family."

In the meantime, Corey had other leads to chase. He had asked for and received from the Birthday Ball Committee a list of the donors attending the ball at the Shoreham Hotel. He had a clerk from the Bureau comparing that list to one of known felons. He also wanted to speak with Joan Roswell, the reporter. Although he didn't suspect her of involvement in the crimes, there was a chance that she had seen someone who might have been.

Corey had also received complete copies of the D.C. and Virginia police files on the case. In both jurisdictions the case was considered open, but both departments had scaled back their efforts to resolve the case when the Bureau had gotten involved. He had been to Dupont Circle where Missy's car had been run off the road and he had personally examined the Chevrolet recovered near Alexandria. Now he decided to back track to the Shoreham Hotel where this whole mess had started.

Joan Roswell had been one of the many reporters calling the Washington office of the Pinkerton Detective Agency.

"Good morning! This is Jane calling from the President's Birthday Ball Committee," Joan had told the woman answering the phone. "I'm tying up loose ends from Thursday night's polio ball and I need to speak to Mitch."

"Good luck, sister," replied the woman. "We haven't seen him since Thursday. We've even got a fellow staking out his apartment. So far, no show. You want to speak to the boss, Mr. Harvey?"

"No, dear, I don't want to bother him. I'm sure he's got his hands full what with how everything turned out and all."

"You can say that again. What do you need Mitch for?"

"Well, you may have heard that Ginger Rogers was our special guest at the ball. Our photographer took a picture of Mitch with Miss Rogers. She is such a dear person," Joan gushed, "she insisted on taking pictures with everyone, even us little people. I'll never miss another one of her movies. Anyway, I've got this handsome photograph of Mitch and Ginger—Miss Rogers—and I just wanted to get it to him."

"Why don't you mail it?" the secretary said.

"But you said he hasn't returned to his apartment."

"Well, he gets his mail down at the post office. We keep a file of the mailing addresses of all our employees— or past employees in Mitch's case."

Joan's stomach fluttered, and she took a deep breath to control the excitement in her voice. "Sure, give me his mailing address. I just hope the post office people don't bend the photograph. You know how they are about stuffing mail into those little boxes."

The secretary laughed and read Mitch's address off to Joan. "Thank you, dear," Joan said. "You've been most helpful."

"Happy to help the polio cause. Don't mention it."

*You can be sure I won't,* Joan thought, hanging up with a smile.

James Carmody was the Shoreham's general manager. He was meticulously neat, from the trim of his thinning brown hair to the cut of his charcoal gray three-piece suit. He was also most concerned for the welfare of his guests, even when those guests were FBI agents investigating a crime.

"Please let me or any member of staff know of anything you need, Agent Wainwright," he said when Corey came calling Monday afternoon. "Although the theft didn't actually occur on our premises, we want to help find those responsible and ensure they receive their just desserts."

Corey was seated in a comfortable bottle-green leather arm chair in Carmody's executive office, tucked away behind the Shoreham's front desk.

"I appreciate your cooperation. I'd like to see the room where the money was counted, and also walk around the ballroom itself, just to get a feel for things."

"Of course."

"I'd also like to take a look at your guest registrations for the entire weekend."

"You'll be discreet?"

"I promise."

"I'll have the ledger brought in. You can use my desk." Carmody stood. "I don't really spend much time in here," he gestured at the surroundings. "My work takes place throughout the hotel, from the suites and bed chambers to the kitchens and grounds and so forth. So, make yourself at home. If you need me, let one of the desk clerks know and they can track me down."

Within ten minutes, Corey had buried his nose deep into a leather-bound hotel ledger listing the names and addresses of weekend patrons. Comparing the ledger to the list of donors Casey Malloy had provided, Corey identified two men in whom he had further interest. One of the two, either Wallace DeWitt of New York or Kevin Dowd of Lancaster, Pennsylvania, was likely the man Joan Roswell had been talking with when Missy summoned her to the counting room.

Corey closed the ledger and left it sitting on top of Carmody's desk. He walked down the narrow corridor and out to the hotel's main reception desk.

"Yes sir," a bright-eyed young man in a blue hotel blazer greeted him with a smile.

"I'm Agent Wainwright with the FBI. Mr. Carmody said to let you know if I needed anything."

"Yes sir. How can I help?"

"I was wondering if Miss Roswell is still staying here. According to your register, she was here over the weekend."

"Oh, yes," the young man replied quickly. "Miss Roswell is still here." He turned and checked the wall of cubbyholes behind the desk. "Her key is in her box, so she must be out at the moment. Would you like to leave a message for her?"

Corey hesitated and then reached into the front pocket of his vest. "Here," he said, handing one of his cards to the desk clerk. "Just give her my card when she comes back."

"Very good, sir."

Corey thanked the clerk and began to wander around the hotel. It was a large building, laid out in the shape of a wide "H" with beautifully manicured grounds which invited a stroll even on these short winter days. He walked into the big ballroom where workers were setting tables and chairs in place for an evening event. He navigated his way carefully through the kitchen and then exited into the hallway and found the room where the money had been counted. It was empty now, the work tables and chairs shuttled off to meet some other requirement in another of the complex's many rooms. Corey stood in the middle of the carpeted floor and looked slowly around. Nothing.

Leaving the room, he headed back into the broad corridor. He'd seen what he'd come to see, but he really hadn't found anything. He rounded the corner to the lobby and there, standing at the reception desk and reaching for her key, was Joan Roswell. Corey waited until she stepped away from the desk and sidled up next to her.

"Miss Roswell," he began, catching her off guard, "Corey Wainwright with the FBI. You may remember me."

Joan flashed her pretty smile. "Of course, I remember you, Special Agent Wainwright." She looped her arm through his and kept walking. "California get too sunny for you? You had to come east for a little winter weather?"

Corey smiled. "I'm here on business."

"Aren't we all? I'm working on a story. Something you might be interested in. I got your card, by the way. I must say I was pleasantly surprised."

"I hoped we could talk for a few minutes. You might be able to help me with my business."

"I'd be delighted to, dear," Joan purred. "You might be able to help me with mine."

Corey wasn't sure how he was going to explain the Shoreham Hotel bar bill on his expense voucher. *Well, Hoover knows Joan; he'll understand.* They had settled into a booth toward the back of the room and Joan had ordered a gin and tonic. Corey had ordered the same, "but hold the gin," he had told the waiter. "I'm working," he had explained to Joan once the waiter had departed.

"Tell me what brings you to the Shoreham?" Joan asked, inserting a Chesterfield into her ebony holder.

"I was in town for an agents' conference and Mr. Hoover pulled me out and assigned me to work on this missing money caper. I spoke with our mutual friend Miss LeHand over at the White House. She told me about the events leading up to the theft and your name came up, Miss Roswell."

"Joan, dear." She reached out and laid her hand on Corey's forearm. "Why would my name have come up?"

"Miss LeHand said you were present for the counting of the money."

"That's right. But she must have also told you that I left before she did."

"She said you mentioned another assignment." He watched as Joan slowly exhaled cigarette smoke. "Did you?"

"Perhaps. I didn't have anything to do with the theft, if that's what you're really asking, dear."

"I've never thought that you did, Miss Roswell."

"Joan, dear."

"What can you tell me about Kevin Dowd?"

"Only that I've never heard of him. Why?"

"He was a donor at the ball."

"There were lots of donors at the ball. I was interested mainly in the official party, Ginger Rogers, Postmaster Farley, and the others. I did get to speak with Mrs. Roosevelt. She's such an... interesting person, don't you think?"

"I really wouldn't know. So, you're telling me you don't know Dowd?"

Joan laughed. "That sounds almost pejorative, dear: 'you don't know Dowd!' But no. I don't."

Corey smiled. He didn't really care for Joan Roswell. She was, in his opinion, something of a bottom-feeder, and her highly embroidered account of the rescue of Missy and Ginger made him distrust her journalistic ethics as well. "How about Wallace DeWitt? What can you tell me about him?"

Joan hesitated for the briefest moment. "More than I can about Dowd, whoever he is. Wallace bought me a drink, two in fact. One before and one after."

"I'm almost afraid to ask," Corey began sheepishly. "Before and after what?"

Joan laughed again, her cheeks dimpling attractively. "His dance with Ginger Rogers, of course. Apparently, the high rollers were thus rewarded for their generosity."

"So, he's a 'high roller?'"

"He certainly appeared to be."

The waiter returned and set their drinks on the table, then quickly retreated. He'd witnessed enough romantic liaisons to know their participants tipped in direct proportion to the amount of privacy they received.

"You were in his company when Miss LeHand summoned you to the counting room?" Corey asked.

"Yes."

"And you left the counting room before Miss LeHand did?"

"That's right. Only the ladies from the White House and Ginger, of course, were still there when I left. And that, dear, was the last I saw of the money."

"Did you see this Mr. DeWitt again?"

Joan paused again, twirling her swizzle stick in the glass and jabbing at the lime slice. "Is this professional curiosity, dear, or should I be flattered?"

Corey kept his gaze even. "Purely professional."

"We spent some more time together."

"How much?"

"Enough that he couldn't have been involved in the theft of the money."

Corey circled back to the beginning and asked different questions. As he listened to Joan's answers, he compared them to what she'd already told him, searching for any discrepancies, looking for any holes that he could wiggle through to uncover some deeper conspiracy. Finally, he concluded that Joan's liaison with this Mr. DeWitt, though far from wholesome, was most likely unrelated to the crimes.

"I need to talk with your Mr. DeWitt."

"He's not mine, strictly speaking, dear. Now let me ask you some questions," she said, lighting another cigarette and signaling to the waiter for two more drinks. Her tone of voice changed, becoming distinctly business-like. "What's going on with your investigation? How many suspects have you got? What's their motive? When do you expect to make arrests?"

"You know I can't answer questions about an ongoing investigation."

"You kept me informed during that little matter on the west coast."

"You were involved as a witness in that 'little matter.' You've just told me you don't know anything about this case."

"I don't, but I need to know, and I intend to find out. I'd be ever so grateful if you would share with me, dear, but I *will* find out one way or another. And this time, Agent Wainwright, I'm not going to let myself be gagged, not by you, not by J. Edgar Hoover, and not by the President." She smiled and sat back. "This has all the earmarks of a great story—it already is a darn good one— and I'm going to see it through. Preferably with your help."

"The best I can possibly do," Corey said after a moment's consideration, "is to exchange information." He stared into Joan's green cat's eyes. "You understand how that works? You give, I give. You don't give, neither do I. And I don't mean Wallace DeWitt's shoe size. I mean information that will help me make this case."

"What if I told you that Wallace DeWitt is in town?"

# CHAPTER 26

Corey stopped by the lab on his arrival back at the Justice Department. The technician working on the case greeted him with a smile. "It's a match all right. The paint from the Chevrolet matches the paint from the Buick."

"Did the evidence team turn up anything else from the Chevy?"

"Two partials," the technician responded, "but I doubt they'll be complete enough for us to match a full fingerprint. Still, matching the paint gives you a good starting point." The tech slapped Corey on the back and returned to his work.

Corey headed upstairs, but when he reached street level, rather than continue to the fifth floor, he exited the building. He was two blocks from the Willard Hotel. *Why not take a chance and see if I can catch up with Mr. DeWitt?*

It was getting dark by the time Corey crossed the red carpet and stopped at the Willard Hotel's reception desk. "Can you connect me with Mr. Wallace DeWitt?" he asked.

The desk clerk motioned him over to a phone sitting on the corner of the reception counter. "Pick it up when it rings, sir."

Corey waited, his eyes scanning the small lobby. The phone emitted a muted ring and Corey lifted the handset. "Mr. DeWitt?"

"Yes. Who is this?"

"This is Special Agent Corey Wainwright of the Federal Bureau of Investigation. I'm in the lobby and wondered if I could speak with you for a few minutes."

"What's this about, Mr. Wheelwright?"

"Wainwright. It's about your attendance at the polio ball Thursday night. I'm sure you're aware that a rather large sum of money was stolen and that two women were kidnapped."

"Yeah. I read about that in the papers, but that's all I know about it."

"I'm not making any accusations, Mr. DeWitt. I'm talking with some people who attended the ball and just trying to piece together what you might have seen with the observations of others who were there."

"I've got some plans this evening, Mr. Wainwright. How much time to you need?"

"Thirty minutes, tops."

"All right. I'll be down in five minutes. Why don't we meet in the bar?"

Wallace DeWitt was a handsome if slightly overweight man, dressed in what Corey took for a custom-tailored suit. Corey guessed he was in his mid-thirties, with wavy, blonde hair and heavily lidded blue eyes, which gave him a look of sleepiness that Corey quickly decided was deceptive.

"Mr. DeWitt," Corey said, standing up from the table and extending his hand. "Corey Wainwright. Thanks for meeting with me."

"Sure. Happy to help, though as I told you on the phone, I don't really know anything."

The two men sat down, and Corey caught the eye of a waiter. "What can I get you, sir?" he asked.

"Scotch on the rocks," DeWitt said.

"Tonic water for me," Corey added. Once the waiter had returned to the bar, Corey sized up his companion. "What got you interested in the Birthday Ball, Mr. DeWitt?"

"Well, it seemed like a fun way to help a good cause. I get to come down to Washington, which I've always thought was a beautiful town, and rub shoulders with the elite." DeWitt smiled. "And who doesn't want to cure polio, after all?"

"A mutual acquaintance of ours said that she talked with you toward the end of the event."

"Who's that?"

"Joan Roswell."

DeWitt eyed Corey warily. "How do you know Joan?"

"Only professionally. We worked on a case together last fall out in California."

"You from California?"

"San Francisco," Corey answered with a nod.

"What brings you to D.C.?"

"I was here for an agents' conference and Mr. Hoover assigned me to this case."

"Hmm." DeWitt nodded. "So, what can I tell you? I was having a drink with Joan. She got up and left with some other lady to go watch them count the money. I finished my drink and then went up to my room."

"But you saw Joan again later, right?"

DeWitt shifted in his chair and leveled his eyes on Corey. The sleepy effect disappeared entirely. "What are you getting at, pal?"

"She said that she was with you again for a time after the counting was done and the money was taken away."

"She was with me for 'a time,' as you say, but I don't know anything about when they finished counting the money or when it was taken away."

The waiter returned with the drinks and set them on the table. "Shall I run a tab?" he asked.

"No, here," DeWitt said pulling a dollar bill from his pocket. "Keep the change." DeWitt turned his attention back toward his questioner. "I'd like to be able to help you, Mr. Wainwright, but I don't know anything about the missing money, or about the kidnapping of those two women. I don't even seem to know very much about Joan, come to think of it. I can't imagine why she would send you hunting for me. She—and you—obviously have the wrong idea about me." DeWitt pushed his chair back.

Corey reached quickly into his pocket. "Like I said, Mr. DeWitt, I'm just talking to people who were there. Here's my card. If you think of anything that might be helpful, please call me."

"What's the big idea sending the FBI after me?" Wallace DeWitt asked Joan Roswell an hour later, after they'd been seated at the Old Ebbitt Grill a few blocks from the Willard on F Street. "What did you tell that G-man?"

"Relax, darling," Joan cooed with a smile. "I only told him what anybody who was there could have reported: you and I shared a couple of drinks, then I left."

"Yeah, but you told him we saw each other later."

"I'm your alibi, darling, don't you see? I vouch for you, you vouch for me. It's really quite convenient."

Wallace poked out his lips and nodded. "I guess it is at that."

"Now relax. We have a big night ahead of us." Joan smiled.

# CHAPTER 27

"Our friend expects a bombshell any time now," Henry Bowman said. It was Monday night, and he and Owen Knox were sitting by the window of the Deacon's room in the Hay-Adams Hotel in Washington. Knox was reviewing the text of a speech he planned to give the next evening at a memorial dinner for Huey Long. Knox had considered Long, the fiery Louisiana politician, to be the most passionate, forceful, and effective advocate for the working man until his assassination the previous fall. Knox often said that society tore down its best while leaving the greedy and corrupt in power.

"What kind of 'bombshell'?" Knox replied, looking up from his pages.

"The kind that will reflect poorly on our adversary."

Knox snorted. "That shouldn't take much effort." He returned his attention to the script, which he continued to edit with the aid of a blue pencil. "I don't understand why the people don't see through Roosevelt's masquerade. He pretends to be the friend of the common man, but he's the richest man to ever hold the office. He has no comprehension of the daily trials real people face."

"That's a good line: 'no comprehension of the daily trials…' You should use that in your speech."

"Maybe I will."

The trip south, despite the warmer weather and the escape from the icy winds lashing Chicago's hardscapes, had plunged the Deacon into a darker mood. Maybe it was confronting the absence of Long or the lack of a satisfying alternative to Roosevelt, Henry thought. He attempted to lighten his boss's mood. "Donations are up," Henry said, glancing at Knox. "Your message is resonating with the public. They're voting with their dimes and quarters and dollars."

"Up how much?"

"Eight percent better than last week."

"How much do we need to run a candidate for president?" Knox stopped his editing and stared at Henry.

Henry let out a slow whistle. "Now that's a question." He scratched out some quick figures in his notebook, squinting through his glasses. "If Long was still in play, we could supplement his campaign pretty effectively."

"Well, he's not."

"Right, he's not." Henry quickly looked up in response to Knox's curt tone and met his eyes. "He's not, so we'd have to realize a ten-fold increase in our donations and we'd have to move quickly to field a candidate and get him on the ballots in enough states to make a difference. You're really talking about a completely different strategy, Deacon. I mean one that would be taking our efforts to a whole new level. Funding Long was one thing. Running our own candidate? Well, that's a much bigger and more expensive undertaking. We'd have to find a pot of big money to go along with the nickel-and-dime stuff we're getting. And we'd have to find a viable candidate. And we'd have to do all of it pretty darn fast."

Knox sat quietly for a moment, staring out the window toward Lafayette Square. "I want to see a plan, Henry." He shifted his gaze to his assistant. "Lay out what we have to do, how fast, and how much it's going to cost. I want to study it on the train."

"I'm not sure I can get that done that fast, Deacon."

"The Lord and I have faith in you, Henry."

# TUESDAY, FEBRUARY 4, 1936

# CHAPTER 28

"Oh my God!" Missy moaned when she saw Page 3 of the *Herald*. She was still in bed, propped up on the pillows. A White House maid had just delivered her morning coffee and orange juice, along with an assortment of newspapers. When she opened the *Herald*, she almost spilled her juice on the pink chenille bedspread.

*How ridiculous*, she thought, *wasting five columns of newsprint on a harmless gag*. But, to Cissy Patterson, Missy knew this was no gag at all—it was hardball politics. The *Herald's* notorious gossip page featured a large reproduction of the photograph taken at the President's private birthday party, the one in which Missy, Grace, and other female members of the staff—not to mention the First Lady—had donned the garb of Vestal Virgins and had been arrayed around the President, himself costumed as a Caesar. It had all been in good fun, but now the fun would be enjoyed by the President's opponents and at Franklin Roosevelt's expense.

She quickly opened the morning's editions of the *Washington Post* and the New York *Daily News*. Fortunately, Missy sighed, their headlines were focused on a debate in the League of Nations about placing an oil embargo on Italy to thwart Mussolini's conquest in Africa. Climbing out of bed, she hastily donned a blue wool dress with white collar and cuffs, pinned her long hair into a roll at the back of her head, dabbed on a bit of lipstick, and headed downstairs, the *Herald* under her arm.

Missy halted in front of the President's bedroom door and shot a worried look at the attending Secret Service agent. "Is he awake, Mike?"

"Yes, ma'am. Irvin went in about five minutes ago." Irwin McDuffie was the President's valet. He had once observed that FDR could work five men to death while never leaving his bed.

Missy knocked on the door. She heard a shout from within and pushed the door open.

"Mr. President?"

"Good morning, Missy!" Roosevelt sang out from his bed. "You're just in time." Irwin stood by the foot of the bed where he had laid out three options from the President's closet. "I'm thinking of going with the blue suit and the red tie. What do you think?"

"I think after you see Page 3 of the *Herald*, you'll be seeing red, all right."

Roosevelt cast a quizzical look at his secretary and held out his hand. Taking the paper from Missy, he snapped it open. Missy waited for the eruption.

Roosevelt let the newspaper fall into his lap. "I'll let you know when I'm ready to dress, Irwin."

"Yes, Mr. President," the valet replied, and quietly left the room.

When the door closed, Roosevelt began to steam. "Now, why would the editor of a newspaper want to run fluff like this? We've got the Italians in Ethiopia, the Japanese in China, and the Germans rattling their sabers at every neighbor they've got, and Cissy Patterson wants to play games with a private picture from an old man's birthday party. What's newsworthy about that?" He slapped the picture with the back of his hand.

"She just wants to make you look bad. She's got her axe to grind. Everybody understands that."

"No, not everybody. Some poor souls will think that because it's splashed across the pages of a newspaper—even if that paper is the *Herald*—that it must be important. And you know just about every paper in the country will pick it up from here." Roosevelt wagged his finger at Missy. "Mark my words, our opponents will be making hay out of this for weeks to come, big bales of it! How did she get hold of this thing in the first place?"

"I don't know, F.D."

"Has Steve Early seen this? Find him, please, and bring him up here to see me. I want to get to the bottom of this. We can't have our trusted associates stealing photographs and giving them to the enemy. I want a full investigation." Missy headed to the door, eager to find the press secretary and turn this mess over to him.

"Missy," the President called out as she put her hand on the doorknob. "You looked lovely in your toga!"

By the time Missy returned with Steve Early, the President had dressed. He'd stuck with the blue suit, but had opted for a jaunty navy polka-dot bow tie.

"Steve," Roosevelt began as soon as Early arrived, "I want an investigation. I want to know how this picture," he stabbed at the newspaper photo with his finger, "ended up in this paper and I want the offenders keel-hauled!"

"I will certainly investigate the leak on our end—it had to come from Mike Wanner's dark room—but I don't think I'm the best person to demand answers from the *Herald*, Mr. President."

"You're the press secretary, aren't you?"

"Yes sir, but my job is to work *with* the press, not police them. If we start digging into this kind of monkey business every time it comes up, we'll never have the time—or the goodwill of the reporters—to promote our message. I can't cultivate trust with these men on the one hand and be snooping around behind them on the other."

Roosevelt paused and stared toward the ceiling. "You're starting to sound like a lawyer, poor soul. I understand your reluctance, but I want you to understand that I mean for this kind of nonsense to stop. It's a distraction at best and if the wrong thing leaked out—

diplomatic negotiations, for example—real damage could be done. I want to know how this got out and who was behind it."

Steve glanced at Missy and shrugged his shoulders. "You know Ambassador Bullitt is old friends with Cissy Patterson," he said hesitantly. "I've heard they have a history that goes way back. Why don't you ask him to pay a call on her? He might be able to sweet-talk some information out of her."

"Missy?" the President said. "Is that okay by you?"

"No objection from me, F.D." she said staunchly. She knew about the ambassador's romantic history with Cissy, which he insisted was old news.

"It's settled then. Work him into my calendar sometime today and let's figure out how to deflect this distraction," the President said, holding up the newspaper. "I needed to see him anyway to hear him rant and rave about the Russians. But, Steve, you've got a leak somewhere in your press office. That photograph didn't just walk out of the White House on its own. I want you and Missy to work on that end of it together."

"Yes sir!" Steve and Missy said.

"Well, here they are," Mike Wanner pointed to a stack of photos covered by a piece of heavy paper on the corner of his desk. "I made a print for each person in the picture, including the President, and then one additional print for my files. I keep one print of a shot unless it's no good. You know, like if I take the President's picture and his eyes are closed or he's got a goofy expression on his face."

"And they're all here?" Steve asked.

"Yes sir, nineteen copies."

"And the negative?"

"In the file cabinet in the dark room. I keep all the negatives, even of the pictures we don't use. You never know, right?"

"Hmmm. And no one's removed a copy? All the prints you made are accounted for?" Missy asked.

"Yes ma'am." *At least as far as you know*, Mike thought.

"Could anyone else have gotten access to the dark room and made a print without you knowing about it?" Missy asked.

Mike stroked his tiny moustache. "Well, I guess that's possible. Theoretically. I mean, I keep the place locked up when I'm not here. I don't want people coming in here and messing around, you know. I've got chemicals and light-sensitive film and paper in there." He jerked his thumb toward the neighboring dark room. "Somebody doesn't know what he's doing could make a real mess."

Missy thought a moment. "Do you have the only key?"

"I doubt it. The head usher has keys to everything."

"I guess we should talk to him," Steve said. "Mike, can you think of anyone who has come to see you, I mean out of the ordinary?"

"Not off hand," Mike said. "I don't get many visitors here. You know I'm kind of a mole in my hole here, unless I'm out taking pictures."

"I'll check with the Secret Service log at the gate," Missy said. "Thanks, Mike, we'll be back to see you if anything turns up. And get the rest of those pictures under lock and key!"

Mike smiled to himself. *A lot of good that will do. That's locking the door after the horse has escaped from the barn.*

# CHAPTER 29

"I have to go to a banquet tonight," Wallace DeWitt said as he and Joan Roswell shared a room service breakfast of bacon, eggs, grits, biscuits, orange juice, and coffee. "You interested?"

"What a romantic invitation," Joan said with a sleepy smile. The couple had shared another energetic night. Joan's hips were still sore. "Can I let you know later? I've got some work to do today and I don't know how long it's going to take."

"Sure," Wallace said, refilling her coffee from the silver decanter. "I'll be out most of the day on business. Just leave a message for me at the desk." He looked into Joan's green eyes. "I hope you can make it. I'd love to see you again tonight."

"Aren't you the Romeo!" Joan tittered.

By 10 a.m., Joan was showered, dressed, and standing in the lobby of the massive marble post office building at the corner of North Capitol Street and Massachusetts Avenue, just across from Union Station. She had donned a plain gray wool coat "borrowed" from the cloak room at the Shoreham, a black beret covered her blonde hair, and she wore her most comfortable shoes. She couldn't know how long she would be on her feet.

From her vantage point in the post office's long lobby, Joan maintained a view of a bank of the building's mail boxes, in particular the wall containing Box 2213, the mailing address of one Mitchell Novak. According to the postal clerk she'd spoken to on the phone the previous day, the box mail was put up every morning between ten-thirty and noon. Joan figured it was unlikely that Novak would show up before that, but who really knew? Rather than run the risk of missing him, she decided to take up watch early.

After leaving Wallace DeWitt's room, she had gone back to the Shoreham to freshen up and change. On her way out, the desk clerk had handed her a Western Union envelope. She'd stuffed it in her pocket; she had a pretty good idea who it was from. Now, standing at a writing counter in the lobby, she pulled the envelope from her pocket and opened it. As she had suspected, it was a message from her boss.

## SEND MORE RE THEFT STOP BILLY

*That's exactly what I'm working on, dear*, Joan thought. If her hunch played out, Joan would have the last laugh. And if it didn't, well, she wouldn't be the only person in America out of work.

# CHAPTER 30

In her West Wing office, Missy opened the black-bound ledger book on her desk. The "Hail, Caesar" picture was taken on Thursday, January 30 and ran in the *Herald* on the morning of Tuesday, February 4. That meant she had to review four days of gate logs maintained by the Secret Service's Uniformed Division. Visitors' names were printed in the left-hand column; their business or government office came next; followed by the office they were visiting within the mansion's complex; the time in; and, lastly, the time out.

On Friday, January 31st, she noted that a Mr. Wallace DeWitt had visited Mike Wanner. Her eyes flicked to the left. DeWitt's business was listed as DeWitt Southern. Wallace DeWitt. Missy's heart jumped in her chest. DeWitt! She was almost sure that was the man she had met talking to Joan Roswell.

She hurried over to the press office and, finding Steve Early gone, knocked on the dark room door. "Mike? Are you in there?"

"Just a minute," came a muffled voice.

When Mike emerged, wiping his hands on a gray towel, she showed him the name on the ledger. "I think I met this man at the Birthday Ball," she said.

Mike stared at the name. "Gee, sorry, Missy, I forgot all about him. I took his picture dancing with Ginger Rogers. He came by the next day to get a copy. He was in and out pretty fast."

"Any chance he could have seen the picture of the 'Hail, Caesar' party or maybe lifted one off the stack?"

"It's like I told you before, I only printed nineteen copies; one for each person in the picture and one for the

151

file. They're all in the file." Mike gestured toward a tall, four-drawer cabinet. "And there they stay until Steve releases them."

"Once they're released, what happens to them?"

"These probably go to the President. I figure he'll sign 'em and then one of your girls will send them out. Once they leave here, I don't really worry about them anymore." *You can ask all the questions you want,* Mike thought with satisfaction. *You're never going to be able to account for one lonely piece of photo paper made into one little print.*

"And you remember this DeWitt?"

"Sure. I can even show you a copy of the picture with him and Miss Rogers if you like. I told you I keep at least one copy for the file."

"That would help, Mike. Thanks."

"The file cabinets are in here," Mike said, leading Missy into the dark room. He flipped on the overhead lights.

"I thought you had to keep it dark in here all the time?"

"Only when we're handling unexposed film or paper," Mike explained. "All that's stored in light-tight boxes and cabinets. As long as everything is put away, we've got no worries." Mike opened a file drawer and began thumbing through folders.

"What's your system for organizing photos?"

"By date. I keep a log of the events I cover each day, so I can refer to that to refresh my memory about what I shot when." He pulled a folder from the drawer. "Here we go." He lay the folder on the counter and opened it. "That's DeWitt and the one in the long dress is Rogers," he joked.

Missy studied DeWitt's face. "Yes, that's the man who was sitting with Joan Roswell. Can you make me a copy?"

"Sure," Mike said. "I'll get it to you in a few minutes."

"Thanks, Mike!" Missy said. "You're a peach. I'll be sure the P knows how helpful you've been."

Mike grinned. "Thanks, Missy. That's awful nice of you." His smile faded as she left the room.

Missy left a note on Steve Early's desk asking him to drop by and see her later in the afternoon, then had a brief chat with the head usher. Predictably, he was somewhat offended to think he or anyone on his staff might have been suspected of slipping into the dark room with a passkey in order to snatch an embarrassing photo of the President, but he promised to speak to his staff.

# CHAPTER 31

"Corey Wainwright." The agent answered his phone on the first ring.

"Agent Wainwright? Robert Trent, D.C. Police."

"Good morning, Inspector. Any news today on our thieves and kidnappers?"

"No, but I do have some information to share on a relevant topic."

"Let me grab a note pad," Corey said, shifting the phone to his left side. "All right, go ahead."

"I'd rather share this with you in person, Agent Wainwright. How well do you know our city?"

Corey chuckled. "Well, I can find the White House, the Justice Department, the train station and the Capitol. Beyond that, I'm at the mercy of whoever is driving."

"Better find a driver, then," Trent said, no trace of humor in his voice. "Meet me down by the D.C. Tree Nursery. It's on the Anacostia River. Tell your driver to cross the 11th Street Bridge by the Navy Yard and then go west on Nichols and right on Howard. I'll see you in about thirty minutes."

The D.C. Tree Nursery sat on a patch of ground right next to the U.S. Botanical Garden on the south bank of the Anacostia River. This time of year, there wasn't much activity at either location.

Corey's driver had let him off at the nursery's gate and elected to remain with the car. Corey, wearing his overcoat and fedora, walked between rows of leafless trees, their naked branches reaching up toward a gray overcast sky. As he walked, he scanned ahead for any sign of human activity. Coming over a shallow rise, he saw the

Anacostia ahead, and on its bank, several men standing over what appeared to be a sheet-shrouded body.

# CHAPTER 32

Joan continued the charade of addressing an envelope, glancing up every time anyone approached the wall containing Box 2213. By eleven-thirty, she was beginning to get sleepy as the sun splashed through the windows, creating bright pools of light on the white marble floor. By twelve-thirty, Joan's fatigue had been joined with hunger. She looked up at the large clock centered above the long service counter. Several dozen people were scattered among five or six lines, all waiting to buy a stamp, mail a letter, pick up a parcel, or transact some other business with the Post Office Department.

The reporter turned her attention back to her surveillance just as a short, dark-haired woman wearing a shabby red coat approached Box 2213. Joan held her breath as the woman reached into her pocket and took out a ring of keys. She selected a small brass key, fitted it into the locked box, turned it to the right and pulled the door open. The woman removed several letter-size envelopes from the box along with what appeared to be a rolled-up newspaper. She pushed the door closed, pocketed the keys, and turned toward the North Capitol Street exit. Joan followed from a distance, her pulse accelerating, her breathing more rapid.

Out on the sidewalk, Joan trailed behind, maintaining a discreet distance and hoping that the red coat would lead her to Mitch Novak. *Then I'll have a story, one way or another*, she thought.

The woman crossed the street and walked directly toward the row of municipal buses queued up outside Union Station. She climbed aboard the second bus. Joan dug through her purse searching for change and followed.

Dropping her fare in the coin box, Joan made her way down the narrow aisle. Halfway back on the left sat her quarry. Joan settled into a seat directly behind the woman and tried to relax. *So far, so good.*

The bus pulled out of the queue, passed in front of Union Station and continued east on Maryland Avenue. Joan leaned forward over the seat back and spoke softly. "I guess you're a friend of Mitch."

The woman flinched as though she'd been slapped. She didn't turn, and she didn't respond.

"It's all right, I'm a friend," Joan said.

The woman turned her head to the right, looking at Joan. "I don't know you."

"My name is Joan, dear. I'd like to talk to Mitch. I'll make it worth your while."

"You're not one of them, are you?"

"One of whom, dear?"

"The Pinkertons. Mitch said they'd come around, that they'd want to talk to him. Maybe to me too."

"And have they?"

"Not yet. Not me, anyway."

"Have they talked to Mitch?"

"I don't know. I haven't seen him since last Wednesday night."

"Where is he now, dear?"

"I don't know. You're not police, are you?"

"No, dear. I'm a reporter. I'll pay you ten dollars for Mitch's story. And I'll keep you out of it. What do you say?" Joan was grateful that Wallace had been covering the costs of many of her meals, leaving enough money from her travel advance to bribe the young woman. "All you have to do is put me in touch with Mitch. Easiest money you'll ever make. How about it?"

"This is my stop." The woman reached up and pulled the cord above her head, ringing a small bell beside the driver.

Joan reached into her purse and took out her card. She scribbled the Shoreham's phone number on it and handed it to the woman. "Call me when you're ready to talk. I promise you complete confidentiality."

The woman stared at the card for a moment. The bus slowed to a halt. She stood and stepped toward the rear door, sticking the card in her coat pocket. The bus pulled away from the curb in a cloud of acrid, gray smoke.

Joan watched through the rear window as the woman climbed up the steps and disappeared inside a nondescript apartment building on West Virginia Avenue.

# CHAPTER 33

Inspector Robert Trent was slightly shorter than Corey, with rounded shoulders and thinning brown hair combed over his bald pate. He had an intelligent face bearing the lines of one who'd seen his share of the inhumanity man could work on his fellow beings.

He shook Corey's hand with a cold, firm grip and guided the agent toward the white sheet. Trent squatted and moved the rock holding the corner of the sheet against the wind from the river. He pulled the sheet back to reveal the pale, bloated face of a corpse.

"Recognize him?"

"No sir," Corey replied.

"No reason you would after he'd spent the last few days in the river," Trent said, returning the sheet and the rock to their places. He stood and dusted off his hands. "That's Mitchell Novak, late of the Pinkertons."

Corey's eyebrows shot upward. "You're sure?"

"About ninety percent. We found an old Maryland driver's license in his wallet. We'll get your boys to check his fingerprints. As a Pinkerton employee, he would have been printed and his record forwarded to your files. Frankly, I'll be surprised if that's not him. He's the link to the theft of that money and may have been involved with the kidnapping as well. Whoever pulled this caper would have wanted him to disappear."

"Did he drown?"

"Probably. The coroner will have to determine the cause of death, but I've seen a few of these over the years. To me, it looks like somebody bashed in the back of his head and then tossed him in for a swim."

"Can you do me a favor?" Corey asked.

"Probably."

"Can you hold off releasing his identity for a couple of days? If the killer knows that we know Novak is dead, he's bound to be a little more cautious. I don't want him to be cautious; I want him to be careless."

"Sure. We'll list him as a 'John Doe' for a couple of days. Any objection to letting the Pinkertons know? They don't need to waste any more manpower staking out this poor guy's apartment."

"No. No objection. What's next on your end, Inspector?"

"Now we get a warrant to search his apartment. See if anything of value turns up there. Maybe he left a detailed log of his dealings with the perpetrators of this outrage."

"You think that's likely?"

"Not a chance. Forgive me, Agent Wainwright. Sometimes I get a little sarcastic."

# CHAPTER 34

Missy returned to her office a little after one. A covered tray sat on her desk, but she had little interest in the cup of broth and crackers under the chrome lid. Dialing Louise Hackmeister, the White House's personable switchboard operator, she asked her to track down Casey Malloy from the President's Birthday Ball Committee.

The phone rang a few minutes later and an eager young man's voice spoke her name. "Good afternoon, Mr. Malloy," she said. "How are you?"

"I will be feeling wonderful if you tell me there's been a break in the case," Casey said hopefully.

"Oh, I wish I could," Missy said. "We've got a very capable FBI agent working on it, plus the local police, but nothing definitive has turned up yet."

Casey sighed. "You don't know what it's like to deal with the women on this Birthday Ball Committee," he confided. "Someone is calling me every five minutes, swearing their reputations are being ruined over this thing and they'll become social pariahs if the money isn't found."

"Oh, dear. I promise I'll let you know as soon as we know something," Missy said. "Actually, I need some help on a different matter. There is a fellow named Wallace DeWitt who was at the ball, apparently a big spender. He was one of the men who got a dance with Ginger Rogers. I need to get in touch with him."

"Mr. DeWitt? Oh, sure. President of DeWitt Southern. He's got an office in New York, at the Empire State Building." Missy heard Casey shuffling papers, and soon he was giving her a phone number.

"Thanks, Casey. And I promise, you'll be the second one to know when we recover the money."

"Who'll be the first?"

"Why, the President, of course."

Missy returned the handset to the phone's cradle, smiling at her little joke, and the phone almost immediately rang again.

"Missy? It's Corey Wainwright."

"Oh, hello, Corey! How are you? Any news?"

"Well, yes, as a matter of fact. Remember that bet we had about the Pinkerton agent? You owe me lunch, if it's not too late in the day. Can we meet somewhere we can speak without being overheard?"

"What about my sitting room?" Missy said. "I'll get the kitchen to send us up some sandwiches. Which do you prefer, tuna salad or chicken salad?"

"Chicken," Corey said. "I'll be there in fifteen minutes."

Missy's sitting room was comfortably appointed with a couch, a chintz-covered slipper chair, a coffee table, desk, and a book case filled with autographed books given to her by visitors to the White House. They ranged from biographies and detective novels, which she devoured, to weighty tomes she would likely never crack, all personally inscribed. When a White House usher arrived with Corey Wainwright, she had just had time to plump the pillows on her couch, freshen her lipstick, and close the door to her bedroom.

"Very nice!" Corey said, looking around. "This is much more pleasant than my place in Frisco. I'll have to hire you as my interior decorator."

Missy laughed. "I'm afraid I don't travel outside my jurisdiction." She looked around the room, giving it a critical eye. "It's very convenient for me to be so close to work since I'm called on at all sorts of crazy hours. It's also kind of a refuge when members of the staff need a place to blow off steam."

They had just gotten settled on the couch when a maid arrived with a tray of sandwiches and two glasses of iced tea. "Thanks, Dorothy," Missy said. "I appreciate the quick response."

The sandwiches were made with soggy white bread and garnished with anemic-looking dill pickle slices. The two looked for a moment at the dismal fare, and finally Corey picked up a sandwich and took a bite. "Well," he said after a moment. "I've had worse."

"Really?" Missy asked. "I can't imagine where."

"On the Italian front during the war," he replied, eyes twinkling.

"Oh, you," she laughed, picking up a sandwich of her own. "Tell me what you've found out."

"Well, if you haven't already lost your appetite, what I've got to tell you may do the job," Corey said. Missy laid down her sandwich.

Corey told her about finding the body of Mitchell Novak. "I hate to collect a bet this way, Missy, but it looks like this guy was in on the heist and was knocked off because he knew too much."

Missy's face paled. "Oh, dear."

"I was down at the river with a detective from the D.C. Police. They'd just fished him out," he explained. "You can see why I asked for the chicken salad instead of the tuna."

That made Missy laugh—a little. "That poor man," she said. "What will you do going forward?"

"Well, the D.C. Police will work with the FBI fingerprint lab to make a hundred percent identification. Then they will search his apartment. They'll undoubtedly question his co-workers, try to find out if he has family or friends, someone he confided in. They'll keep me in the loop," Corey said, picking up his sandwich again. "They aren't going to release his name for a couple of days, so keep this under your hat. Oh, and we did get a match of the paint sample from your car. It was definitely a stolen vehicle, found abandoned in Virginia, that ran you off the road. It's a gray Chevrolet."

"I wish I could say I remember the color and make," Missy said, shaking her head, "but it was such a shock and it happened so fast, plus it was dark. I just didn't take it in."

The two sat quietly for a few minutes, chewing their sandwiches. Missy thought about confiding in Corey about the investigation she was making into the "Hail, Caesar" party picture, but decided to keep it to herself. It wasn't a criminal matter, after all, and best kept within the White House "family."

Corey eyed her over his sandwich, admiring her graceful figure and the lovely line of her neck, the quick upturn of her face when he spoke. Then Missy's stomach growled. "I'm sorry," she giggled. "This sandwich is just inedible."

"Do you have dinner plans?" he asked.

# CHAPTER 35

By the time Ambassador William C. Bullitt walked into the Oval Office late that afternoon, evening newspapers all up and down the eastern seaboard were running the picture of "Franklin Caesar."

"Bill, what can be done about this?" the President asked, holding up that morning's edition of the *Herald*.

"I could go talk to Cissy, if you like, Mr. President."

"That's right, you're old friends with her, aren't you?"

"Yes sir, I knew her way back before she emptied all the brains from her head and became a Republican," Bullitt said.

Roosevelt chortled. "I see I've called the right man to the task." He leaned forward, lacing his hands together on top of his desk. "Now, listen, Bill. I want this handled quickly and quietly. It can't look like a witch hunt against the press—or even a certain witch in the press—as appealing as that sounds. I want to find out how she got the picture. Our objective here is less about silencing critics than it is about plugging leaks. I'm appointing you as my chief plumber!"

Bullitt's face split into a toothsome smile. "I'll go find a plunger and get right to work!"

"Now, tell me about the Russians," the President said. "It sounds like Stalin is showing his true colors, and I don't just mean red."

The ambassador's smile disappeared, and he spit out his words like bullets. "I think Stalin intends to eat like a cancer through Europe and that he hopes in the end Germany will go Bolshevik and France and England will follow. I have no doubt he is already making plans for our side of the Atlantic."

"Do you really think he's planting agents here, on our shores?" Roosevelt asked.

"He stated it plainly at the Third Communist International meeting—the Comintern—during the summer," Bullitt said. "The new plan is called the Popular Front. He's got agents, both American and Russian, infiltrating harmless organizations here and turning them bright red. Trade unions, for example. Any group that professes to be anti-Fascist and anti-Nazi. Even that American Youth Congress the First Lady is so fond of."

The President grunted. He wasn't a fan of the American Youth Congress.

Bullitt paused. "Mr. President, I wouldn't put it past the Russians to try to influence the election this year. They could try to oust you in favor of someone farther to the left. Or even someone on the far right, an extreme isolationist, for example. They'd back anyone they could use as a rallying point for a violent overthrow of the government of the United States."

FDR tapped his newspaper. "Maybe I should look at this photo leak as something more than a nuisance. Do you think the Russians could have something to do with that, trying to make me look bad as part of their strategy?"

"I wouldn't put it past them," Bullitt said. "They are devious people and Stalin has shown he'll stop at nothing to achieve domination."

The two men stared at each other across the President's desk, then Bullitt slapped his knees and stood up. "Time's of the essence," he said. "I think I'll go by Cissy's house tonight, catch her early before she's had too many martinis."

"Ha!" the President said. "It might be a better idea to catch her after she's had a few. Might make her more likely to let something slip."

"True," the ambassador said. "By the way, where is Missy? I went by her office a few minutes ago but she wasn't there."

"I don't know, Bill," the President said blandly, knowing perfectly well that Missy had gone out to dinner with Corey Wainwright. "I've kept her pretty busy trying to track down how that Caesar picture got out of the White House. I'll let her know you asked."

# CHAPTER 36

Joan Roswell was standing in front of her bathroom mirror appraising her eyebrows when the phone rang. She set down her eyebrow pencil and crossed the bedroom.

"Hello."

"Is this Joan?" a woman's voice asked.

"Yes. Who's speaking?"

"We shared a bus ride today."

Joan froze for a moment. "Yes, of course, dear. You've considered my offer, I take it?"

"I need to see you. Right away." The woman's voice quavered.

"Why, that would be lovely, dear. Would you like to come to my hotel? We could sit in the bar."

"No. There's a Forsman's Pharmacy at the corner of Seventh and L. Meet me there at six-forty-five, at the soda counter. And come alone. You promised everything would be confidential."

"It will be, dear. You have my word." The call was disconnected, and Joan stared at the handset for a moment. *So much for my date.* Joan pressed down and then released the receiver. The hotel operator answered.

"Connect me with the Willard Hotel, please." When the Willard front desk answered, she asked to be put through to Mr. DeWitt's room.

"Hello."

"Wallace, darling, it's Joan. I hate it when work gets in the way of a good time, but I'm afraid I'm going to have to stand you up tonight."

"Sorry to hear that," Wallace replied, and Joan was pleased that she could hear disappointment in his voice.

"Any chance we can meet up later, catch a late drink or something?"

"It's the 'something' I'll look forward to, darling. I'll call you later. In the meantime, behave yourself."

The seat next to Wallace at the banquet table was empty, but Constitution Hall was otherwise filled to capacity. Wallace had enjoyed the company of the three couples at his table, including an attractive brunette from Virginia who had entertained him with her stories of living on a peanut farm. Round tables like theirs filled the hall, which was draped with red, white, and blue bunting. A ten-piece band had played patriotic music during dinner, but now Deacon Owen Knox stood upon the dais, his fists striking the lectern as he thundered forth criticism after criticism, complaint after complaint concerning the current occupant of 1600 Pennsylvania Avenue.

"...He has no comprehension of the daily trials of the very people he professes to govern! He sits just blocks away in the People's House, a palace that further insulates this scion of wealth and privilege from the common citizens of our republic. He attends lavish formal dinners while so many among us scramble desperately to scrounge a loaf of bread for our children. He is attended to by a staff of hundreds, by a bureaucracy of thousands, and to what end? So that he can make life better for those ravaged by this economic disaster? Or for the speculators and money-changers who caused the disaster, the same people who now lift up his candidacy for a second term?"

Applause from an excited audience interrupted the tirade, allowing Knox a moment to sip from a water glass hidden on a shelf of the lectern.

*He's pretty good*, Wallace had to admit. When Al Smith had suggested that Wallace attend the dinner, he had been less than enthusiastic. "You'll enjoy the show,"

Smith had said, grinning. "Who knows, maybe you'll pick up something we can use."

"You're not suggesting we work together with Knox, are you, Al?"

Smith had laughed. "I don't think we'd find much common ground with that socialist. The only difference between him and Stalin is that he believes in Jesus."

"And he doesn't have people shot," Wallace had added. But as Wallace now sat, toying with his chocolate cake, he appreciated the passion and the power of the Deacon's message.

Knox was holding up a newspaper, presenting it to the crowd. "Now comes Franklin Caesar, surrounded by his sycophants, already preparing his bid to become dictator. It isn't enough that Caesar appoints his supporters to government jobs in every community across the country—"

Wallace's ears perked up.

"—he then diverts their time and energies away from official duties to plan social activities, events to which his people, his affluent supporters, are invited...are invited to dance the night away in splendid ballrooms while their neighbors, proud men and women who desire nothing more than an honest job, huddle around a fire, their bellies growling as they watch their children sleep wrapped in a blanket on the ground and ponder how they will feed these children when they awaken.

"And they dance—and he gloats. And they drink—because Caesar, like his predecessors of ancient Rome, has a fondness for the mind-numbing, soul-destroying vice of alcohol. And they party—dressing in their silly, frilly costumes that mock the condition of the multitudes."

Al Smith had been right: Wallace was enjoying the show.

"'But, Deacon,' you may argue, 'these parties, they raised money to help stamp out a dreadful disease, one that brings misery and suffering to thousands. Surely,' you say, 'surely this is a worthy cause. Surely we should look beyond callous frivolity to the good that results?' I say: what good? What good resulted from this bacchanalian extravagance—an orgy of self-congratulation and deception?"

Wallace snorted, then covered his reaction with a cough. There hadn't been any orgy at the Shoreham event.

"Yes, friends! Deception. Where, oh great Caesar, is the money? It was stolen by thieves? Truly? Stolen from under the nose of the most powerful man in the country? Stolen from the first American dictator? Stolen—or dumped into Caesar's growing campaign chest?

"My friends, we cannot sit idly by and let Franklin Caesar march on our country as Julius Caesar marched on Rome. We cannot allow him to sweep aside his political foes under an avalanche of agencies that exist to consolidate power in the hands of the government—in his hands!" Knox was pounding his left fist on the podium as his words reverberated around the hall.

"Every day that we rest, every day that we delay, every day that we wait for a new hero to arise, brings us a day closer to the death of individual liberty. Friends, we must unite to stop Caesar! We must form a united front to resist the concentration of so much awesome power in the hands of one man, one corrupt and venal man." Knox fell silent. He mopped his high, pale brow with a white handkerchief. The great hall was so quiet that for a moment, Wallace had the wild notion that he was alone.

"We, my friends," Knox resumed quietly, his voice barely audible, "we must put a stop to the machinations of this power-hungry egomaniac. And we will begin by asking one simple question: Where's the money, Mr. President? Where is it? What have you done with it?"

Knox paused again, his wide eyes sweeping the audience. "Will you join me? Will you rally to the banner of freedom? Will you stand and take back our country? Will you ask the question?"

The crowd began to stir, to rumble.

"Where's the money, Mr. President?" Knox thundered. "Where's the money, Mr. President?"

The crowd picked up the chant as men and women rose from their seats around the banquet tables. People began clapping their hands and stomping their feet in time with Knox's cadence. "Where's the money, Mr. President?"

The phrase was repeated over and over, faster and faster, flushed faces beaming at the sweating figure on the dais. The words began to tumble together, tripping over each other until all that Wallace could discern was a throaty roar, like the crashing of a hundred waves on the beach.

*I'll bet they can hear this at the White House,* Wallace thought with a bemused grin.

The band members at the side of the stage picked up their instruments and launched into a tune. Wallace could only pick out the highest notes at first, and many in the wailing sea of faces were unaware that the band was even playing. Eventually the peanut farm woman opposite Wallace began to sing. After a few measures, the others at his table joined in.

"...Christ, the royal Master, leads against the foe, forward into battle, see his banners go. Onward, Christian soldiers marching as to war, with the cross of Jesus going on before."

*Hell of a show,* Wallace thought.

# CHAPTER 37

An accident had snarled traffic at Thomas Circle. Joan, fidgeting in the back seat, had finally paid off the cabbie and stepped out of the taxi. Rather than run the risk of missing her appointment, she decided to walk the last six blocks. She walked as quickly as her black heels would allow, jaywalking across two intersections as she kept a wary eye on her watch.

Despite her exertions, it was almost seven o'clock by the time she walked into Forsman's Pharmacy. Joan strode toward the lunch counter at the back of the store, breathing heavily and perspiring lightly. She reached the end of an aisle and saw the stools standing in front of the service counter. Empty.

Joan fought panic. *If I've lost this story...* From the corner of her eye, Joan saw movement. She looked to her right. The dark-haired woman, wearing the same shabby red coat, was sitting in a small booth to the right of the counter and staring at her. Joan took a deep breath, smiled, and walked over to the booth. She sat down opposite the woman.

"Good evening, dear. Shall I order us something to eat?"

The woman's brown eyes were red-rimmed and underlined by purple pouches. "I'm not hungry, but I'll take a Coca-Cola if you're buying."

"I'm buying." Joan motioned to the young man behind the counter. "Two Cokes, please." She turned her attention back to the woman. Joan removed her black gloves, opened her purse and pulled out a pack of Chesterfields. "Cigarette?"

"Don't smoke, but you go ahead."

Joan lit the cigarette with a match from the book Wallace had given her and surreptitiously studied the face of the young woman. *She's pretty, in a way. Maybe if she smiled. That's a bad blemish near her hairline, though.* "I want to repeat what I told you on the bus," Joan began, inhaling. "You share your story. I pay you ten dollars. I protect your privacy. No one knows about you from my story. Do we have a deal?"

"Deal."

The waiter set two pale green bell-shaped glasses of Coke on the table. "Get you ladies something to eat?"

Joan looked up and smiled. "Not right now, dear, thank you." The waiter lingered for a moment enjoying his pretty customer and her orange and jasmine scent, and then retreated to his counter. "Now then, let's start with something simple. Tell me your name, dear."

"Penny. Penny Jeter. My real name is Penelope but that's so old-fashioned."

Joan reached her hand across the table. "It's nice to meet you, Penny Jeter. Now tell me your story."

Penny Jeter said she had met Mitch Novak two months earlier at a YMCA Christmas dance. They'd danced a couple of times and he'd bought her a cherry Coke and they'd talked until the dance closed down. He'd asked her to the pictures and she had gone. They had dated once or twice a week since then and, according to Penny, their relationship had been "progressing."

"We weren't doing anything wrong, you understand," Penny said, a blush appearing on her face.

"I would never have thought so, dear."

"Well, on Wednesday night, we went to see that new movie, *Top Hat.* Anyway, before the show starts, he says that he's going to be working Thursday and after that he might be gone for a couple of days, but he'd get in touch..." Penny's voice faltered, her eyes staring down at the laminated table top.

"It's all right, dear. Take your time."

Penny took a tiny sip from her Coke. When she looked back up at Joan, she had tears in her brown eyes. "I haven't heard anything from him since and I'm afraid something's happened."

"Now, dear, I don't know Mitch, of course, but I know about men. They're not always as thoughtful of us women as they should be. Why, they get involved in work or they get busy living their lives and sometimes we're not at the top of their minds."

"Mitch isn't like that," Penny said, pouting. "He's very thoughtful and very considerate."

"Has he ever gone more than a few days without calling you?"

"Yes, of course, but this is different."

"Why, dear?"

"Well, he said that after Thursday, he would have enough cash that he wouldn't have to work for Pinkerton any more. He didn't really like the work."

"What didn't he like?"

"He said it was boring. He was a security guard. He'd stand around all night waiting for nothing to happen. That's what he always said, 'waiting for nothing to happen.'"

"And he thought he'd quit after Thursday?"

"Yes. He said he was going to get a bonus." Penny paused.

"What's the matter, dear?"

"He said not to tell anybody, about the bonus, I mean."

"And he expected to be paid this bonus for his work Thursday night?" Penny nodded. "And his assignment was the big polio ball at the Shoreham Hotel?"

"That's right."

"Why did he expect to get a bonus?"

"I asked him, and he said he was doing an extra service for Smith."

"'Smith'?"

"That's what he said."

"Who's 'Smith'?" Joan asked.

"I don't know. I don't even know if Mitch knew. Like I said, he told me he would be gone for a couple of days and that he'd write to me at his post office box. That's why he gave me his box key. He said when he saw me again we'd celebrate, you know, go somewhere nice for dinner or something."

"Did you ever see this 'Smith'?"

"No. I never went on any of Mitch's jobs. I never met any of the people he worked with. Not that he really worked much with anybody. Pinkerton would tell him where to go and he'd show up. It was usually just him by himself, walking around a warehouse or a motor pool or a factory all night, chasing away drunks and stray dogs."

Joan listened to Penny Jeter for another forty-five minutes, occasionally interrupting her narrative to ask a question or clarify a comment. By eight o'clock, Joan had the address to Mitch Novak's apartment—and his spare key—which he'd given to Penny for safekeeping.

"A deal's a deal," Joan said, reaching into her purse. She pulled out a ten-dollar bill and laid it on the table. Penny reached for the bill, but Joan kept her hand on top of the banknote. "When you hear from Mitch, you contact me. If anybody else calls you about Mitch, you contact me. If the police contact you, you contact me. Agreed?"

"Yes." Joan released the money. Penny slid it off the table and stuffed it in the pocket of her coat.

A few minutes later, Joan stood in front of the pharmacy and watched as Penny boarded an east-bound bus. She thought back to the previous autumn when, by being in the right place at the right time, she'd found herself in the middle of a breaking story—a story with far-reaching ramifications and great human interest, a story she had been forbidden to tell.

Despite what had happened later, a news blackout imposed by President Roosevelt himself, Joan could have broken the story of the kidnapping of Shirley Temple if she'd only had a corroborating source. Her editor, Billy Bryce, hadn't been willing to run the story on her word alone.

Now, as Joan stood on the cold street corner lighting another cigarette, she found herself in a similar position. Billy would never approve the story based on a single interview with Penny, no matter how credible Joan judged her to be. Joan had to find an additional source. Fast.

# CHAPTER 38

"Mr. DeWitt?" Wallace felt an arm on the sleeve of his brown suit jacket and turned to his left to look into the eyes of a young man in glasses. "I'm Henry Bowman, Deacon Owen Knox's assistant." Wallace shook hands with the conservatively dressed young man. "I wanted to introduce myself and make sure you got one of these." Henry held out a small white button with KNOX printed on it in bold, blue letters.

"Thank you," Wallace said, immediately pinning the button to his lapel. "Goes well with my suit, don't you think?" He smiled.

"I do, I do." Henry, his hand still on Wallace's sleeve, led him toward a corner of the still crowded hall. Out of the mingling throng of the Deacon's supporters, Henry adopted a more casual tone of voice. "I also wanted to thank you for your very generous gift of five hundred dollars. I can't tell you how meaningful your donation is or at what a good time it arrived." Henry leaned closer, turning his lips toward Wallace's ear. "Owen Knox is seriously considering a run for the Democratic nomination. Roosevelt simply isn't going to do what must be done to create economic and social justice in our country."

Wallace knew he had a role to play, but when he heard words like "economic justice" he thought about the "justice" of the government paying farmers not to grow crops, or about the "justice" of the government adjudicating contracts between business and labor. "He certainly can't stand on his record," Wallace agreed.

"Exactly! At any rate, I wanted to tell you 'thanks' on behalf of Deacon Knox and I wanted to invite you to join us for dinner next time we're in New York."

"I'd enjoy that. I'd like to meet the Deacon. I've listened to him on the radio so much, why I almost feel as though I know him."

"We're up to New York in the morning, meeting with the networks. Mutual carries our broadcasts now. They've been very good to us, but their reach is rather limited. NBC or CBS would put us in every large and medium-sized city in the country. Our message would be heard from coast-to-coast."

"I'd be happy to put in a good word with Bill Paley," Wallace offered. "We've served together on a couple of boards."

"That would be wonderful," Bowman said with a smile. "CBS would help us reach so many more Americans."

"How long will you be in the city?"

"Two nights, then back to Chicago."

"I'd be proud to stand you for dinner," Wallace said.

"We're open Thursday evening. We catch the train Friday morning."

Wallace reached into this jacket and pulled out a slender pocket calendar. "Thursday it is. Eight o'clock at Jack Dempsey's?"

"We'll see you there," Henry said, shaking Wallace's hand.

# CHAPTER 39

A butler answered the door at Cissy Patterson's imposing white mansion on Dupont Circle. He invited Ambassador Bullitt into the hall and asked him to wait while he presented his card to Mrs. Patterson. Bullitt lit a cigarette and regarded the pedestals holding busts of Scipio Africanus and Caesar Augustus. *I bet she'd love to add Caesar Franklin to that collection*, he thought. Then he glanced up at the staircase, where the heads of several big game animals were mounted on the walls. *Or that one.*

Cissy Patterson collected newsmakers, and Bullitt was certainly a newsmaker. He had been the youngest member of President Wilson's delegation at the Paris Peace Conference after the Great War, had served as a foreign correspondent, and had been attracted to the violent social experiment under way in the nascent Soviet Union. In fact, he had married Louise Bryant, the beautiful, radical widow of American communist journalist John Reed, fathered a daughter with her and then divorced her because of her all-consuming romance with alcohol. Living in Europe in the mid-1920s, he had met Cissy Patterson, who was ten years his senior, and the two had engaged in a short but torrid love affair. Even if Bullitt wasn't believed by most everyone to be the President's eyes and ears in Europe, Cissy had reasons to want to see him.

When the butler ushered Bullitt into Cissy's living room, the two connected as old friends.

"Cissy! How lovely you are looking," Bullitt said, kissing her three times on the cheeks. He detected a strong scent of gin.

"Bill! How Russian you've become," said Cissy, who had spent part of her youth in what was then called St.

Petersburg. "Did you learn that from Stalin? What would you like to drink?"

From there, the two settled on a sumptuous silk-upholstered couch for an evening of reminiscing that eventually turned to public affairs.

"Bill, how can you bear living in Moscow with all those horrid Bolsheviks?" Cissy said. "I know you have stars in your eyes about them, but really, haven't you wised up yet?"

"I have indeed, dear lady," Bullitt said. "You are looking at a sadder but infinitely wiser man. Stalin is eating his own as fast as he can stuff them into his mouth. Everyone in his government is absolutely terrified to talk to me or anyone on my staff. Tens of thousands of people in Leningrad have simply disappeared. I was just briefing the President on it this afternoon."

Cissy sat up straight, spilling part of her drink on the carpet. "That Man in the White House," she spat. "Or perhaps I should say, that Caesar in the White House. Did he enjoy today's Page 3?"

Bullitt smiled thinly. "Not especially," he said. He looked down nonchalantly. "How'd you come across that picture, anyway? Must have cost you a pretty penny."

"Not a penny, not a dime, not a dollar," Cissy proclaimed. "And I'm not going to tell you how I got it, so you might as well change the subject. How about dinner? As you've adopted all these continental manners, I'm sure you haven't eaten yet, and my chef is a wonder."

"I'd be delighted," Bullitt said.

Cissy eyed him speculatively. "Behave yourself and I might even invite you to stay for breakfast."

# CHAPTER 40

Mitch Novak lived in a garage apartment behind a house on Evarts Street in northeast Washington. Joan took a taxi to a house on Bryant Street, paid the driver and stood on the sidewalk until he drove away. Then she walked a block north and searched for the address Penny Jeter had given her.

The garage was just off a narrow alley that bisected the block, houses backing up to it on either side. It seemed like a fairly nice neighborhood of family homes. Several had cars parked along the sidewalks out front or in driveways running alongside the houses.

Joan wished she was more properly attired for the work at hand—sleuthing—but a girl had to do what a girl had to do. She cinched her gloves, buttoning them tightly around her wrists. She stood in the alley in the shadow of the garage for fifteen minutes, scanning the area, listening to its sounds. Occasionally, a car would flash past the end of the alley, but none turned down its narrow path. Finally, with her hand clutching the key in her coat pocket, Joan crept toward the wooden steps leading up to the apartment. She climbed slowly, putting her foot on each step and gradually shifting her weight to the next. A step creaked. Joan froze. When she finally reached the door at the top of the staircase, she hesitated for a moment.

*No turning back now.*

Working as quietly as she could, Joan inserted the key into the slot beneath the lock and turned. The bolt slid back, she twisted the knob and pushed the door open, its squeaky hinges protesting, and stepped inside.

Carefully, silently, she pushed the door closed, then turned and looked at the apartment. It wasn't much. A curtain separated what Joan supposed was the "bedroom" from the area in which she stood. In the darkness, she could make out a wooden table with two unmatched chairs, a countertop containing a sink and a two-burner hot plate, and a lumpy, stained sofa.

Joan walked slowly across the wooden floorboards, treading lightly. She reached the curtain and cautiously pulled it back. A single bed, rumpled and unmade, was against one wall. At the foot of the bed stood a low table, a round-topped three-legged stool tucked beneath it.

On the low table was a lamp with a torn shade, a Bible, a notebook of some sort, and several opened envelopes. Joan reached into her purse and retrieved her matchbook. She struck a match, careful to keep her body between its flame and the bedroom window. She rifled through the envelopes. They appeared to be letters. The match burned down to her fingers and she shook it out. She dropped the expended match into her purse and struck another. She opened the notebook. Its unlined pages were filled with writing. She flipped over to the last completed page, noting a date at the top. *A journal?* The match burned down.

In the dark, Joan held the Bible up by its covers and gently shook it over the table. When nothing fell out, she laid it back in its place. She heard the sound of a car outside and her heart began leaping inside her chest. The sound faded as the car continued down the alley.

Joan returned to the table. She stared down at the notebook. She picked it up.

By the time Joan hiked to New York Avenue, caught a cab and got back to her room at the Shoreham, it was nearly midnight. The lure of Wallace DeWitt flashed through her mind as she peeled off her suit and slipped into one of the Shoreham's plush robes. Wallace would have to wait, because Billy Bryce wouldn't. Joan figured she had about twelve hours left before her editor pulled the plug on her job and left her in the unemployment line with nine million other Americans.

She ordered a pot of coffee from room service and settled onto her bed with Mitch Novak's notebook on her lap. It had no cover other than front and back pages of thick paper. Joan had changed from her leather winter gloves into a more flexible pair of cotton ones, conscious that she had filched a piece of evidence. She didn't want to adulterate it as well. With an eye on the clock, she started from the back, quickly reading the scrawled handwriting.

> *Date with Penny last night. Went to see* Top Hat *with Ginger Rogers and Fred Astaire. Penny loved the picture and that made me glad. She let me kiss her, but that was all. She likes me though, I can tell. Mr. Harvey has assigned me to do security for the Birthday Ball at the Shoreham Hotel. He says some people from the White House will be at the ball so maybe I'll get to see the President or First Lady. That would be swell.*

Joan scanned the next entry, written a couple of days later, and gasped with satisfaction.

> *A chance to earn some extra money! I met a guy today who said he has a special job for me at the Birthday Ball. All I have to do is show up for the job and then make myself scarce. No questions asked. Guy didn't give me his name, but said I should just call him "Smith." Like John Smith, I asked. He thought that was pretty funny and said he could tell I was smart—too smart to be walking in circles all night waiting for nothing to happen. He's right about that! He said he'd also give me a train ticket, that I'll need to disappear for a few*

*days.     With the money I've got coming, disappearing will be no problem.    Then I'll send back for Penny.*

"You've disappeared all right," Joan said aloud. She turned the pages, working backwards, but that was the only mention of "Smith." Still, it was all the corroboration she needed. By the time her coffee ran out at 3 a.m., she had roughed out an article. She spent the next hour editing, weaving the few facts she knew into the fabric of a story telling what she believed had happened. By four-fifteen, the reporter was exhausted. She rolled over and switched off the bedside lamp, but not before setting her alarm clock for 9 a.m.

# WEDNESDAY, FEBRUARY 5, 1936

# CHAPTER 41

The Los Angeles *Standard* was a morning paper. Billy Bryce typically arrived at his office between 11 a.m. and noon and then worked until the morning edition was "put to bed," usually around a quarter to midnight. Since Joan was on the east coast, she already had a three-hour head start on her boss.

At eleven o'clock Washington time, Joan placed her first long distance call to the *Standard's* downtown office. "Los Angeles *Standard*. How may I direct your call?"

"This is Joan Roswell calling long distance for Billy Bryce, city desk."

"Hi, Joan, it's Ethel," the operator said. "You know he won't be in for two or three more hours. Want me to take a message?"

"Yes, dear. Tell that bastard that while he's been sleeping, I've been cracking the biggest case in Washington since Teapot Dome and if he wants to keep me on his payroll, he better move fast. Got that, dear?"

Ethel's giggle came through clearly from the other side of the country. "Got it! But I left out the b-word."

"Tell him to call me as soon as he gets in. I'm still at the Shoreham Hotel, Columbia 5401."

"I'll give him the message," Ethel said and rang off.


"So, you've been working while I sleep, huh?" Billy Bryce's voice crackled over the phone. "Given how little I actually sleep, that's not saying too much."

"I've got a lead on the stolen money from the President's Birthday Ball," Joan said.

"Tell me all about it."

"There was a security guard assigned to the ball Sunday night. He was there at the beginning of the dance, but when it was time to take the money to the bank, he couldn't be found. I figure he's the key to the story, so I call his employer, the Pinkerton Agency. I ask to speak to Mitch Novak, that's the guy's name."

"The missing link?"

"Right. The girl I talk to says he's disappeared, but that they're watching his apartment. I'm trying to get his address, so I tell her I have something to mail to him. And then she says, I can give you his post office box number, that's how he gets his mail."

"Go on."

"So, the next day, I stake out the post office. A woman checks his box and I follow her and convince her to talk to me. She's worried, because she's sweet on the guy but she hasn't heard from him since Wednesday, the day before the ball."

"Then what?"

"She tells me a story about Mitch making a deal with a mysterious 'Smith,' that's what she says Mitch calls him, 'Smith.' She says that Mitch says that 'Smith' is going to pay him a big bonus for an extra job. And get this: Mitch tells her he'll have to disappear for a few days."

"Pretty intriguing story. How do you know she's on the up-and-up? She could be a nut job out for publicity."

"No, no. Woman's intuition, Billy. She's legitimately worried about this Mitch guy. I can read her face. Besides, she made me promise to keep her out of the story. She's a pathetic, love-sick kitten. She just wants to find the guy."

"It's interesting, Joan, but you've got to have more than a 'love-sick kitten' to build a story around. Can you dig up another source?"

Joan smiled. Billy had walked right into her trap. "I've got documentary evidence that her story is legit."

"What kind?"

"Mitch Novak's journal."

"Is it signed and notarized?"

Joan laughed. "Come on, Billy! It's a journal, like a diary."

"How do you even know it's his? The girl could have written it and pawned it off on you."

"The girl didn't give it to me. I found it myself."

"Where?"

"In the guy's apartment, Billy!"

Silence, broken only by the static from the phone line, filled Joan's ear. "I see," Billy said after several seconds. "I guess you have been working late. I thought you said they were watching his place."

"They weren't last night. The journal corroborates the girl's story, Billy. It mentions 'Smith' and the money and a train ticket so Mitch can 'disappear.' And he has."

The line was quiet again. Joan could picture Billy sitting behind his desk, chewing on an unlit cigar, weighing the strength of her facts. "Write it up," he said.

# CHAPTER 42

## Onboard the *Crescent Limited*

"I'd say it was a successful event," Henry Bowman said. He and Owen Knox were riding in a private compartment aboard the *Crescent Limited* from Washington to New York via Philadelphia. "We raised twelve thousand dollars, which would make it worthwhile by itself. But we also had some students out in the crowd as it was breaking up. They were handing out these," he showed the Deacon a "Knox" button, "and asking 'Would you consider voting for Knox for president?'"

"With what results?"

"Seventy-eight percent answered, 'yes.'"

Knox sat back in his leather seat and stared at the brown fields and barren trees of the Pennsylvania countryside as it slid past the window, wrinkling his high, pale forehead and pursing his lips. "Of course, that's an audience already favorable to our message," he said sourly. "How would that extrapolate to the population at large?"

"Well, that's the question, isn't it? The answer will eat up about five thousand of those dollars we just raised. We can purchase a four-state survey from a guy in New York who does what he calls 'public opinion surveys.'"

"How's it work?"

"This guy, George Gallup, calls people up at random and asks who they'd vote for. I'm sure his methods are a little more sophisticated than that, but that's the basic idea."

"How much?"

"Five thousand, plus some administrative costs on our end."

"What would those be?"

"We'd have to set up a dummy organization to authorize the polling. This Gallup fellow won't poll for a political party."

"We're not a political party. We're a ministry."

"You're right, Deacon, but as soon as you start exploring a run for office—especially this office—we're playing a whole new game."

Knox continued to stare out the window as grazing cows flew past and the train rocked along its rails. He shifted his eyes to Henry. "Get it started."

"I already have."

# CHAPTER 43

## Washington, D.C.

Late Wednesday afternoon, Missy, Steve Early, and Ambassador Bullitt met with the President in his private study to compare notes on the missing photo. As usual, FDR took drink orders and used the silver shaker with his initials engraved on the side to combine the gin and vermouth for martinis for himself and Bullitt. Steve Early asked for an old fashioned, Missy for Scotch and soda.

"Well, where are we in our investigation?" the President asked as he plunked olives into his glass. "Missy, ladies first."

Missy summarized her conversation with Mike Wanner, with Steve interjecting a comment or two, then her follow-up with the head usher and the security guard's ledger. "The only person from the outside who had visited Mike during the days between the Caesar party and the *Herald's* publication of the picture was a man named Wallace DeWitt. He came over last Friday to get a photo of himself taken with Ginger Rogers. I have tried to reach this Wallace DeWitt in New York, but he's been out of town and his secretary won't give me a number for him. She promised she'd ask him to call when he got back to New York, though."

"Seems pretty unlikely he had anything to do with it," the President said.

"That's what Mike said," Missy conceded. "He just keeps insisting that he printed nineteen pictures and none of them are missing."

"Is that the skinny little photographer with the small moustache?" Bullitt asked. "I've never liked him. Every time he takes my picture with you, Mr. President, my eyes are closed in the print your press office releases."

"Well, as long as I look good, that's all that matters," the President said with a laugh. "Any luck with Cissy Patterson?"

"Not a bit," Bullitt said, glancing toward Missy. "I spent the evening with her at her home, and enjoyed a very good dinner, but she was tight as a clam about where she got the picture."

"Where does that leave us?" the President said.

"I'll keep a close eye on Mike Wanner," Steve volunteered. "He's a good photographer—except when Ambassador Bullitt is the subject," he joked, making the others smile. "But you never know. He may have gambling debts or some other money problems that would make him susceptible to a bribe."

"I will keep trying to reach this Mr. DeWitt," Missy said.

"Well, I've done my duty for my country," Bullitt said. "You won't find me darkening Cissy's door again. But as I told the President the other day, I wouldn't put it past the Russians to have a hand in this affair. They could even be trying to influence the election. For that matter, I wouldn't put it past them to have been involved in the theft of that Birthday Ball money."

The President's eyebrows shot up. "Good God, Bill! You've said these people will stoop to anything. You really think they would steal money from polios?"

"Stalin would steal money from his own mother and laugh all the way to the bank," Bullitt said.

The conversation from there turned to lighter subjects, and at around six the President shut down the bar. Bill Bullitt pulled Missy aside in the corridor outside the study. "You know my leave will be over next week," he said. "Let's have a nice evening out together before I go. What are you doing Saturday night?"

She smiled at the handsome ambassador. "I guess I'll be spending it with you," she said.

"Excellent!" He smiled. "Let's have dinner and go dancing at the Shoreham. It's been so long since I spun you around on the floor. Wear your prettiest gown."

"That sounds lovely," Missy said. *And maybe I'll pick up some new clues!*

# CHAPTER 44

### MISSING GUARD BRIBED TO VANISH; MYSTERY MAN PROMISED DOLLARS FOR DISAPPEARANCE

WASHINGTON, D.C., February 5 (AP)—by Joan Roswell, Los Angeles *Standard*—

Mitchell Novak, the Pinkerton Detective Agency security guard assigned to escort the money raised at Thursday's President's Birthday Ball at the Shoreham Hotel, was paid to 'disappear,' according to confidential sources. Novak, twenty-five years old, lives on Evarts Road in Northeast Washington and had been employed at the agency for six months.

According to sources, a man identified only as "Smith" offered Novak a "bonus" of an unknown amount for making himself "scarce." Novak was also given a train ticket, so he could leave the city for "a few days."

The identity of "Smith," if known by the authorities, has not been released to the public. More than $20,000 donated for polio treatment and research was stolen as the money was being transported to the bank by motion picture star Ginger Rogers and presidential secretary Marguerite LeHand. Unescorted by any security force, Misses Rogers and LeHand were abducted by thieves, but later released unharmed near Alexandria, Virginia.

The theft, involving such a large sum of money, a Hollywood star, and a member of the President's personal staff, has garnered national attention and raised questions about the careless handling of money given for a charitable cause. D.C. Police officials say that Novak is wanted for questioning, but they declined to name him a suspect in the crimes.

"Get Joan Roswell on the phone," Corey Wainwright said, gritting his teeth. He didn't know how she knew what she knew, but he planned to find out—and in a quick hurry. Director Hoover had made it clear that he was watching this investigation with special interest, that it had the potential to secure the Bureau's reputation with the President. The flip side, Corey knew, was that a botched effort could damage the close ties that currently existed between Hoover and the President—and earn the Director's wrath. *If I don't get a handle on this fast, I'll be the special-agent-in-charge in Anchorage, Alaska.*

Corey's intercom squawked, and he flipped the switch. "Miss Roswell on the line."

Corey snatched up the handset. "Miss Roswell, this is Special Agent Corey Wainwright."

"Good morning, dear. So nice to speak to you again."

"I read your story in the paper this morning. I have to compliment your detective work—and I have to know how you developed your theory."

"It's more than a theory, dear. My story is based on corroborated facts."

"I'd like to hear all about them. Maybe we can share information."

"I tried that once before with you, Agent Wainwright. I held my tongue on a story even bigger than this and, in the end, all I got was a gag order and two paragraphs on Joan Crawford." Corey winced. Technically, she was right. Hoover had promised Joan the inside story on the Shirley Temple case. When the President had clamped a total press blackout on the story, Hoover had slipped her an inconsequential gossip piece about the wedding of Crawford to actor Franchot Tone.

"Obviously, there's been no effort to censor the press on this case," Corey began, thinking as he talked. "I mean your story is already out there—and on the news wire, no less."

"That's because I didn't consult with you before publication, dear. You had no opportunity to bury my story."

"Well, I'd still like to talk to you. What harm can it do?"

"And you promise you won't hinder my reporting?"

Corey swallowed hard. Joan was an annoyance at best, a career-killer at worst, but smarter to keep her close than leave her free to do further damage to his case. "Sure, I do. I might even have some information you can use."


"Do you carry a gun?" Joan Roswell asked two hours later as she sat down in the wooden chair in front of Corey Wainwright's desk. She placed her small satchel on the floor next to her feet and kept her lizard-skin purse in her lap. She was smiling, in a playful mood, and not at all intimidated by the sturdy, utilitarian atmosphere of the FBI headquarters.

"Yes. All agents carry weapons." Corey closed the office door.

"Can I see yours?"

The agent pulled back his suit coat to reveal a brown leather shoulder holster snugged under his left arm.

Nestled in the holster Joan could see the hand grip of a pistol.

"Have you ever fired it?"

"Many times—on the firing range. And I got my share of shots off in the war too." Corey perched on the front edge of his desk and stared into her green cat's eyes. "As soon as I read your story in this morning's paper, I knew we had to talk. Candidly, you know some things that we don't. You can imagine how big this story is."

"I certainly can. I can imagine that the White House is all in a dither. I read Deacon Knox's speech from Tuesday night. He's using the theft as a sledge hammer against the President's integrity." Joan tittered. "Imagine, a politician being accused of having any of that to start with!"

"The Bureau stays out of politics, Miss Roswell."

Joan laughed. "Surely you don't believe that. Why, your Mr. Hoover is nothing if not a political animal. Grant you, he's very good at his job, but he keeps a careful eye on the political winds and their frequent shifts. I wouldn't be surprised if he didn't assign you to this case because of your contact with Miss LeHand out in San Francisco." Joan watched the agent's face, looking for any signs that her barb had hit a target.

"What really matters, Miss Roswell—"

"Joan, dear."

"—is that we bring the criminals who perpetrated these crimes to justice. It doesn't matter to me what the money was donated for or even where it ended up. What matters to me is that someone, we think it was three men, drove a car off the road, kidnapped two women, and stole the money. It's a simple case of bad people doing bad things, and my job, our job," Corey swept his arm toward their surroundings, "is to capture these bad people and turn them over to the judicial system."

"Bravo!" Joan said, clapping her hands. "I hope you succeed."

"And I'm hoping you will help me, help us. I'm really very impressed with what you found out about this 'Smith,'" Corey said, leaning back and crossing his arms over his chest. "How did you do it?"

Joan leaned forward, looking up at the agent. "A little intuition, a little luck, and a lot of work." She sat back and smiled.

Corey smiled in return. "Tell me how you did it. What was your first clue?"

"I started with the newspaper reports of the theft. In one of the articles, you mentioned the Pinkertons and this elusive Mr. Novak."

"Go on."

"I started making phone calls to see what I could find out."

"And?"

"And I discovered sources that seemed to have been overlooked by the…" Joan started to say FBI, but hoping to avoid offending her host, said, "…authorities."

"Who's the source?"

"Sources. They're confidential, dear."

"You have multiple sources?"

"I do."

"Listen, Joan," Corey leaned forward, his hands on his thighs, "I think you're an excellent reporter. I was very impressed with the work you did on the Temple case. And, like I said, I'm impressed by your reporting on this case. You've found out some things we didn't know, things that could help us crack this case. Will you please tell me how you found out about this 'Smith'?"

Joan snapped open her purse, removed a cigarette and struck a match. Corey reached behind him and handed her an ash tray.

"What do I get?" Joan asked, blowing smoke toward the ceiling.

"I'll share what I know that won't compromise the case. You'll have it shortly before we release it to the rest of the papers through the Bureau's press office."

"How do I know you won't rescind your agreement like last time?"

"Last time was different. We were dealing with international political issues."

"How do you know we're not dealing with those same kinds of issues this time, dear? We've got the White House involved. You're going to have to show me yours, before I show you mine." Joan smiled and put the cigarette back to her lips.

Corey sighed. "Do the words 'obstruction of justice' mean anything to you?"

"Do the words 'freedom of the press' mean anything to you, dear?" Joan flicked ash into the ash tray. "Why don't *you* tell *me* something that *I* don't know. I've already done some work for you. You admitted it earlier, said you were 'impressed' by it." Corey stood and walked over to the window, his hands in his pockets. Joan stared at the agent's back. "Give and take. In that order."

Corey turned and squeezed behind his desk. He opened the center drawer, removed a brown folder and slid it across the desk. Joan scooted forward, setting the ash tray on the desk. She opened the folder and cringed. A black and white photograph of a pale, bloated corpse stared up at her.

"Meet Mitchell Novak."

Joan looked into the agent's face, then back at the picture. "When was this taken?"

"Two days ago, down at the Anacostia River. The D.C. Police confirmed the identification yesterday afternoon. We haven't released the information yet because, quite frankly, we thought the bad guys might be a little more cautious if they knew we had a body."

"And I can run this?"

Corey shook his head. "Give and take, Joan. Now it's your turn."

Joan hesitated. She looked back at the gruesome picture. So, this was poor Penny Jeter's boyfriend. No reason to drag that sad girl any deeper into this. Joan took a drag on her cigarette and leaned over. She unsnapped the flap of her satchel, pulled out an unbound notebook and tossed it on the desk.

"What's this?" Corey asked.

"Mitch Novak's journal."

# CHAPTER 45

## New York

"The guy can carry a crowd," Wallace DeWitt said, smiling and shaking his head. "He had everybody in the building stomping their feet and chanting. They were really fired up. It was a great show."

"Find anything we can use?" Al Smith asked, leaning back in his chair at his Empire State Building office and lighting his cigar.

"I picked up some enthusiasm for a Knox candidacy. A couple of people, after the banquet was over, were working the crowd handing out Knox buttons. They didn't say 'Knox for President,' just 'Knox,' but I think maybe he's putting some feelers out, you know, testing the waters. But Knox would be a disaster. It's one thing to make a fiery speech and get people excited, but there's nothing in this guy's background to suggest he has any executive ability. Plus, his policies would torpedo the economy. We'd end up with economic chaos."

"We've got that now," Smith said, exhaling a plume of smoke. "One in five workers can't find a job and this is three years into Frank's administration. He's making matters worse. This Depression would have been over by now if he'd get the government out of the way and let business lead the recovery."

"Yeah, well I wouldn't hold my breath."

"So, what *would* you do?"

"I don't know, Al. I'm just a humble businessman trying to make my own small contribution to the betterment of society by making sure we never run out of toilet paper." Smith laughed appreciatively. "What do you think? Is the Liberty League going to be strong enough to make a difference?"

The smile eased from Smith's face. Since his bombastic speech, donations to the League had actually decreased. Smith, Wallace thought, had gone too far in aligning the President with the communists in Moscow. His hard line had backfired.

"Ah, but politics is a fickle business," Smith said. "I'm of a mind that we might be better off pinching Frank from both directions—us from the center and Knox from the left. If we can get Knox to commit to a race, we can throw a monkey wrench into the convention. If we can keep Frank from a first ballot victory, wiser heads can prevail, and we can put up a candidate who can lead the country out of this mess instead of making it worse."

Wallace had an opinion too, but he didn't share it with Smith.

# CHAPTER 46

## Washington, D.C.

*Why did it have to be "Smith"?* Corey Wainwright asked himself, as he walked down the stairs toward the sub-basement of the Justice Department building. In his hand was an evidence envelope inside of which rested the journal Joan Roswell had given him. Of the one hundred thirty million people in the United States, Corey figured two million were named Smith. His one-man task force would have a tough time tracking them all down. *It's probably just an alias anyway*, he consoled himself.

Corey walked along a sterile cinder-block corridor scanning the labels on the wooden doors which opened off each side of the hall. When he reached one marked "Documentation," he pushed the door open.

A middle-aged man with graying hair and wire-rimmed glasses looked up from his work. He was wearing thin, white cotton gloves and a light blue lab coat with "FBI" stenciled in gold on the breast pocket. "Help you?"

"I'm Wainwright. Working a case for Mr. Hoover. I wonder if you could take a look at something for me." Corey opened the envelope and tipped it down, so the journal slid out onto the technician's desk. Joan Roswell had probably already compromised any fingerprints that might have been found on the journal, but why take the risk of additional corruption? "Can you check this for prints and any other identifying marks, just work your usual magic?"

"For Mr. Hoover, you say?" the technician asked, looking up.

"Right. This is part of that polio ball case that's been in the papers. The White House and all that stuff. Mr. Hoover wants it resolved and fast." *I do too*, Corey thought.

The technician laid aside a file and a set of magnification lenses he'd been working with and removed his gloves. He reached for a stack of forms next to his desk lamp and meticulously inserted a sheet of carbon paper and piece of cardboard between two of the forms. "OK, tell me what you got," he said, picking up a pencil.

As Corey described the journal and its author, the lab man noted the relevant information on the form. When he was finished, he reviewed the form and, satisfied that he'd recorded the information he would need, turned it around so that it was facing Corey.

"I need you to sign right here," the technician directed, pointing to a blank space at the bottom of the form. "Then print your name and your telephone extension underneath. I'll call you as soon as I finish the analysis." He removed the carbon and handed Corey a copy of the evidence receipt.

"How long?"

"Well, for you, about two weeks." The technician grinned. "But for Mr. Hoover, I'll try to have something by Monday afternoon."


Joan Roswell was also pondering the identity of "Smith." Maybe "Smith" had seen the dearly departed Mitch Novak as a conduit to an easy score—easy money and a lot of it. There had to be plenty of rats in a rich city like Washington, low-life just looking for ways to burrow through the cracks and pick up some crumbs. But who would want to steal money from the polio charity? It was almost like stealing from the church.

Maybe "Smith" had other motives. Joan sat at the small writing desk in her hotel room staring at the blank piece of paper in front of her. In addition to plenty of money, which made Washington similar to all big cities, the capital had in abundance what no other American city possessed in more than very limited quantities: political power. Perhaps "Smith" was playing some kind of political game. Rather than making off with the purse, maybe "Smith" had been trying to embarrass the host of the ball, the man who had lent his prestige—his political power—to the event. Maybe "Smith" was attempting to weaken the President on the eve of a reelection campaign.

# THURSDAY, FEBRUARY 6, 1936

# CHAPTER 47

## POLIO CASE MURDER! MISSING GUARD'S BODY RECOVERED AT ANACOSTIA RIVER

WASHINGTON, D.C., February 7 (AP)—by Joan Roswell, Los Angeles *Standard*—

Washington, D.C. police confirmed today that the body of missing security guard Mitchell Novak has been identified. It was recovered from the Anacostia River on Tuesday.

Novak, the Pinkerton Agency guard assigned to last week's President's Birthday Ball at the Shoreham Hotel, had been missing since Thursday night. Police are treating Novak's death as a homicide.

It is now believed that Novak accepted a bribe, or the promise of a bribe, to desert his post at the ball, which was sponsored by the President's Birthday Ball Committee to raise funds for polio treatment. Novak's duties included escorting funds donated at the ball to the Riggs National Bank.

When he failed to appear for escort duty, screen star Ginger Rogers, attending the ball as the special guest of the committee, and presidential secretary Marguerite LeHand transported the money. On the way to the bank in downtown Washington, Miss LeHand's car was violently forced from the road. She and Miss Rogers were abducted along with the money. While the two women were rescued near

Alexandria, Virginia a short while later, the money and their abductors remain at large.

D.C. police are asking any persons with knowledge of Novak or his assailant(s) to contact Inspector Robert Trent at police headquarters.

*Not bad,* Joan thought. *Two page-one stories in three days. That ought to keep Billy at bay for a few more days. Poor Penny. But I kept her out of the story, just as I promised.*

Even when Corey had pressed her for her other sources, Joan had refused to divulge Penny. Besides, the FBI agent hadn't offered any more information. *I guess he thought a dead body was sufficient.* The poor girl was going to suffer enough. Joan hated to think of the sad young woman reading about her boyfriend's murder in the newspaper.

Thanks to the briefing Corey had given Missy LeHand, Joan Roswell's scoop about Mitch Novak's corpse didn't cause much consternation at the White House. It was more than overshadowed by a front-page editorial in Thursday's Washington *Herald* written and signed by Cissy Patterson.

## WHAT DOES FRANKLIN CAESAR KNOW?

It has now been almost a week since the heist of an estimated $20,000 collected at the Shoreham Hotel for the President's Birthday Ball, and little progress solving the case has been reported.

Thanks to a photo published in the *Herald* on Tuesday, we do know that helping children suffering from polio wasn't uppermost in the

President's mind that night. Rather, he was masquerading as a Roman Caesar, enjoying the adulation of his staff, family, and friends, who were arrayed in rather eyebrow-raising costumes.

Or was it a masquerade?

Why has Franklin Caesar been so tight-lipped about this sordid affair?

Why was his private secretary, Marguerite LeHand, involved in not only the counting of the money, but also the ill-fated delivery of said funds to the bank, without proper security detail?

Why hasn't J. Edgar Hoover, who has the vast resources of the FBI at his fingertips, been able to crack this case?

Is it incompetence? Or has he been told to hold his firepower?

Think, dear readers, on the consequences of the money remaining lost. Or is it lost?

We make no accusations. Still, one wonders.

Missy's face was ashen as she read her newspaper in bed that morning. The phone on her bedside table rang.

"My dear Lady." It was Bill Bullitt. "I can't believe what that bitch Cissy Patterson has written, dragging your name through the mud. I could just shake her until her teeth rattled."

"Thanks, Bill," Missy sighed. "It hasn't given my morning a great start, that's for sure. I know Mrs. Patterson hates F.D., but I have always had cordial relations with her. She's even invited me to parties at her home."

"She's a complicated woman," Bill said. "I've known her to sit across a tea table from someone she was planning to destroy in the next morning's edition and butter wouldn't melt in her mouth. She probably took lessons from Stalin. Come to think of it, she could probably teach him a thing or two."

Missy giggled a little. "Thanks, Bill. You always make me laugh."

"Lady, let me know if I can do anything more. I am so looking forward to going dancing with you at the Shoreham tomorrow night. There's a wonderful orchestra in the Blue Room. I'll come by around six and we'll have lots of time for drinks and dinner too."

"That sounds heavenly," Missy said.

She had barely laid the phone down before it rang again.

"Missy?" It was the President. "I am so sorry you have been accused of complicity in this Birthday Ball matter. It's so unfair. I have broad enough shoulders to handle this sort of abuse, but I won't have you being attacked by that vixen in Chanel. I want to get with you and Steve at nine o'clock sharp to plan a statement from you to issue at today's press conference."

"Thanks, F.D.," Missy said. "I appreciate that very much."

The phone rang a third time. It was Corey Wainwright.

"Corey? Oh, I'm so glad it's you," Missy said, and burst into tears.

# CHAPTER 48

Missy had recovered her usual composure when she and Steve Early joined the President in his office at 9 a.m. FDR was smoking a cigarette in his ivory holder, laughing over an editorial cartoon. It depicted him as a king in a crown, holding the Constitution in one hand and a dripping ink pen in another, having just written, "Cancelled — FDR."

"Steve, I think this crown suits me even better than the laurel leaves I wore as Caesar," he said. "Keep it in mind for next year's Cuff-Links Gang reunion."

Missy and Steve smiled weakly.

"I know. Not very funny," the President conceded. "Let's come up with a statement for Missy to make, Steve. Something categorically denying she had anything to do with the heist, explaining that her work at the ball was strictly voluntary. And make it clear that she should be considered a heroine in this affair, not a criminal. She might have been killed during that heist!"

"Yes sir," Steve said. "I'll have a draft ready for you by nine-thirty."

"Thanks, Steve. Anything new on your photographer?"

"No, Mr. President," Steve said, frowning. "After our meeting Wednesday, I asked him a few more questions, trying to catch him in a lie, but he keeps saying the same thing. He printed nineteen photos, and they are all there. We don't inventory individual sheets of photo paper, so he's the only one who could know. He's a good photographer; I don't want to fire him just on suspicion."

"No, no, of course not," said the President, who never wanted to fire anyone. He always delegated that job to someone else. "I'll let you get to work on that masterpiece you are going to write for Missy."

When Steve had left the room, Missy said, "F.D., Corey Wainwright is in my office. I wondered if we might bring him into our meeting? He might give us a few tips to further our investigation about the missing photo. Steve and I don't seem to have gotten very far."

"By all means," the President said, eyes twinkling. "I want to meet this paragon from the west coast."

Missy walked to the doorway between the Oval Office and her own and beckoned to Corey. He quickly crossed the carpet and offered the President his hand. "It's an honor, sir," he said. "I was proud to vote for you in 1932 and will be proud to vote for you again this November."

"Grand!" FDR said, smiling around his cigarette holder. "Let's get these twin mysteries cleared up so I won't be run out of town on a rail before then. Missy has been keeping me up to date on the heist, and I feel certain you and the other law enforcement officers are doing your best. Surely with the recovery of the missing Pinkerton agent there will be a break in that case soon."

"I agree, sir," Corey said. "I've been quite impressed with both the D.C. Police Department and the Virginia State Police. And, of course, Mr. Hoover has made it clear I am to avail myself of any resource the FBI has. He was very upset about the front-page editorial in the *Herald* this morning, as you can imagine."

"I can indeed," the President said. "Well, let's move onto the case of Franklin Caesar, which seems to be more of an internal matter, but one where we could use some advice."

Missy outlined to Corey the efforts made by Ambassador Bullitt, herself, and Steve Early with respect to Cissy Patterson and Mike Wanner. "Our photographer insists he made nineteen prints and none of them are missing," she said. "He has the negatives under lock and key. But a print somehow got into Mrs. Patterson's hands. He says the only visitor he has had out of the ordinary is a man who danced with Ginger Rogers at the Birthday Ball. He came to pick up a picture Mike had taken of them." She pulled the black-and-white photo from a manila envelope in her lap. "I got his telephone number in New York from the Birthday Ball Committee, but unfortunately, he's been away from his office and I haven't been able to reach him. His name is —"

"Wallace DeWitt," Corey said.

"Yes!" Missy said, astonished. "How do you know that? Have you met him?"

"Yes, I have," Corey said. "I talked to him earlier in the week, sort of a routine interview because he had been one of the people near the counting room. He was a little prickly, but nothing that got my antenna up. You know what they say, though, fool me once, shame on you, fool me twice, shame on me. If there's a link between our two mysteries, Mr. DeWitt may just be that missing link. I'll get his phone number from you and give him a call."

The President shook his head. "I am beginning to believe that everything Hoover says about the FBI is true," he said.

# CHAPTER 49

**New York**

Wallace Dewitt had reluctantly arrived at a conclusion. Based on the negative reaction to Al Smith's Liberty League speech—both in popular opinion and in fundraising—Wallace had determined that a Smith candidacy for the Democratic nomination would be dead on arrival at the Philadelphia convention, now just four and a half months away. Although Wallace considered himself a political neophyte, he was confident that too little time remained to field a more competitive pro-business Democrat.

"I really like, Al," Wallace said, staring out the window of his twenty-second-floor office in the Empire State Building at a blowing snowstorm, "but he's not going anywhere. You were right, Jim, he's a has-been."

"Let me get a stenographer in here to memorialize that last statement," James Eustace replied.

"That Smith is a has-been?"

"No. That you acknowledged I was right about something." He stood and headed over to the sideboard, pulling the heavy glass stopper from a decanter of Scotch. "That's worthy of a drink!" He poured Scotch into two tumblers and carried one to Wallace. "Cheers." Eustace lifted his glass and nodded toward Wallace.

Wallace took a sip and set the glass on his desk. He'd become a good customer of the Pennsylvania Railroad, traveling frequently between the city and Washington over the past week. While he continued to recognize his lack of political experience, he'd come to the realization that he had to be involved in the process. If you aren't at the table, Eustace had advised, you're likely to find yourself on the menu.

"So, if Smith isn't the answer—and I agree that he isn't—what are you going to do?" James asked.

"First of all, I don't want Smith to know that he's not the answer. I like the guy too much." Wallace watched as snowflakes swirled by his window. "There's no benefit to dumping the guy and walking away, but I don't want to waste any more of our money on him. Well, maybe token amounts, just to keep our hand in the game."

"OK. So where does that leave us?"

Wallace turned toward his counselor. "We go in the opposite direction. We start supporting Knox."

Eustace whistled. "That's the opposite direction, all right." He wagged a stubby finger at his employer. "I can feel the gears turning between your ears, but I haven't the slightest idea what they're about to crank out."

"Sure you do. What's the problem with Roosevelt?"

"He's too far left. He believes more government is the key to solving our economic problems."

"Right, but he carried all but six states and kicked Hoover's ass in the electoral college too. A landslide victory, popular *and* electoral. So, what does that tell you?"

Eustace stared at the ceiling for a moment. "That people wanted a more aggressive approach to the Depression than they were getting from Hoover. And that since he's been in office, Roosevelt has moved to the left. I mean he didn't start out as a socialist, did he?"

"No, because Americans—even fed up with Hoover—wouldn't have voted for a socialist or a communist."

"I agree, but I still don't see where you're headed."

"We need people to see the real Roosevelt, the one creating agency after agency and bloating the rolls of

216

federal employees. We need them to see that when he runs low on money, he just prints up some more. He's not like the rest of us who have to make do on what we earn—that is if we even have jobs."

"So how do you get a chameleon like this guy to show his true colors?"

"Put pressure on him from the left. Knox revs up his populist nonsense about nationalizing key industries, you know, put the government in charge of everything for the benefit of the people. It sounds a lot like communism, right? Feed Knox so he gains traction, builds his following. What's Roosevelt going to do? He's going to move to the left. He can't let Knox chip away at his base."

"And then he starts losing votes from the center?"

"And the right."

"Where his support was never more than lukewarm."

"Check. So, we shift our political budget from Smith to Knox, at least until the Republicans put up a candidate who can actually win. Then we switch again."

"What if our support of Knox makes him a viable candidate?"

"The stronger he gets, the more political capital Roosevelt has to spend and the better chance a pro-business candidate—Democrat or Republican—has of breaking into the race."

"It's a long shot, Wally."

"It is, but I don't want to be on the menu—I want to set the table."

# CHAPTER 50

**Washington, D.C.**

"Agent Wainwright?" the familiar-sounding voice had come over the telephone as soon as Corey arrived at the Justice Department. "This is Major Bishop, Virginia State Police. We've got someone in custody I think you ought to talk to."

Corey had listened for a couple of moments before hanging up the phone and hurrying to the Bureau's motor pool. Within forty-five minutes, he was seated in Bishop's office at the state police barracks in Alexandria.

"One of our troopers responded to a single-vehicle accident last night on Route 50 near Fairfax," Bishop said.

"Where's that?"

"About fifteen miles west of here. The driver was inebriated, but other than a bruise over his eye, seemed to be unhurt. Unfortunately for him, he'd run into a utility pole and damaged it. Didn't cause an outage, but the power company's going to have to repair or replace the pole. That being the case, the trooper brought him in and had him booked for destruction of property and driving while intoxicated. In the course of the booking process, his personal items were catalogued and stored." Bishop reached to the right corner of his desk and picked up a large, manila envelope. He unwound the string holding it closed and carefully poured its contents on to the top of the desk.

Corey watched as a leather wallet, a wrist watch, short plastic comb, pencil, address book, and a couple of dollar bills and loose papers piled up. Bishop lifted what looked like a check from the top of the pile. "This is what I wanted you to see." He extended the paper toward Corey.

Corey took the paper. It was indeed a check: a check made out to the President's Birthday Ball Committee.

Carter MacBride stood with his hands on the bars peering out into the dusty corridor of the Alexandria City Jail. He'd been in worse places—lots worse. State-run facilities were usually a cut above local jails. Still, a jail was a jail and, except for prison—or the Western Front during the Great War—the last place he wanted to be. Especially now.

MacBride had slowly sobered up through the course of the morning, the yellow sunshine casting a splash of brightness on the dingy cell floor. He had recalled the sequence of events that had landed him in his current trouble. Every time he touched his sore forehead, he remembered why he should never drive after spending the evening at the Cherry Tree Tavern on Alexandria's waterfront.

*Ah well, I'll be out afore too long.*

# CHAPTER 51

## New York

Wallace was seated in the rear of the restaurant, one booth away from the double swinging doors that led from the low-lit, comfortable dining room to the bright, bustling kitchen. He had arrived early and with the help of the maître d' settled on an inconspicuous spot for his dinner date with Henry Bowman and Owen Knox. The last thing Wallace wanted was for Al Smith to get wind of his meeting. He had pondered switching the dinner to a more obscure restaurant, but this was New York, after all, where even the most famous could walk the streets in relative anonymity.

"Why'd they stick you way back here in the corner?" Wallace looked up from his Scotch to see the ruggedly handsome face of the restaurant's namesake.

"What'd you say, Champ?" he asked, standing and shaking former world heavyweight champion Jack Dempsey's hand. "Looks like business is pretty good." The dining room was full except for a couple of tables marked "reserved."

"You been bad or something, sitting back here?"

"No, well, I haven't exactly been good, but you know how that goes." Wallace chuckled, and Dempsey joined in. "I'm meeting a couple of guys on business. I thought an out-of-the-way table might be best."

"So, you bring 'em to the most famous restaurant in the city so nobody will see 'em? Great strategy, Wallace."

"This isn't Delmonico's."

Dempsey laughed. "A real wise guy. I'll stop by later and say 'hello' to your guests."

"That'd be great, Champ." Dempsey wandered off to another table of Friday evening diners and Wallace sat back down. He checked his watch. Ten past eight. Out-of-towners were often late, unaccustomed to the city and the masses of people moving about. He took another sip from his drink and watched Dempsey pose for a picture with a well-dressed couple. It was hard to tell who was more excited, the man or the woman. *Maybe it's their anniversary.*

Through the large plate-glass window looking out on Eighth Avenue, Wallace could see the red cheeks and noses of curious passersby staring in at the swells and their ladies eating and drinking like royalty. The rain had let up, but it was still cold and the light from the cabs and streetlights was sparkling on the wet pavement. He was glad to be on this side of the glass.

Wallace had finished his drink by the time he saw Knox and Bowman enter the restaurant and remove their overcoats. His eyes followed them as the maître d' led them through the tightly bunched tables of the dining room toward Wallace's booth. Wallace reached into his coat pocket, pulled out his KNOX pin and hastily stuck it on his lapel.

"Hello, Henry," Wallace said, standing, smiling and extending his hand.

"Mr. DeWitt," Henry replied, smiling and regarding Wallace through his steel-framed glasses. "Allow me to introduce Deacon Owen Knox."

"Mr. DeWitt," Knox said, with a nod of his head, shaking hands. "A pleasure to meet you."

"The pleasure's all mine," Wallace said. "Please sit down." He motioned toward the black leather upholstered bench opposite him. Wallace was struck by the contrast between the bombastic preacher he'd heard on the radio, the fiery orator he'd observed at Constitution Hall, and the very ordinary-looking man now standing before him, his straight brown hair combed back from his pale, high forehead. *Looks like a clerk in an insurance office*, he thought.

"I'm sorry we're a little late," Henry said, sliding into the high-backed booth. "I underestimated how long it would take us to get here."

"That's easy to do in New York. The length of a journey is dependent on so many factors. And on a night like this..." Wallace shrugged. "How has your visit been so far?" he asked, looking directly at Knox.

"Favorable, I'd say. We had a good meeting at CBS. Henry tells me you put in a good word for us."

"I just called an acquaintance, that's all. Happy to help."

"A rather influential acquaintance."

A waiter wearing a black jacket and bowtie over his starched white apron arrived at the booth. "Would you gentlemen care to start with a cocktail?" Wallace motioned toward his guests.

"Ginger ale," Knox said primly.

"Same," said Henry.

"Mr. DeWitt, another?"

"Sure," Wallace said with a nod.

Once the waiter had withdrawn, Knox picked the conversation up where it had left off. "I gather you have a lot of influential friends, Mr. DeWitt."

"My work brings me into contact with interesting people, just as I'm sure yours does."

"Not many of the people Henry and I meet own radio networks," Knox replied, his brown eyes fixed on Wallace, "or major paper companies either."

The waiter returned and set their drinks on the white cloth-covered table. He took their orders and disappeared through the swinging doors and back into the kitchen.

Knox resumed, fixing his eyes on Wallace. "Mr. DeWitt, I wanted to personally thank you for the most generous contribution to our ministry. We're doing important work, reaching millions of people every week and helping them understand how to apply the Gospel of the Lord Jesus Christ to this sad world in which we find ourselves. Your donation helps us sustain and expand our ministry."

"That's my goal, Deacon Knox. I want your ministry to grow and, as I've told Henry here, I'd like to see it expand in new directions. That's why I made the call to Mr. Paley's office at CBS. I'm not a fan of the President's. I'd like to see someone else win the nomination and win the presidency."

Knox continued to stare at Wallace. "I would have thought an overt capitalist like you might have favored someone from the opposite end of the political spectrum."

Wallace sipped his Scotch. *Careful now.* "In an ideal world, maybe so. But, as you mentioned a moment ago, this world is less than ideal. Candidly, if I could pick a perfect candidate, he might not be you. But he most certainly isn't Franklin Roosevelt either. I'd like to see Roosevelt beaten, preferably at the convention, and, if that isn't in the cards, then in the general election."

"Tell me about your political philosophy, Mr. DeWitt. How do you see my candidacy benefitting you and your business associates?"

"Deacon Knox, you and I diverge on some economic issues. I'm not keen, for example, on nationalizing industries."

"But these industries—coal, railroads, big oil—are abusing workers, grinding them down to faceless, nameless units of labor. This inhumanity has to be stopped, Mr. DeWitt."

*At least he didn't mention the timber industry,* Wallace thought. He chose his next words carefully. "I'm in favor of better treatment for all workers, Deacon Knox, but I'm not so naïve as to believe for a second that government ownership would be an effective agent for change. You simply swap one set of ills for another. Plus, you remove the profit motive which promotes greater efficiency, lowers the cost of goods and results in a higher standard of living."

"I see I was correct about your capitalistic beliefs."

Wallace grinned. "You were. And while we may disagree on the issue of nationalization, we do agree on the need for a more equitable business environment. Believe it or not, capitalist that I am, I concede that there is a place for government regulation. The government should set boundaries, if you will, within which business should operate. These should be broad in nature and based on our shared values."

"Our Christian values?"

"We're a secular nation, Deacon Knox. We have to arrive at our values in our own way. That's what the Founding Fathers guaranteed in the First Amendment."

"For the overwhelming majority of our citizens, these values come from the Bible, from the Ten Commandments, and the Gospels of Jesus Christ."

"What's this, a debate?" a deep voice growled. Wallace, Knox, and Bowman looked up at the grinning, rugged face of Jack Dempsey.

"Champ, meet my friends Owen Knox and Henry Bowman."

"Delighted to meet you," Dempsey said, smiling and shaking hands. To Knox he said, "I've heard you on the radio."

"I hope you enjoy listening," Knox replied.

"I don't get too involved in politics. I keep pretty busy around here." Dempsey made small talk with his guests. Wallace could tell that mingling with his clients came easily to the retired boxer.

By the time Dempsey strolled away from their booth, their orders arrived, borne by an attendant balancing a tray above his shoulder and following their waiter.

"Spanish mackerel for you sir," he said placing a dish in front of Deacon Knox. Roasted Long Island duck was set before Henry, and a sirloin steak and baked potato were served to Wallace.

Wallace picked up his fork, then hesitated when he felt Knox's eyes staring at him.

"Henry," Knox said, still watching Wallace, "would you return thanks for us?"

"Bountiful Lord, who has given us so much, we thank Thee for Thy mercy, for our many blessings and for this food. May we use it to serve Thee and to expand Thy Kingdom on earth as it is in heaven. In Jesus' name, Amen."

"Amen," Knox repeated.

They continued to talk as they ate, Knox circling warily, trying to determine the sincerity of Wallace's support. Henry leaned forward throughout the entire meal, much like a sprinter eager to spring from the starting blocks, the prospect of more checks from DeWitt Southern floating always just beyond his reach. With the contacts that DeWitt could bring to Knox's nascent campaign, Henry wouldn't have to worry about funding.

It wasn't until dessert was served—apple pie á la mode—that Knox finally began to warm toward his host. "We both believe more in the individual than in institutions," he said, forking a tiny bite of pie redolent with cinnamon into his mouth. "The greatness of Jesus was that, while he recognized our innate sinfulness, he also treated everyone as an individual. He didn't lump us all together into one bucket and assume that we all had the same problems and that one solution would work for us all."

"Exactly," Wallace said. "Government on the other hand, this one in particular, sees humanity as a mass. It doesn't see that we all have talents. Some, like yours, Deacon, and Henry's and mine too, are greater than those of other people. Some, no doubt, are greater than ours. But the government wants to pull everybody down to one common level. I believe that's wrong. You take the story of the rich, young ruler who asks Jesus what he had to do to reach heaven. Jesus told him to give away all his possessions. Now the rich guy didn't want to do that, but what if he had? You know there are a lot of people who do just that: they make a lot of money and they give a bunch of it away. And I'm not talking about taxes either. I'm talking about giving to the local Community Chest or the Salvation Army where the money actually gets to the people in need. That's the kind of culture we need to promote, one where people can employ their talents and make their fortunes and where *they* decide how that money gets shared, not the government."

They finished their coffee. Wallace would have ordered an after-dinner drink, but he knew he'd be drinking solo.

"This has been a most enjoyable evening, Mr. DeWitt. I hope we'll have a chance to resume our discussion another time," Knox said, fastidiously wiping his mouth with his napkin.

"I look forward to it." Wallace laid twelve dollars on the table and the three stood and shook hands.

As Knox led the way through the now mostly empty dining room, Henry Bowman hung back with Wallace. "He seems to like you," Henry said.

"Good. Maybe we can help each other out."

"Yes, well, in fact, I was wondering if I might impose upon you for a few minutes in the morning. I know eight-thirty is a little early for Friday morning, but there is something you might be able to help us with."

Wallace shook hands with Henry again and said, "See you at eight-thirty."

# FRIDAY, FEBRUARY 7, 1936

# CHAPTER 52

## Alexandria

Carter MacBride heard the key rattle in the heavy metal door at the end of the hallway and the tumbler clunk into place. The jailer who had brought him burned toast and tepid coffee for breakfast now led a man in a suit and another in a trooper's uniform toward his cell.

*Now what?*

"Mr. MacBride," the suit said, stopping just short of his cell door, "I'm Special Agent Wainwright of the Federal Bureau of Investigation and this is Major Bishop of the state police. I wonder if we might ask you a few questions."

"Sure, I guess," MacBride said, stepping back as the jailer unlocked the door and pushed it open.

"Have a seat," the FBI man said, pointing to the cot behind MacBride. MacBride sat.

The jailer remained out in the corridor, leaning against the wall and reaching in his pocket for a cigarette. The FBI man and the trooper sat on the cot on the opposite side of the nine-foot-wide cell.

"Mr. MacBride, Major Bishop informs me that you have been apprised of your right to an attorney, is that correct?"

"Yeah, I guess so." His two interrogators looked at each other and nodded.

"Major Bishop and I are part of a team investigating a crime that occurred last week. We thought you might be able to help us."

"Always happy to help law enforcement. My brother-in-law is a deputy sheriff down in Culpepper County," MacBride said.

The FBI man pulled a rectangular piece of paper out of his pocket and unfolded it. It was an envelope—no, it was a check.

"I wonder if you could tell us how you came to have this check in your possession, Mr. MacBride," the G-man said.

MacBride leaned forward and squinted his eyes to get a good look at the check. He remembered it well. "Sure. I picked it up in a card game. Some old boys and me was playing a friendly game and one of them wanted me to have it."

"Why's that?" the trooper asked, but MacBride wasn't worried; gambling would be a local beef, not state, and certainly not federal.

"Let's just say we was keepin' score. You get my drift?"

"We get it." It was the FBI man again. "Major Bishop tells me that they've checked your record and that, apart from some traffic and public intoxication issues, you're an upright citizen. That right?"

"Yep." MacBride's head was starting to hurt again as he tried to figure out what these two wanted with him. "It's like I already told you, my brother-in-law is a deputy sheriff. He'll vouch for me. I married his sister, don't you see?"

"Yes sir, we see. Mr. MacBride, when you accepted this check here," the man in the suit held it up in his hand, waving it like a fan, "you took possession of stolen property. That's a felony in Virginia."

MacBride sputtered. "Well, how did I know it was stole? That fella didn't say nothing about it being stole. He just said he owed me and so here take this and I took it. I didn't steal it. I can take you right back over there and prove it."

"Where exactly were you?"

"The Cherry Tree. You can nearly always find a game there if they know who you are."

"I'm afraid we're going to have to charge you, Mr. MacBride."

"Now just wait a minute, fellas. Like I said, I didn't steal nothing. Seems to me that what you really want is the fella I got this from. Now, ain't that right?"

The G-man spoke again. "Well, sure, that would be best, but how would we find him?"

MacBride smiled for the first time since the interrogation had started. "Why, I'll take you right to him. I remember the fella."

"And you think he'll be there?" the trooper asked.

"Sure, he will. He's in there pretty near every night."

# CHAPTER 53

**New York**

"Mr. Henry Bowman is here, Mr. DeWitt."

"Thanks, Margie. Would you show him to my office?" Wallace said into his intercom, setting aside a production report from the company's Georgetown, South Carolina mill. He stood and greeted his guest at the door. "Hello, Henry. How's the campaign this morning?"

"Good morning, Mr. DeWitt. Thank you for seeing me on such short notice. I told the Deacon I had an errand to run and that I'd meet him at the station." Henry seemed excited.

*Maybe he likes riding the train*, Wallace thought. "I would offer you a drink," Wallace said, grinning, "but it's still a little too early even for me."

Henry chuckled. "Perhaps another time. I'm careful around the Deacon. I don't want to offend him, but I'm not exactly a teetotaler."

"Sit down, Henry." Wallace motioned to the leather chair in front of his desk. "You realize it's a little early to come looking for another contribution just yet."

"Oh, no, no, I completely understand. I was hoping you could help us with another matter."

"How can I be of assistance?"

"Well, I think I mentioned that I had a meeting with CBS. They're willing to sell us fifteen minutes each Tuesday at 10 p.m. as long as we can find sponsors to pay for it."

"How hard will that be?"

"A challenge, but a surmountable one. Deacon Knox, despite what he might lead you to believe, knows a lot of people. Millions, in fact, who tune into this program each week on Mutual. By shifting to CBS, we'll reach tens of millions. It's a perfect platform from which to launch the campaign. I'm reasonably confident that we'll be able to fund the radio program from increased contributions. So, what we really need is a sponsor for just two or three weeks. After that we can carry it ourselves."

"Impressive. But DeWitt Southern as a corporation doesn't endorse candidates or fund campaigns."

"That's not why I'm here."

"Oh. Why are you here, Henry?"

"I hope you won't take this the wrong way, Mr. DeWitt, but the Deacon and I consider you to be a very successful and sophisticated businessman."

"No offense taken." Wallace grinned.

"No, of course not." Henry reddened. "You see, we have a challenge. You might call it an opportunity. We have received a rather large donation."

"How large?"

"More than eighteen thousand dollars."

"That is rather large," Wallace agreed, impressed. "If you don't mind my asking, who's it from?"

"Well, uh, that's the opportunity, you see. It's not really one donation; it's a, well sort of a confederation of smaller donations that add up."

"I see," Wallace said, but he didn't really.

"The donations are in the form of checks, you see." Wallace nodded, waiting for Henry to continue. Henry was silent for a moment. "We need your help getting the checks into our account."

"Why don't you just take them down to the bank? You've got banks in Chicago, don't you?" Wallace chuckled.

"You see, that's just it. We do have a bank, a good one. But they require any checks we deposit to actually be made out to us. These aren't."

Wallace leaned forward. "The checks aren't written to your account? I'm sure your bank doesn't require them to be precise. Just call your branch manager if you're having trouble with a teller. Sometimes the tellers have more common sense, but they don't always have the authority they need."

Henry stared at his hands. When he looked back up, Wallace could tell he'd reached a decision. "It's not that simple. The checks weren't originally intended for the ministry."

Now it was Wallace's turn to hesitate. "Who were the checks intended for?"

"The President's Birthday Ball Committee."

Wallace felt his heart turn a flip. *What the hell have I gotten myself into?*

# CHAPTER 54

## Alexandria

Corey Wainwright and Detective Miller Pappas of the Alexandria Police were sitting on stools, one on each end of the Cherry Tree Tavern's L-shaped bar, beers in thick glass mugs before them. Behind them, at one of the pub's small round tables, sat two more detectives, also nursing beers. A radio was playing a jazz concert. *Maybe Bob Crosby*, Corey thought.

From his spot at the bar, Corey could see the entire pub by looking into the long smoked-glass mirror covering the wall behind the bartender. Not only could he make eye contact with Pappas, he could also see the other two agents as well as the front door. He checked the time: 9 p.m.

As scheduled, Carter MacBride walked through the front door at the top of the hour. Without acknowledging Corey, the only one of the law enforcement officers he'd met, he approached the bar and ordered a beer, paying for it with a quarter. He took a sip and turned, leaning his elbow on the varnished wooden surface of the bar. He scanned the tables and the booths that lined the back wall.

Over the next forty-five minutes, MacBride talked to the bartender, sat down for a few minutes with an acquaintance and drank a second beer, but he never loosened his tie, the signal that he'd identified the check passer.

Shortly before ten o'clock, MacBride left the bar. Corey sighed. It looked like a wasted night. By prearrangement, Corey would leave first, followed ten minutes later by the detective at the bar. The pair at the table would follow ten minutes after that.

Corey lay a quarter on the bar and slipped off his stool. He considered delegating future stakeouts to Pappas and the others. He had too many things to do to sit on his ass for three hours for no result. Corey pulled his fedora and his overcoat from the rack by the front door that opened out onto Union Street.

At that moment, a blast of cold, damp air swept into the tavern as the door opened and MacBride, his arm across the shoulders of a huskily built man of about twenty-five, came back inside.

"Gus!" MacBride shouted to the bartender, "set us up a couple!"

Thinking quickly, Corey pretended that he'd just come inside himself. He hung his coat and hat on the rack and gave a pretend shiver, rubbing his hands together and blowing into them. He headed back to the bar.

The bartender served MacBride and his friend, then headed toward the end of the bar where Corey had resumed his seat.

"What can I get you this time?" the bar man asked with raised eyebrows, a white towel in one hand.

"A beer," Corey replied looking the man in the eyes. "And a little discretion," he added quietly.

MacBride was laughing and gesturing, his companion smiling and nodding. As the bartender set Corey's fresh beer in front of him, MacBride loosened his tie. Corey caught Pappas's look in the mirror and gave a barely perceptible nod. He took a sip from his beer and stood, slipping another quarter from his pocket and placing it beside his glass. Pappas, at the other end of the bar, stood and approached the two men to his right.

Corey watched as Pappas drew the attention of MacBride and his colleague. The other two detectives formed a cordon between the tavern's door and the men at the bar. MacBride stopped talking, the other man stopped smiling. Pappas removed from his jacket pocket the leather wallet that contained his badge and held it up for both MacBride and the other man to see. "You're under arrest for possession of stolen property. I advise you that whatever you say can be used as evidence against you and that you have the right to the representation of an attorney. Please stand and place your hands on the bar."

Because he'd been coached, MacBride complied immediately. It was the intention of Pappas and Corey that the other man, whom MacBride only knew as "Ed," not realize that MacBride had fingered him. Ed hesitated, glancing over his shoulder. When he saw the other two detectives, their hands at the ready, he stood and placed his hands on the bar.

# CHAPTER 55

## Washington, D.C.

Missy had chosen a red chiffon evening gown for her date with Bill Bullitt. It was a color that went well with her silver hair and blue eyes, and she had carefully selected an Elizabeth Arden lipstick and nail polish to match her dress. When Bill arrived at the White House Saturday night, he gave her an appreciative wolf whistle, which made her blush and laugh.

The evening that followed reminded her again why she had come to care for Bill and how much she missed him during his long absences abroad. He was charming and attentive, relating hilarious stories about his experiences in Moscow, mimicking Stalin, and listening closely when she spoke of her work for the President. They compared notes on the Stalin government, how it was affecting the Russians, and how it was perceived in Washington.

*He's such a wonderful dancer too,* she thought, as Bill expertly led her in waltzes and slow fox trots to popular songs such as "Cheek to Cheek." He knew faster tunes made her breathless and didn't want to aggravate the heart condition that was an unwanted souvenir of her childhood bout with rheumatic fever. With her heels on, they were exactly the same height and truly could dance cheek to cheek. "I love your perfume," he murmured. "Is it the L'heure Bleue I sent you?"

"Yes," she said. "You always remember my favorite."

Late in the evening, seated at their table, Bill pulled a small box from his tuxedo pocket and handed it to Missy, moving the candle on the table closer so she could see it better. "It's been awhile since I added anything to your charm bracelet. Open it."

Missy lifted the lid and plucked out a tiny red enameled Easter egg. Wishing she had a pair of glasses in her purse, she peered at it in the candlelight. There were daisies on one side and the letters XB on the other. She looked at him quizzically.

"Stalin has outlawed religion in Russia, but the people still have their traditions," he explained. "The letters are Slavic for 'Christ is Risen.' The daisies are for Marguerite, which, as you know, is French for daisy."

"It's lovely, Bill," she said, smiling at him. "You're so thoughtful. I'll get it to the jewelers next week and add it to my bracelet."

"I hope this will be my last trip to Moscow," Bill said, leaning back in his seat and lighting a cigarette. "The ambassador in Paris, Mr. Strauss, is quite ill, and I hope the President will appoint me to take his place." He regarded Missy through the smoke. "Paris is much closer to Washington, and the trans-Atlantic phone service is infinitely better. I would love to entertain a certain special Lady at the embassy there."

Missy smiled. "You know I love Paris," she said. "It's my favorite city. I'll put in a good word for you with the Boss." Inside, her stomach clenched a little. *There it is again. Always a favor to ask. Does he really care for me at all?*

He covered her hand with his own. "I know you will. Thanks, Lady."

As the pair was leaving the Shoreham through the motor lobby, Missy involuntarily shuddered.

"Cold?" Bill asked, putting his arm around her.

"I guess a rabbit ran over my grave," she said. "I was just thinking about the last time I was here." She paused, suddenly remembering her last encounter with Mike Wanner the night of the Birthday Ball. *Why had he been hanging about the lobby still, a half-hour after he said he was leaving? Had he really forgotten his movie camera?*

# CHAPTER 56

## Alexandria

"This is Special Agent Wainwright with the FBI, Mr. Wardlaw. I think it's safe to assume that his presence here is a signal that you're in big trouble." Ed Wardlaw had been booked, his personal effects confiscated. He had declined to make a phone call and now sat in an interrogation cell at Alexandria's police headquarters. Pappas was standing, one foot on the floor, the other on a folding chair, his elbow propped on his knee, a cigarette between his lips.

Wardlaw sat quietly for a moment. "What is it that you think I stole?"

"We didn't say you stole anything." Pappas glanced at Corey. "Did we say anything about him stealing?"

"I don't believe you did." Watching local cops work was always like watching a variety show. It could be brutal or tedious or sometimes even entertaining.

"Did you steal something, Ed? You got a guilty conscience that might be searching for absolution? If so," Pappas straightened and clapped his hands together one time, "you've come to the right place!"

"No, it's just that you said I had something that was stolen."

"I think he's right," Pappas said to Corey. "I think we did say something about something that was stolen." He turned back toward Wardlaw. "So, what did you steal?"

"Nothing."

"What stolen property was in your possession?"

"I don't know what you're talking about."

"Hmm. You sit right there a minute," Pappas said. He opened the doorway to the cell and disappeared into a dark hallway. Corey stood silently in the corner of the room staring at the accused. Two minutes later, Pappas was back in the room, waving the check in front of Wardlaw's nose.

"This look familiar? I've got a witness says that you gave it to him to pay off a gambling debt."

Wardlaw stared at the check. He looked back up at Pappas, but said nothing.

Corey stepped closer. "Mr. Wardlaw, we've got you dead to rights on possession of stolen property. That's a local beef. You're a relatively young man. I'm sure you can do the time. No big deal. But before you decide not to cooperate with Detective Pappas, I want you to understand that your possession of that check—which Detective Pappas can prove beyond all reasonable doubt—ties you to certain more serious crimes."

"Like what?"

"Like kidnapping and violation of the Dyer Act, both of which are federal crimes. Federal time is a little tougher, Mr. Wardlaw, but it's your call. Maybe you could tough it out. Maybe." Corey stepped back toward the corner. Then he stepped forward again. "Oh, there's one more problem that check creates for you."

Wardlaw snorted. "Another federal case?"

"No, it's not federal. You wouldn't go to Leavenworth if you were convicted. Not sure exactly where you'd go, to tell the truth. Do you know, Detective Pappas?"

"I think it's downtown in the courthouse."

"What is?" Wardlaw asked, his face wrinkled with confusion.

"The electric chair," Corey answered. "Murder is a capital crime, Mr. Wardlaw, and that check locks you in like a strait jacket." Corey watched as perspiration popped out on Wardlaw's forehead. "What crime do you prefer to go down for, Mr. Wardlaw: local, federal, or capital?"

# SUNDAY FEBRUARY 9, 1936

# CHAPTER 57

**Washington, D.C.**

"What brings you back to Washington so soon, dear?" Joan Roswell asked as Wallace DeWitt held the chair for her. Joan was dazzling, as always, her green eyes animated and sparkling, her blonde hair perfectly coiffed under a fetching feathered hat. They had returned to the Old Ebbitt Grill, convenient to the Willard Hotel, where Wallace was once again staying.

"A combination of business and pleasure," Wallace answered with a smile.

"And which is this, dear?"

"A combination of business and pleasure," Wallace repeated with a laugh. "I've got a meeting with Congressman Gasque Monday afternoon. We've got a paper mill in his district. We want to enlarge it, invest in some new equipment, create a few new jobs. I'm hoping he can help us with the lay of the land down there. And, of course, this is the pleasurable part of my trip right here."

"Wallace DeWitt, you are a shameless flirt!"

"How come you're still in town? I was sure you would have decamped back to Hollywood by now and that I would have been left to wander the halls of power in lonely solitude."

Joan flashed her dimpled smile and leaned forward, placing her hand on Wallace's forearm. "My editor has actually been impressed for once. Oh, he doesn't say it outright, that would crack his tough-as-nails-newspaper-editor façade, but he's finally recognizing what I can do. Hopefully, I'll be able to hang around until this polio case is cracked." She cocked her head and added, "I may just do some of the cracking."

Wallace looked down at the leather-trimmed menu resting at his place. He pretended to read the evening's entrees, but he was really trying to reach a decision, trying to determine his next step. After a moment, he looked up and said, "I may be able to help you."

"And you're sure he was talking about the missing checks?" Joan asked a few minutes later, chewing a forkful of Caesar salad.

"He was specific. He said, 'The President's Birthday Ball Committee.'"

"What did you do?"

"I tried not to choke! I was quiet for a second and then I told him to let me think on it and get back to him with a plan."

"And have you?"

"Of course not. I'm not going to jail for Deacon Knox, no matter how much I want him to succeed," Wallace said, adding to himself, *which really isn't that much.* "What I'm really thinking is that I should call that FBI fellow and tell him what I know."

"You should definitely do that, dear," Joan's eyes flashed, "but not until I have the whole story!"

"I've pretty much told you what I know. If you write the story now, it'll spike Wainwright's investigation. Knox and Bowman will just dump the checks somewhere, burn 'em probably, then you don't have a story and Wainwright doesn't have a case."

Wallace sipped his Scotch. Joan stared down at her salad. "How about this," she began slowly, looking up. "How about I take you to see Wainwright? I sit there while you tell your story. I get first access to the FBI's investigation for bringing you in." Wallace's eyebrows shot up. "So to speak, dear."

Kelly Durham and Kathryn Smith

# CHAPTER 58

**Washington, D.C.**

Ed Wardlaw had been a juvenile delinquent, petty grifter, and small-time muscle, but he was no fool. When the FBI agent had dangled a murder charge in front of him—a murder about which he knew nothing, by the way—Ed had decided to take the path of least resistance. He knew he'd goofed up by passing that check off to the old drunk with the big mouth. Ed knew the cops had him dead-to-rights on that charge. His best play under the circumstances was to cut a deal.

By Sunday night, Wardlaw had informed his court-appointed lawyer that he wished to cooperate with the feds. Wardlaw intended to plead guilty to a single count of possession of stolen property in exchange for the dropping of kidnapping, auto theft, and all other charges, including the murder he knew nothing about. In addition, the feds had to agree to inform the judge of his cooperation—if his information helped resolve the case. And that was a big "if," because, while Ed had passed that check and had been among the crew that had stolen it and had, temporarily at least, driven those two women across the state line, Ed had no idea for whom he had been working.

# MONDAY FEBRUARY 10, 1936

# CHAPTER 59

Corey Wainwright had been only too happy to schedule an interview with Wallace DeWitt first thing Monday morning. It seemed that everywhere Corey had looked recently, DeWitt's name had popped up. That Corey also had to accommodate Joan Roswell was less pleasing. Nonetheless, he had hustled up an extra chair and squeezed it into his tiny office, so he could maintain his "give and take" relationship with the annoying reporter.

"Did you actually see such a check, Mr. DeWitt?"

"No sir, but he was very clear about who the checks were made out to."

"Did he say how the checks had come to be in his possession?"

"No, and frankly, I was too startled to ask. I asked him to let me think the matter over and told him I'd call him this week."

"Are you willing to cooperate with the Bureau on this matter, Mr. DeWitt?"

Wallace looked bemused. "I thought that's what I was doing."

"I'm speaking of something a bit more involved."

"Like with the Temple case?" Joan interjected.

Corey shot her a look that could have thawed Niagara Falls in winter. Wallace was now confused. Rather than answer Joan's question, Corey continued. "Would you be willing to meet with Henry Bowman and accept the check or checks from him and then testify in court? If we can catch him with the checks, we put another piece of this jigsaw puzzle in place. We come closer to catching the thieves and kidnappers and hopefully a murderer as well. What do you say, Mr. DeWitt?"

Wallace poked out his lips and thought it over. The idea appealed to his sense of adventure. Heck, he might even enjoy a little action for a change. Business was rewarding, but not often exciting.

"I'll help you out, Mr. Wainwright, on one condition."

Corey's brow wrinkled. "And that is?"

"Joan gets the story first: all the way from the White House to the ball to the theft to the capture and arrest of the men behind it." Wallace glanced over to his lady friend to find her beaming. "I'm sure she'll agree not to write anything prejudicial to your legal restrictions, right, Joan?"

Joan's smile slipped away, but she nodded in agreement. "Right, dear."

"It's a deal," Wainwright reached across his desk and shook hands with DeWitt.


"Who hired you for the job?" Corey Wainwright asked Ed Wardlaw. They were in an interview room at the federal courthouse jail.

"I don't know. He didn't exactly offer me a resume, you know."

"He didn't give you a name?"

Wardlaw shook his head. "No, no name."

"Smith, maybe?"

"No name."

"Can you describe the guy—it was a guy, right?"

Wardlaw laughed. "Yes, it was a guy. Maybe a year or two younger than me. He spoke well. Dressed nice. Not bad looking—not that I was interested."

"What was he wearing, do you remember?"

"Brown suit, white shirt, striped tie."

"Hair? Eyes?"

"Yes," Wardlaw said and then laughed again. "He had both." Corey waited, staring at Wardlaw.

"This is no joking matter, Wardlaw," Corey said, slowly and quietly.

"OK, geez, I'm making a joke. Loosen up."

"What color was his hair?"

"Light brown. His eyes were green."

"Would you recognize him if you saw him again?"

"I think so."

"Did you see him again? Was he present at the theft and kidnapping?"

"No. It was two other guys working that night."

"Describe them."

"They were older than me, late thirties, I guess. Both were about five foot, eight or nine. Stockier than me too. Darker hair, but I only saw them in the dark. Then for part of the time, we had masks on."

"Any names?"

"Gehrig, Ruth, and Lazzeri."

"Come on, Wardlaw!" Corey slapped the top of the table, causing Wardlaw to flinch. "Quit cracking jokes!"

Wardlaw held up both hands in front of him. "No, listen, that's what we called each other. Like on the Yankees, right? I was Lazzeri. The other two guys were Ruth and Gehrig."

"Where did you meet them?"

"The guy who hired me told me to meet them in front of the Chinese restaurant on M Street near Connecticut at ten o'clock that night. He said they'd drive up to the corner and ask directions to Ford's Theatre. That's what happened."

"What was the plan after that?"

"We were to go to the Shoreham Hotel and wait outside. Ruth and Gehrig were in the front seat of the car and I sat in back."

"This was the gray Chevrolet?"

"Right. So, we sit there for, must have been a couple of hours. I'm about to nod off and finally Gehrig says, 'There's the signal.' I look up but I don't see anything looks like a signal. So, I'm not sure what's happening, but I just do what I'm told. Gehrig cranks up the car and we sit there a few more minutes and finally see these three women walk out to a Buick coupe. They're carrying bank bags and I'm thinking, 'Here we go.' One of the women goes to the car, puts her bag in the front and then goes back inside the hotel. The other two get in and crank up and we're off to the races."

"What were your instructions about the women?"

"My job was to listen to Gehrig and do what he said. We were to stop their car, grab the money and put them in our car and haul ass out of there as fast as possible."

"What were you supposed to do with the women?"

"Just what we did: turn 'em loose."

"Why take them in the first place?"

"So we'd have a head start on the cops; you know, get out of town before they were wise to us. That's what we did. Then we kicked 'em loose. We never had any plan to hurt them, and we didn't."

"What about the money?" Corey asked. "What was the plan for the money?"

"The guy who hired me told me to stay with Ruth and Gehrig until we got to Lorton. That's where we split up."

"That where you got paid off?"

"Right. Let me give you a tip, Mr. G-man: never split up until after you've been paid off or you won't ever get paid off."

"Thanks," Corey said, scribbling a note on his pad. "How much was your take?"

"Two hundred bucks." Corey whistled. Wardlaw grinned. "Pretty good for three hours work, huh? Bet your hourly rate's a little less, huh?"

Corey nodded. "Pretty good until you consider that you had over twenty thousand dollars in those bank bags." Wardlaw's face fell. "Not quite as good a deal as you thought. What happened to the rest of the money?"

"You'll have to ask Ruth and Gehrig—if you ever find them."

"We'll find them, Mr. Wardlaw. Haven't you heard? We always get our man—or men, as the case may be."

# CHAPTER 60

Wallace hung up the phone beside his bed and exhaled. *Well, that's done.* He had called Henry Bowman from his room at the Willard Hotel to arrange a meeting.

"I've got to be back in Washington tomorrow to meet a campaign advisor," Henry had said.

"Sounds serious."

"He's definitely going to run," Henry had replied. "But don't tell anybody yet. We want to get a big push from the press coverage when he formally announces. Keep it on the Q-T until then."

"Sure," Wallace had taken a deep breath and added, "maybe we could continue our discussion from our Saturday meeting. I think I've got a solution worked out."

Henry had been silent for a moment as though he was trying to remember the Saturday conversation. "Yes. That would be helpful."

"I'm in Washington on business now, and I can stay over a day. We'll set a time and place to meet once you get here. Oh, and make sure you bring those documents with you," Wallace had said before hanging up.

*Seventy-five cents for a three-minute long distance call. No wonder the Willard could afford to put these nice robes in every room.* Fortunately, local calls were cheaper, only ten cents. Wallace pushed down on the telephone's cradle and released it.

"Operator. How may I connect your call?"

Wallace looked down to the card in his hand. "Atlas 7680, please." Wallace listened to the clicks on the line as the operator made the connection and the phone on the far end began to ring.

"FBI, Special Agent Wainwright."

"It's Wallace DeWitt. I've got a meeting set up with our man tomorrow."

"How did he sound?" Corey asked.

"Fine. He told me he was coming into town on business, so I just suggested we meet then."

"Did you set a time and place?"

"No, I thought maybe you'd want to be in on that."

"You bet I would!"

Ed Wardlaw lay his head back on the blue ticking pillow and read the sports page. One of the jail guards had turned out to be a decent Joe. He'd grown up in Manassas, not far from where Wardlaw had lived as a kid. He had shared with Wardlaw the newspaper once the guys in the day room were done with it. The guard, Dutton was his name, also left the hallway door open when he was working nights, so Wardlaw and the other "guests" could listen in on the radio.

Wardlaw wasn't much interested in a bunch of college boys playing basketball, but pitchers and catchers would report to spring training in a couple of weeks and Wardlaw was hoping 1936 would be a better season for the Senators. They'd finished twenty-seven games behind Detroit the previous year, but there were a couple of hot young players in the Senators' farm system that Wardlaw thought might get called up.

He closed the paper and folded it, letting it rest on his chest. *That takes care of this morning,* he thought, looking up toward the ceiling. *What should I plan for this afternoon?*

"Can you keep a secret?" Wallace asked Joan as they waited for their roast beef sandwiches to arrive. They were seated at a small table in the Willard's restaurant. It was midday and the place was nearly full of well-dressed businessmen, lawyers, and lobbyists plotting how to get a piece of the ever-expanding federal pie. Joan was one of only three women in the place, and, Wallace thought, the most attractive by a mile. He had noticed with a sense of pride how she turned the heads of most of the men in the place when they'd walked in.

"Can I keep a secret? Why, darling, I'm a reporter. That's what I do." She batted her eyelashes at him theatrically as she pulled a cigarette and its holder from her purse. Wallace pulled out a book of matches imprinted with the hotel's stylish "W" logo and lit her smoke. "Why do you ask, dear?"

He shook the match out and dropped it into the glass ash tray in the center of the round table. "Henry Bowman will be back in town tomorrow. We plan to meet."

"Where? When? I want to be there!"

"You'll have to be inconspicuous. If you mess up Wainwright's case, he won't be very nice about it."

"Oh, don't you worry, dear. I can handle Corey Wainwright. Why's Bowman coming to town? I thought you were going to have to go to him."

Wallace stared into Joan's green cat's eyes. "He's meeting with a campaign advisor. Knox is going to declare for the nomination."

"When, when, when?" Joan asked. She was leaning forward as though she was about to be fired out of the big cannon at the circus.

"I don't know. I'll try to find out, but you don't run with any of this until I say so. Agreed?"

Joan slumped backwards and pouted. "All right, all right. People are always telling me things I can't print. It's a wonder I ever get a scoop."

"Just be patient. You'll get your story."

# CHAPTER 61

Missy had first gotten to use a home movie camera in Warm Springs in the late 1920s, when FDR's advisor Louis Howe had suggested taking films of Warm Springs Foundation patients to demonstrate their progress in order to solicit donations from wealthy philanthropists. "Perhaps just one showing them doing a hundred-yard dash or shoveling coal or something another after treatment, together with the statement that, when they arrived, it required two stretchers and an ambulance to get them down to the pool," he had said. George Eastman, founder of Eastman Kodak, had given Franklin Roosevelt one of the first home movie cameras his company had made for this very purpose. As the devices became less expensive, Missy had been able to afford one of her own. She often used it to shoot activities such as picnics at Hyde Park and boat trips on the Potomac. She'd even gotten some film of Eleanor Roosevelt on ice skates the winter before.

"I'm going to see Mike Wanner for a minute," she told Grace Tully early Monday afternoon. "Will you listen out for the President's buzzer?"

"Sure," Grace said, looking pointedly at the movie camera in her hand. "Are you going to shoot a movie of him?"

"No, I'm going fishing," Missy said mysteriously.

When she reached Mike's office, he was sorting some photos on his small wooden desk. He glanced up, smiling a bit warily.

"Good morning, Mike!" Missy said sunnily. "Mind if I pick your brains for a few minutes about movie cameras?"

"Of course not," Mike said. "But you may know as much about them as I do. I do far more still work than movie work."

"I bet you got some footage of Ginger Rogers dancing at the Birthday Ball," Missy said. "I thought the President would enjoy seeing it since he didn't go to the ball himself."

"Sorry, I didn't bring my movie camera with me that night," he said. "I just shot stills."

Although Missy quickly dropped her eyes, Mike realized immediately that he had slipped up. He'd used the excuse of a movie camera for hanging around the Shoreham, saying he had forgotten to pack it with his other gear and had to go back into the hotel. "Oh, that's too bad," she mumbled. "F.D. will be disappointed. Well, I better get back to my office. See you!"

"Yeah, sorry I couldn't be of any help," Mike said, watching her walk away. *Now what do I do?*

As soon as Missy got back to her desk, she placed a call to the FBI office, trying to reach Corey Wainwright to tell him of her hunch about Mike Wanner. The receptionist said he was on another call and she would leave a message for him. "Thanks," Missy said, drumming her fingers. "Please tell him it's rather urgent."

# CHAPTER 62

Wardlaw had traversed his cell one hundred and seventy-five times. He figured the cell was about ten feet long, so he'd walked about a third of a mile. *I'm getting more exercise in here than I do on the outside,* he thought with a grim smile. He reached down to his cot and tossed the newspaper out of his way as he sat down.

He glanced at the front page and then looked away, toward the yellow, winter sunlight streaming in through the window. Wait a minute! Wardlaw picked up the newspaper and stared at the pictures on the front page. Under a headline proclaiming PRESIDENT'S CRITICS EYE DEM NOMINATION were two photographs. One of them featured that radio preacher, Deacon something. The other one showed an older looking guy with a cigar and a big smile.

But what caught Wardlaw's eye was the man in the background; a younger man, nicely dressed and smiling at the potential candidate. *That's him! That's the guy!*

"Dutton! Hey, Dutton!" he called out to the friendly jailer.

Dutton waddled out of the guard's dayroom. "What's all the racket for? I'm right here. Gee, you'd think the place was on fire or something."

Wardlaw stood at the barred door to his cell gripping the paper in one hand. "I need to talk to Mr. Wainwright at the FBI."

"Sure you don't want me to just get J. Edgar Hoover on the phone?" Dutton smiled.

"I'm serious. This is important."

"I'm sure Agent Wainwright is already working on important stuff. I'm sure he don't need you bothering him on a sunny afternoon."

"C'mon, Dutton. This is about the case me and him are working on. There's something in the paper that he needs to see."

"I dunno. You already had your one phone call. This isn't the Mayflower, you know. We don't have room service and we don't shine shoes."

"Dammit! I ain't playing games!" Wardlaw held up the newspaper. "I've got evidence right here that he needs to know about—that he wants to know about. You don't get me to the phone, I'm gonna make sure Wainwright and Hoover both know it was you caused this case to crater."

Dutton stared at his prisoner. He seemed truly agitated—and sincere. "I'm not supposed to let you make personal calls."

"It ain't personal! I'm not calling my mama. I'm not calling my lawyer. I want to talk to Agent Wainwright at the FBI. Do I have to draw you a picture?"

Dutton hesitated. *What kind of trouble will I get into if I let him use the phone? And what if I don't?* He reached to his belt and removed a pair of handcuffs, sticking them between the bars. "Put these on."

The knock on his door caused Corey to look up. "Agent Wainwright?" Standing in the door frame wearing his blue coat was the technician from the documentation laboratory.

"Hey! Come in," Corey said, standing up behind his desk. He glanced at his watch. It was only two o'clock. "You're ahead of schedule."

"Well, we don't get many opportunities to work on a project that has Mr. Hoover's direct interest, if you know what I mean."

The technician sat down in the single wooden chair in front of Corey's desk and handed across the same envelope Corey had walked downstairs the previous Wednesday. "Quite an interesting document, as you'll see in the report. I put a copy inside the envelope." Corey opened it and pulled out a carbon copy of a three-page typewritten report with a photostat paper clipped to the back. Corey flipped through the pages quickly, his eyes settling on the signature at the bottom of page three.

"What did you find, Leo?"

"To begin with, the journal itself is interesting. The binding and paper stock is not of a style you would normally find. It's made from amate, a type of tree bark. You'd see it in some high-end shops in Mexico, but not typically around here. I was a little surprised that a night watchman would be keeping a diary in an expensive journal like this. I also wondered what might have happened to its cover."

"It's cover?"

"Yes, normally the binding here," Leo pointed to the glued spine of the journal, "would be hidden inside a leather or a fabric cover of some type. But that's not the only curious thing. I contacted the Pinkerton office where you said this fellow worked and got a copy of his application—his handwritten application. Guess what."

"What?"

"The handwriting on the application bears no resemblance to that in this diary. Look at the copy included at the back of my report. When we analyze handwriting, we compare the shapes of letters first. See how he loops the 'L's in 'Mitchell'? Now look at the diary. The 'L's there are straight, single lines, not loops. In fact, almost none of the letters written in the diary match the decedent's handwritten letters on the application."

"So, what are you telling me?"

"It's a phony. The whole diary is a fake. Not even a very good one. You've hooked a red herring."

Corey sighed and looked toward the ceiling. *Wait till I get my hands on Joan Roswell!* He offered Leo a tight smile. "I'm going to make sure the source of that journal feels my wrath. And I'm going to make sure Mr. Hoover knows what good support you've provided this investigation."

Leo beamed.

It felt like it was taking forever, but finally Dutton handed the telephone to Wardlaw. "Agent Wainwright?"

"What is it, Wardlaw? I don't have time for monkey business."

"No sir. I know that. You asked me if I could identify the guy who paid me to take part in the heist."

"Yes, I remember. The man with no name." Wainwright's voice betrayed his impatience.

"Well, he's right there on the front of the newspaper."

"What paper?"

"This morning's *Herald*. He's standing right behind the guy at the microphone." Wardlaw heard Wainwright cover the receiver, heard a muffled voice. Then, "Hang on a minute. We're finding a copy."

Wardlaw heard a clunk as Wainwright set the phone down. He heard footsteps, then silence. Dutton was standing by the desk, waiting, glancing at his watch, and growing more impatient and nervous with the ticking of each second.

"Hurry up," he whispered.

Footsteps again; a swishing sound and then Wainwright was back. "OK, Wardlaw. I'm looking at the paper. Front page?"

"Yeah. You see the guy at the microphone?"

"I see him." Wainwright looked at the bright eyes and broad smile of Al Smith, the former New York governor.

"Well, look right behind him! The guy in the suit. That's the guy!"

Wainwright's eyes shifted to a man standing behind Smith's shoulder, a well-dressed man whose face was already well-known to him: Wallace DeWitt.

*How could I have been so stupid?* Corey had hung up the phone in a rage, not at Wardlaw for calling him, but at himself. *I should have listened to Missy! She told me this guy was up to something. And now I've let him play me and the Bureau like a prize mackerel.*

He looked at his watch. Two-thirty p.m. He needed to pull DeWitt in and have a chat before his meeting with Henry Bowman. *What the hell is going on?*

# CHAPTER 63

By the time he arrived at the Willard Hotel, Corey Wainwright's uncertainty over Wallace DeWitt was swirling through his mind like leaves scattered before an autumn wind. Why had DeWitt come to Corey with his tale of the stolen check—which he admitted he hadn't seen—if he was behind the theft of the polio funds in the first place? Was this some elaborate political scheme to discredit Knox? Had Henry Bowman ever really gone to see DeWitt? No matter from which angle he examined the question—and he'd looked at it from front and back, above and below—Corey couldn't come up with an answer that made sense. Absent a logical conclusion, he'd decided to confront DeWitt directly.

The other thing bothering him was the phone call he'd gotten from Missy while he was on the phone with Wardlaw. When he called her back, Grace Tully had picked up and said Missy was in the President's office and couldn't be disturbed. He didn't have time to sit around. *I'll have to call her back later.*

Corey asked the front desk clerk at the Willard to ring him through to DeWitt's room. He picked up the house phone at the end of the registration desk and turned to face the small lobby. His fingers played along the edge of the folded newspaper in his coat pocket. He didn't want DeWitt to sneak past him while he waited for him to answer his phone.

On the third ring, a voice answered, "Hello?"

"Mr. DeWitt, it's Corey Wainwright. I'm down in the lobby. I wonder if you've got a minute to talk?"

"Sure. I've got an appointment on the Hill in a couple of hours, but we can talk until I need to leave."

"I doubt we'll need that much time," Corey replied, but, truthfully, he wondered if Wallace DeWitt would still be a free man in a couple of hours. "I'll meet you in the bar."

"Be down in ten."

"Drink?" Wallace DeWitt asked as he sat down across the small round table from the FBI agent. He waved his hand to attract a waiter.

"No, thanks. On duty," Corey answered.

"Scotch on the rocks," Wallace said when the waiter reached their table. Turning to Corey he asked, "Tonic water or something?" The G-man shook his head.

"So, what's up? I didn't expect to see you so soon. You decided where you want my meeting with Bowman to take place?"

"Right now, I'm trying to decide if I still want that meeting to occur."

Wallace frowned. "I'm not sure I follow you."

Corey reached in his pocket and laid the newspaper on the table. He tapped the picture of Al Smith with his finger and observed Wallace's face. "I've got a suspect in custody who says you paid him two hundred dollars to steal the polio money." Either Wallace was a consummate actor, or he was truly shocked, because he otherwise couldn't have expressed the combination of confusion and anger that quickly transformed his face into a furious mask.

"That's bullshit! Why would I have come to you if I was involved in this mess?" Wallace leaned forward, his fists clinched, his face flushed.

"That's what I want to know, Mr. DeWitt. I know you can vouch for your whereabouts at the time of the robbery, but that doesn't mean you weren't somehow involved in planning the crime."

Wallace held up his hand. "I'm done talking to you. You start accusing me of things and you can start talking to my attorney." He pushed his chair back, just as the waiter returned with his drink. He paused to take a gulp and set the glass back on the table with a sharp whack.

"Wait a minute," Corey said, hesitant to let Wallace leave. If he was involved in this thing, letting him out of sight seemed like a poor strategy. If he wasn't, maybe there was an easy way to find out. "I've got an idea."

Wallace had objected at first, but had yielded to Corey's entreaties. He wanted to get this thing cleared up and this might be a quick, easy way to do so. If it didn't work, he figured he'd be no worse off. He had finished his drink as Corey stuffed the newspaper back into his pocket. They'd left the Willard and taken Corey's Bureau car to the federal courthouse.

Corey had left Wallace in the company of one of the bailiffs and had gone to the jail cells in the basement. He talked with the sergeant of the guard and arranged for Ed Wardlaw to be taken to one of the viewing rooms from which he could observe a line-up of suspects. Then, Corey had returned to Wallace, who was now third in a line of six men. Two of them were clerks working in the building, one was a security guard, one a reporter covering a case on recess, and the other was a repairman summoned to fix a leaky radiator in the chief judge's chambers.

Wallace nervously watched the clock. It wouldn't do for him to miss his meeting with the congressman— especially if his absence was due to his arrest by the FBI. Finally, the bailiff led the "suspects" into a narrow, brightly lit room. They were told to turn and face a large mirror mounted on the wall opposite them.

Wallace wondered who was on the other side watching him.

Meanwhile, Ed Wardlaw wondered who the men were in the line-up. They were staring at him—or rather at the large one-way window that appeared to them like a mirror.

"Recognize him?" The FBI man asked.

"Recognize who?" Wardlaw asked, looking away from the window at the agent.

"The guy from the paper. The one you said hired you."

"Nope. It's not any of these guys."

"But you said..." Corey stopped. He tugged the newspaper from his pocket and held it up for Wardlaw. He pointed past Al Smith's shoulder at the dimmer image of Wallace DeWitt. "You said that guy hired you, paid you two hundred smacks!"

Wardlaw smirked, shaking his head vigorously. "No, not that guy." He snatched the paper out of Corey's hand and flipped it over. "That guy!" He jabbed his finger at a different picture, a picture of Owen Knox, behind whom stood the smiling, bespectacled Henry Bowman.

# CHAPTER 64

Corey hadn't said ten words since he'd pulled Wallace away from the other "suspects" and offered to drive him to his appointment. Wallace had fumed as the government car carried him along Pennsylvania Avenue toward the Capitol.

"My meeting's in the House Office Building. You know where that is?"

"I know it's around here somewhere."

"Turn right on Third, then left on Independence. You can let me off at the top of the Hill."

Corey followed the directions before coming to a stop in front of a large marble-clad building just south of the Capitol.

"Thanks for the lift." Wallace reached for the door handle.

"Mr. DeWitt, I apologize for not being squared away back there. I should have been more diligent before I started making accusations and dragging you through all that." Corey bit his lip, staring at his passenger.

Wallace exhaled, then chuckled. "It's OK. I guess I've been called worse, I just can't remember when. No harm done. It makes me all the more determined to help you bust this thing open, though, I can tell you that."

Corey extended his hand and Wallace shook it. He winked at the agent and said, "But now you and Mr. Hoover owe me a drink."

"Agreed," Corey said with a laugh, "under one condition."

"What's that?"

"You tell me how to get back to the Justice Department."

"My meeting with Bowman is set for tomorrow night," Wallace told Joan. "I'm meeting him for dinner at the Mayflower."

Joan smiled and exhaled blue smoke. Lying in his bed wearing nothing but a pair of jade earrings, she brought to Wallace's mind the image of a seductive and beautiful dragon. "I'll be there."

"You might want to clear it with Wainwright."

"Not a chance. I'm not going to let him cheat me out of the story this time."

"He cheated you out of a story? When?"

"Last autumn in San Francisco. I would have won a Pulitzer, but Wainwright's boss pulled the plug." She tapped ashes into the tray resting on the top sheet. "I helped them out any way. I'm such a good little girl when I want to be."

Wallace laughed. "Which isn't very often, I suspect."

Joan punched him playfully on the arm. She took a long drag on her cigarette. "You know what I need?"

"What?"

"I can land this story on the front page of every daily in the country if I have a good photograph. Click, flash—snapped right at the moment he hands over the incriminating evidence!"

"I think it'd be better if you waited for Wainwright to make the arrest. Catch the startled look on Henry's face as the FBI slaps cuffs on him." Wallace cocked his head and raised his eyebrows. "That'd be pretty dramatic."

"If I only had a photographer!"

"Wait a minute." Wallace picked up his billfold from the bedside table and thumbed through its contents. "Here," he said, pulling a business card out and handing it to Joan. "Call this guy."

"The White House?"

"He took the picture of me dancing with Ginger Rogers. He said he did some freelance. If he's not available, maybe he can suggest someone."

"Wallace DeWitt, you're simply the best!"

# TUESDAY FEBRUARY 11, 1936

# CHAPTER 65

Missy was applying her signature to a stack of letters when she got a call from the security guard that Corey Wainwright wanted to see her. She hastily smoothed her hair and touched up her lipstick, using a mirrored compact she pulled from her desk drawer. When Corey entered, she greeted him with a bright smile and offered him coffee.

"It's been a busy few days since I saw you and I wanted to get you up-to-date on all that happened," he said, taking a seat in front of her desk. "I tried to call you back yesterday, and you were in with the President, then we had some interesting developments in Virginia." He quickly outlined the arrest of Ed Wardlaw and the revelation about Henry Bowman, leaving out his embarrassing mistake about Wallace DeWitt. "Mr. DeWitt is fully cooperating with us. He's having dinner with the suspect at the Mayflower tonight, and we will arrest him as soon as he hands over the checks."

Missy stared at him, stunned. "This is so much more complicated than I thought," she said. "I have never cared for Deacon Knox, he's such an insufferable, sanctimonious character, and he says such horrible things about the President, but I never dreamed he'd be involved in this."

"We're not sure he is," Corey cautioned. "It may just be that Bowman has gotten over-zealous about raising money for him. If that's the case, there's a question in my mind about whether Bowman is being manipulated himself."

Missy looked down at her fingernails for a moment and then leveled her blue eyes on Corey. "You may have heard that I see Ambassador Bullitt when he's back in the States," she said. "He took me dancing at the Shoreham Saturday night and we had a long conversation about the Russians. He's shared his views with the President too. He believes they are trying to influence the election this year. I know it sounds crazy, but could this be part of their strategy?"

Corey stared back, trying to take in both Missy's confession of a romantic relationship and Ambassador Bullitt's concern about Russian interference. His ears turned red at the tips. "I don't think it's far-fetched at all," he said, "and I know Mr. Hoover won't." His mind began to race.

"Another thing about Saturday night," Missy said. "When we were leaving, I suddenly had a memory from the Birthday Ball night." She told him about Mike Wanner's excuse for re-entering the building and her conversation with him Monday about the movie camera. "That's what I was calling you about yesterday, but it sounds like you had much bigger fish to fry."

"I think your hunch is more than a hunch," Corey said seriously. "We know someone had to have signaled the car that went after you on Dupont Circle. It could have been the photographer. Have you shared this with the President or Steve Early yet?"

Missy shook her head. "The President is covered up with appointments today and Steve's out of the office until late this afternoon. I plan to bring it up during our Children's Hour today."

"Children's Hour?"

"That's what the Boss. calls the daily cocktail party in his study," Missy giggled. "I thought you knew."

The President was energetically shaking martinis in his silver shaker and Missy was arranging a tray of small slices of toast to be topped with caviar when Steve Early strode through the door of the study.

"You wanted to see me, sir?" he asked.

"Yes, Steve," the President said. "Old fashioned?"

"That would be wonderful," Steve said gratefully. "It's been quite a day."

"Tomorrow won't be any better," Missy said. She quickly told him about the White House photographer's subterfuge regarding the movie camera at the Birthday Ball.

"I don't think there's any choice but to confront him first thing in the morning," the President said. "This is serious stuff. And on top of that, I never have bought his line about none of the pictures being missing, and now this…You know I'll stick out my neck for anyone who is loyal, but this fellow has gone too far, even if he does take good pictures."

"I totally agree," Steve said. "I'll talk to him first thing tomorrow."

"I've asked Corey Wainwright to arrive at nine," Missy said. "He's going to take him in for questioning."

"Yes, it's far more than a personnel issue," Steve said. "We'll come at him from all angles."

"Good! Glad that's over," the President said. "Oh, here's Grace. Come in, Duchess! I meant to tell you this morning how nice you looked in that blue dress. Did you know it's my favorite color? Now, did I ever tell you children about the time …"

# CHAPTER 66

"Not quite as good as Jack Dempsey's, is it?" Wallace asked Henry Bowman with a smile. They were seated in the Mayflower Hotel's main dining room. Ornate gold-leaf trim reflected light from the chandeliers, casting the wide room in a glow of yellow light. A narrow mezzanine level lined two of the dining room's sides, offering additional space for overflow diners. Wallace glanced up. Only one couple was seated up there on this cold evening, and while they looked like they might be celebrating an anniversary or a birthday, Wallace knew their purpose had more to do with what was happening at his table than at theirs. They were part of Wainwright's back-up detail.

"Not quite as exciting, no," Henry agreed with a smile, "but probably more to the Deacon's liking. He felt a little out of place at Dempsey's. The whole alcohol and prize-fighting atmosphere is a bit different than his usual environment."

"Yeah, I guess not many of his followers order drinks when they come to hear him preach. He doesn't drink, right?"

"The most I've ever seen him take is a small glass of sherry, and that only infrequently. You know he was an early supporter of Roosevelt, but he really struggled over the whole Prohibition issue. He finally went along with repeal because he felt alcohol was the lesser evil when compared to the way Prohibition was strengthening organized crime."

"I guess you had your share of that in Chicago, huh?"

"Oh, I could tell you stories," Henry said, green eyes glinting behind his glasses, and proceeded to do just that. As he talked, Wallace's eyes strayed around the room. He caught a glimpse of Corey Wainwright and another man—probably another agent—two tables to his right. He wondered how many other agents were waiting for him to stand and shake Henry's hand, the signal for them to move in.

Mike Wanner wasn't nearly as handsome an escort as Wallace DeWitt, but then this was only a one-time gig. Once Joan got her photograph, she wouldn't have to deal with the skinny, sloppily dressed man with his ridiculous little moustache again. *Honestly, you'd think a grown man could at least wear an ironed shirt and a clean suit to dinner. And I'm having to pay!*

Joan had been cautious about the timing of their arrival. She knew the action wouldn't take place until Henry Bowman handed over the stolen checks. She also knew that Corey Wainwright would throw her out of the building if he saw her before she saw him. She had waited until the other characters in the drama should have been in place. Then, while Mike waited in the hotel lobby, she had climbed to the second floor and reconnoitered the dining room from one of the doors leading to the mezzanine. She had quickly located Corey Wainwright, seated at a table near Wallace's. She'd gone back downstairs and tipped the maître d' two dollars to seat them at a table behind Corey's back and out of his view.

"Now, Mike, darling, pretend that we're a couple. Act chivalrously, even if you're not accustomed to doing so. And keep your camera bag under the table for now."

"But you're paying the check, right?"

"Yes, dear, but I need you to play the man. Understand?"

"Sure, sure." Mike was swinging his head around like a kid at Coney Island. "I've been here before, you know. Not to eat, of course, but to balls and big events and things."

"Good," Joan replied, her gaze level. "Then you should know how to get a good action photo, yes?"

"Action? What kind of action?"

"There's going to be an arrest here tonight. You're going to take a picture of the suspect as he is clapped in irons, so to speak. I expect you to move fast, dear. Miss the shot and you'll miss your paycheck." Joan smiled.

"There won't be any shooting or anything, will there?" Mike asked with a frown. "That would change our agreement."

"I'm sure the FBI will have the situation under control, dear."

"FBI?"

"Yes, dear." After that, Mike was quiet, for which Joan was grateful.

Wallace picked at the remnants of his roast beef. Henry had devoured half a chicken.

"Not bad, not bad at all. You know, Mr. DeWitt, you pick good places to eat."

"Why don't you call me Wallace, Henry."

"It's good to have you on our team, Wallace."

Their waiter returned. "Would you gentlemen care for coffee and dessert?"

Wallace nodded toward his companion. "Apple pie, please," Henry said.

"Chocolate cake with a cup of coffee for me," Wallace said.

Once the waiter departed, Henry reached into the inside pocket of his suit coat and pulled out a thick envelope. "To business, Wallace," he said, sliding the envelope across the table.

"Just so I have this straight," Wallace began, "you want me to find a way to convert these," he patted the envelope with his hand, "into cash and return it to the Knox campaign."

"That is correct, as we discussed in your office."

Wallace picked up the envelope and studied it for a moment. He hoped Wainwright and his associates were watching. Joan too. He stuck his finger under the flap and lifted it open. He pulled out dozens of checks. He recalled Wainwright's instructions. He had to receive the stolen items directly from Henry Bowman. Check. Bowman had to confirm that the checks were to be converted into cash for the use of the Knox campaign. Check. And Wallace had to verify that the checks were in fact payable to the President's Birthday Ball Committee. He quickly thumbed through the stack. Check.

"It's a lot of money, Henry. It will take a couple of weeks. That OK?"

"That's fine, Wallace. I appreciate your help. The Deacon would too, but he doesn't really keep up with the financing of the campaign."

"He doesn't know about this?"

"No, and I'm trusting you to keep it that way, Wallace."

Wallace put the checks back in the envelope and stuffed it in his coat pocket. He reached over the table and shook Henry's hand.

"Thank you, Wallace," Henry said, smiling. Henry's smile flickered as Wallace stood up, still holding his hand. Confusion wrinkled his brow, then consternation as four men in dark suits suddenly rushed the table, shouting, flashing badges, and brandishing pistols. Before he understood what was happening, his arms were jerked behind him. Bright lights flashed in his face. Handcuffs bit into his wrists. All around, people were standing at their tables, staring wide-eyed at the commotion surrounding him. A fair-haired man with blue eyes was squatting next to him, holding a badge next to his face.

"Henry Bowman," the man said, "you are under arrest for possession of stolen property, kidnapping, robbery, and violation of the Dyer Act. Any statements you make can be used as evidence."

A waiter balancing a tray stopped a few feet away, glancing from Wallace to Henry to the squatting man. "Do you still want your dessert, sir?"

"Did you get that, dear?" Joan asked over the mounting cacophony in the dining room. Everybody in the place, from the couple at their table on the mezzanine— who had abandoned their romantic pretense and drawn service revolvers—to the wait staff and frantic maître d' to the agents now lifting the hand-cuffed Henry Bowman to his feet were chattering, issuing orders and shouting directives.

"I got a couple of good ones," Mike answered. "I think you'll like them so well that you may even want to give me a bonus for hazardous duty."

"Ha! Your bonus was the free meal and my company, dear." Joan was smiling, watching two men leading Bowman between the tables and out of the dining room. He looked stunned, his eyeglasses askew. The waiters were moving from table-to-table reassuring their guests. Corey Wainwright was shaking hands with Wallace. Then the FBI man turned and headed straight toward her. *Uh oh*, Joan thought, *he doesn't look very happy*. "You'd better run along, dear," Joan said quickly to Mike.

"Miss Roswell, I need you to come with me, please." Corey reached out to take her by the arm, but Joan pulled away.

"Now, now, it's 'Joan.' We've had this conversation before." Joan kept her smile fixed in place.

"You very nearly compromised a federal investigation, Miss Roswell! If I'd seen you before we moved in to make our arrest, I would have had you forcibly removed." Corey snapped, his face flushed, biting off his words. "I ought to throw you in the back of the car with Bowman. First you throw that phony journal at me and now you almost gum up our arrest!"

"Phony?"

"Phony! Did you know? Have you been playing me all along, Miss Roswell? Because if you have—"

"What do you mean, 'phony'?"

Corey took a deep breath, trying to regain what little composure he had left after the heady adrenalin rush of the arrest. "Our experts said none of the handwriting matched Mitchell Novak's. You gave me that diary to throw me off."

"I did no such thing, Corey Wainwright. I gave you that out of a sincere desire to help you with this case."

"To help yourself, you mean! And picture-taking in the middle of an arrest! I ought to charge you with obstruction of justice and every other crime I can think of!"

"It didn't get fouled up," Wallace DeWitt said from over Corey's shoulder. "Everything went just like we planned it. Besides, you agreed that Joan could have the inside story, remember?"

"This is the outside story! We had weapons drawn!" Corey looked from Wallace to Joan. "Don't either of you understand how dangerous this could have been?"

"Well, dear, you're the one who selected a public place—a crowded one at that," Joan said, glancing around the dining room. A few of the patrons were still staring, but most had gone back to their steaks and lamb chops.

"Relax," Wallace said. "Everything worked out just fine."

Corey shook his head. "I want those pictures. I decide when they can be released."

"What pictures?" Joan asked.

"The ones your photographer took," Corey snarled, looking around for the camera man.

But Mike was gone.

Kelly Durham and Kathryn Smith

# WEDNESDAY FEBRUARY 12, 1936

# CHAPTER 67

## FBI MAKES ARREST IN POLIO CASE
## G-MEN NAB SUSPECT AT D.C. HOTEL

WASHINGTON, D.C., February 12 (AP)—by Joan Roswell, Los Angeles *Standard*—

Agents of the Federal Bureau of Investigation arrested a key member of Deacon Owen Knox's staff Tuesday evening at Washington's storied Mayflower Hotel.

Henry Luther Bowman of Chicago, Knox's personal secretary and a man many see as the organizational and financial genius behind Knox's ministry, is being held at the Federal Courthouse in this city pending arraignment on charges of accessory to kidnapping, wire fraud, and possession of stolen property.

Federal officials refused comment, but this reporter has learned that Bowman may also be charged as an accessory in the as-yet-unsolved murder of security guard Mitchell Novak. It was Novak's absence from his post on the night of the President's Birthday Ball at the Shoreham Hotel that led to the kidnapping of motion picture star Ginger Rogers and presidential secretary Marguerite LeHand and the theft of more than $20,000 donated for polio treatment.

Another by-line, another break in the case. Joan smiled over her cup of room service coffee as Wallace slumbered beside her in his bed at the Willard. She was rather enjoying her stay in the capital and she knew that scoops like this one were the currency by which her trip could be extended.

Joan had enjoyed another night of energetic amour with Wallace, fueled by the excitement of their involvement in the arrest at the Mayflower. She had hated to crawl out of his cozy bed, but she knew the sooner she got the photographs from Mike, the better.

Missy LeHand picked up the receiver of her desk phone and smiled when she heard the voice on the other end. But her face turned serious almost immediately.

"Missy, you saw the headlines this morning about the arrest at the Mayflower Hotel?" Corey said, all in a rush. "I'm headed your way to talk to Mike Wanner. He turned up there last night with Joan Roswell, and it's just one coincidence too many."

"He was there?" Missy said. "With Joan? Of all things!"

"I think you've hit on something about his actions the night of the robbery, especially regarding that phantom movie camera. Can you round up Steve Early and be sure Mike doesn't leave the White House grounds? Get some Secret Service backup, too."

"Of course, Corey," Missy said. "I'll get right to it. How long before you get here?"

"Not more than ten minutes," Corey said. "I'm leaving right now."

After she hung up, Missy tried without success to get Steve on the phone. Finally, she jumped to her feet and peeked into the Oval Office. The President hadn't arrived yet. "I'm going to run down to the photographer's office for a minute," she said to Grace as she headed out the door.

"If the Boss comes in shouting for me, tell him I'm on FBI business! Oh, and if you should see a Secret Service member, send him over there pronto!"

"With Bowman in custody, it's only a matter of time before they're on to me. He's weak and he won't be able to stand up to their interrogation," the woman in Mike Wanner's office said, her British voice clipped in its urgency. "I suggest you execute your relocation plan immediately."

"Oh, c'mon. This isn't like it is in Moscow. They don't use those kinds of techniques here," Mike hissed back. He could tell she was really angry. The scar on her forehead always darkened when she was.

The woman shook her head and pursed her lips. "You idiot," she said contemptuously. "Naivety will get you killed, there, here, anywhere."

Mike heard footsteps in the hallway and put his finger to his lips.

Missy was out of breath by the time she reached Mike Wanner's office, and she hadn't seen a single Secret Service agent in the halls. *Oh, well, it's just Mike. I don't think he'd put up much of a fight,* she thought. The office door was closed, and Missy wondered if the photographer was in yet.

She put her ear to the door, and hearing voices inside, rapped on it sharply. "Mike? It's Missy LeHand. Can I have a word?"

She heard scuffling from the other side and the sound of a door opening and closing. After a few moments, Mike swung the door open, looking harassed.

"Hi, Missy," he said. "What's up?"

Missy walked into the tiny office and looked around. "Are you alone?" she asked. "I thought I heard you talking to someone."

"Oh, I was just on the phone," he said.

"I didn't know you had an intercom," she said, eyeing him strangely. "I thought I heard a woman's voice."

The door of the dark room swung open behind her and Missy quickly looked over her shoulder. A short woman in a red coat was standing there, and she held a pistol in her hand.

"Mike? Who is this woman?" Missy demanded.

"You better do what she wants," Mike said.

With a curt nod, Penny motioned Missy into the dark room. With Mike blocking her exit, Missy had no choice.

Inside the dark room, the woman directed Missy to a metal stool, never saying a word. She pulled a soiled handkerchief from her pocket and stuffed it into Missy's mouth. Mike grabbed some rags on the counter by the developing tray, tore them into strips and tied the secretary's hands behind her back and her ankles to the legs of the stool. He left the dark room and the door clicked shut.

With her back to the door and the gun trained directly at Missy's head, the woman said quietly, "Make one sound and the President will be short a very good private secretary. Understand?"

Missy nodded.

Joan presented her AP credentials to the uniformed guard outside the White House and was directed to the West Wing. Finding Mike's office, she bustled in, all smiles. "Good morning!" she trilled. "How did the photographs turn out?"

The photographer seemed anxious, preoccupied. Working his tiny moustache with his lower lip, he reached into a desk drawer and handed her a manila file folder. "I think you'll be pleased," he said.

"Let's see what you got," Joan said. She pulled two pictures from the folder and laid them out on the desk. In the first one, Henry Bowman's head was turned so that his face was only partially visible. But the second photo, the one Joan knew instantly she would use, showed Bowman with the expression of bewilderment akin to a three-year-old whose lollipop has just been snatched from his sticky little hands.

"This will do nicely, Mike," Joan smiled, shuffling the photos back together and returning them to the folder. "Next time I need an ace photographer, I'll give you a call."

"Please do," Mike replied. *It'll be a long-distance call.*

Joan was halfway to the security gate when the thought occurred to her that she probably would want to use Mike's services again, and what better way to assure his availability in the future than to give him a tip? She poked around her purse, finding a crumpled two-dollar bill, and turned back toward his office. As she reached the photographer's office door, she met Steve Early and Corey Wainwright coming from the opposite direction.

"What are you doing here, Joan?" Corey asked, scowling.

Joan smiled at him. "Just dropping in on my friend Mike Wanner, to thank him for the lovely dinner last night," she said archly.

"Stay out of the way, Joan," Corey growled. "This time I really will lock you up."

"And I'll revoke your press credentials," added Steve Early.

The photographer's office door was closed again, and Steve pushed it open without knocking. "Mike, oh sorry, I didn't know you had a visitor," he said, seeing the back of a woman in a red coat. "Ma'am, we need a few private words with Mr. Wanner, so I'll have to ask you to leave."

Mike's eyes opened wide, and the woman stood stock still, her back to Steve, Corey and Joan, who was peeking over the men's shoulders.

"Ma'am, are you all right?" Corey asked. The woman turned slowly toward him.

Joan gasped. "Penny?"

Penny Jeter bolted from the doorway, pushing between the men and slamming into Joan like a running back hitting the line. Joan stumbled and fell backwards, landing hard on the floor. "Ow!" Joan looked up at Corey and shouted, "The phony journal! She gave it to me!"

By the time Joan's words registered with Corey, the woman had reached the exit door at the end of the corridor. She pushed through the door, but the belt of her red coat snagged on its handle, spinning her around. Before she could free herself, Corey had closed the gap, grabbing her by the back of the collar.

"You're under arrest for obstruction of justice and accessory to murder. If you say anything, it can be used as evidence." Corey reached in his coat pocket for a pair of handcuffs. As he did, the woman spun from his grasp, slipping her arms from the coat. Steve reached the pair in time to kick the woman's foot, causing her to trip and fall on the sidewalk.

By then, one of the White House uniformed policemen had arrived from the gatehouse. He knelt in the middle of the woman's back until Corey could get the cuffs snapped on her wrists. "Thanks," Corey said to the policeman. He turned to Steve. "We really need to question Wanner now. And where's Missy? I called her before I left the Justice Department. I thought she was meeting us in his office."

Together, they turned back toward the West Wing, Joan limping determinedly behind them. When they reached Wanner's office, there was no one in sight, but a ruckus was coming from the dark room. It took another ten minutes to summon the chief usher with a key to let Missy out.

Corey pulled the gag out of her mouth and used his pocket knife to cut the strips of cloth binding her wrists and ankles. "Are you okay?" he asked.

"I think so," Missy said, rubbing her wrists together. "But Children's Hour can't come any too soon for me!" She looked around. "Where's Mike?"

It was a question no one could answer. Mike was gone.

Within fifteen minutes, an unmarked van had arrived. The woman, who had been searched, still refused to speak. She was placed in the back of the van with an escort and driven to the federal courthouse.

In Steve Early's office, Missy settled for a fortifying cup of black coffee instead of a dry martini. "I need you to provide a written statement, Missy," Corey said. "Write down everything you saw and heard, especially when that woman held you hostage in the dark room. And you," he said turning to Joan, "I need a written statement from you going all the way back to how you got hold of that bogus journal. And don't play that 'confidential sources' card with me either. You cross the line one more time and I'm going to charge you!"

"With what, dear?" Joan smiled. "Upholding the First Amendment? I'll plead guilty."

"Come along, Miss Roswell," Steve said. "I'll find you a desk where you can work."

Joan followed Steve down the hall. She held on to the folder Mike had given her, hoping that neither Corey nor Missy would suspect what was inside.

# CHAPTER 68

Half an hour later, Corey was walking Joan through her statement.

"I staked out Mitch Novak's post office box," Joan explained.

"How did you know it was his?"

"The receptionist at the Pinkerton's office gave it to me. I never met her, just spoke to her over the phone." Joan recalled.

"Go on," Corey said.

"Well, that woman, she called herself Penny Jeter, emptied the box. I followed her onto the bus and started talking to her. She was wary at first, but she called me later that day and agreed to meet me. She told me about the existence of 'Smith,' and that he'd offered money to Novak to disappear from his assignment."

"Did she give you the journal?" Corey asked.

"Not exactly, dear. She gave me a key."

"A key to what?"

"Novak's apartment. So, after my meeting with Penny—or whatever her real name is—I went to the apartment and stood in the shadows for a while. I didn't see anybody watching the place—"

"That's because we knew Novak was dead by then."

"So, I took the key she gave me and went inside. I found the journal and took it back to my hotel. I went through the whole thing and found entries that confirmed what Penny had told me. Two sources," Joan said, shaking her head.

"Which were really only one?"

"Unfortunately, yes. And which turns out now to have been a total fabrication. I'm sorry I led you astray."

"Well, look on the bright side, Joan," Corey said, calmer now than he had been in the dining room the previous night or at the White House earlier that morning. "You identified a key person in this mess. I've contacted the lead agent in the counterespionage department at the FBI. He and Inspector Trent from the D.C. Police are going to join me this afternoon for an interview with Miss Jeter."

"Why the D.C. Police?"

"Murder's a local charge. Mitch Novak's body was found in the District. We think she had something to do with the murder—in fact, she might even be the murderer."

"Goodness!" Joan said, a thrill going up her spine. *She seemed so harmless!* "So, why counterespionage?"

"According to Missy, Ambassador Bullitt thinks there may be more to this case than meets the eye."

"Can I quote you on that, dear?"

# CHAPTER 69

Missy sat down at her desk with a feeling of satisfaction, though only partial satisfaction, as she quickly typed out a statement for Corey Wainwright. Penny Jeter and Henry Bowman were under lock and key now, and the mystery of the stolen money was on its way to being solved. Unfortunately, Mike Wanner had given them the slip, and with him went any hope of figuring out who had spirited the picture of the Hail, Caesar party out of the White House.

Finished with that task, she began looking through a stack of letters that had arrived in that day's mail, special mail that had been winnowed from the routine stuff. She had a staff of fifty clerks whose task was answering the 50,000 letters the President received each week from American citizens. Many were routine and repetitive. Would the President send an autograph, for example, was a common request, which was answered with a polite no, the President was far too busy to send autographs, but sends his best wishes and thanks for the friendly thought in requesting one. Occasionally, a letter would announce the birth of a baby named after the President—there were little Franklin Delanos all over the country now—and these proud parents received a small handkerchief embroidered with the words "Happy Days!"

A half-hour into her labors, Missy found a letter addressed to her; the envelope bore the return address of the Washington *Herald*. She quickly sliced it open, pulling out a hand-written note and two clippings from Cissy Patterson's newspaper. One clipping bore the Hail, Caesar picture, the other a picture of Al Smith that had appeared on the front page of the Monday paper. The unsigned note read:

*Dear Miss LeHand,*

*I admire you very much. In fact, you inspired me to enter the secretarial field, and I hope to one day become a private secretary just like you. I was so distressed by the editorial that tried to implicate you in the heist of the Birthday Ball money, I wanted to help you solve a mystery that has probably been troubling you.*

*If you are still wondering how the* Herald *got the picture of Mr. Roosevelt's private birthday party, I suggest you look for the man in the photo with Al Smith. His name is Wallace DeWitt. He came to see Mrs. Patterson at the* Herald *last Monday, with a large envelope in his hand. When he left the building, the envelope was gone, and the picture ran on Page 3 the next day.*

*Please do not let anyone know I shared this with you. I do not like my job very much, but I need it until something better comes along. We working girls have to stick together, don't we?*

Wallace DeWitt!

Missy picked up her phone and quickly dialed Corey's number at the FBI.

# THURSDAY, FEBRUARY 13, 1936

# CHAPTER 70

"We first learned about Miriam Adler from Sanchez, the special-agent-in-charge at the embassy in Mexico City," Corey said. It was Thursday afternoon, and he was updating Director Hoover on the case. "The *Federales* had compiled a pretty thick dossier on her for what they called 'revolutionary activities.'"

"If anybody would know about 'revolutionary activities,' it would be the Mexicans," Hoover said. "Go ahead, Wainwright."

Corey resumed his briefing. Working with agents from the FBI's counterespionage department and its Latin American desk, as well as Inspector Trent from the D.C. Police, Corey had pieced together a bewildering Russian scheme to tip the coming presidential election toward an isolationist candidate, one which it perceived would lack Franklin Roosevelt's internationalist outlook.

"Miss Adler, who used the alias of 'Jeter' in her contacts with Joan Roswell, is a British national. She's from a Jewish Bolshevik family, a 'cradle Red,' so to speak. She spent 1928 and part of '29 in Leningrad. From there, she went to Mexico City, which is where Sanchez first noticed her. She was a real mover and shaker within the Bolshevik movement there—had a reputation for powerful oratory, and a real gift with languages. She speaks fluent Spanish, Russian and American-accented English— that we know of. We think Mexico is where she met Henry Bowman. According to the State Department, he was in Mexico in the summer of '29. Adler got into a couple of tough scrapes down there with the *Federales* and they finally ran her and the rest of the Bolsheviks out. From there, she came to the States—"

"Naturally," Hoover injected.

"—and started working as a labor organizer in Chicago. We think she and Bowman may have hooked up again in Chicago. I think when we lay out what we know for Bowman, he'll come clean. He's been wavering the last couple of times we talked."

"Put the pieces together for me."

"Yes sir. Adler, or Jeter, was working a couple of angles and seems to have been the lynch pin of the whole operation. First, she wanted to funnel money into a competing campaign, the one with the best chance of unseating the President."

"From the Republican side or the Democrat side?"

"Ideologically, I doubt she cared, but we think she already had an in with the Knox campaign. Working through Henry Bowman, Knox's secretary, she set up the theft of the money from the Birthday Ball. We're still cooperating with Inspector Trent here in D.C. on the murder of Mitchell Novak, the Pinkerton security guard. When I called Trent down to the lock-up to see the girl, his eyes lit up like a pinball machine. He recognized her immediately as the secretary from the Pinkerton office, where he had gone as part of the murder investigation. According to Trent's murder investigation, Adler—or Jeter—had gotten pretty cozy with Novak. Apparently, she also kept the duty roster for Mr. Harvey, the Pinkerton boss. Presto, she penciled Novak in for the assignment at the Shoreham. We can already make a pretty strong case that at the very least Adler is an accessory after the fact, probably before the fact as well. She may even have been the killer. Then she set up Joan Roswell to feed us that bogus journal."

Corey paused. He was enjoying his story, and it was obvious Hoover was too. "There's another angle as well. There's a real shadow of suspicion around a White House photographer named Mike Wanner. He was working the ball the night the money was stolen. Wanner left after the money was counted, but when Miss LeHand was carrying the money out to her car, Wanner was on his way back into the hotel. He said he'd forgotten his movie camera."

"They took movies of the ball?"

"Actually, they didn't. That's what brought Wanner to our attention. When Miss LeHand asked him about the footage, he said he hadn't taken his movie camera to the Shoreham. That's a red flag by itself, but there's more. Before the ball, Wanner took a picture of the President and a group of his friends and cronies all decked out in Roman garb."

"I saw it," Hoover interrupted. "It was in every major daily in the country."

"Yes sir. Well, Wanner claimed that all the prints were accounted for, but he would have been the only source for that picture unless somebody else had access to his negative, which doesn't seem likely."

"So, how did Cissy Patterson get the picture?"

"Our best guess is that Wallace DeWitt gave it to her. Miss LeHand got an anonymous tip that DeWitt had visited Patterson the day before the picture ran. He also visited the photographer's office at the White House a couple of days before that. It's very circumstantial, I know, but my best guess is that DeWitt engineered that whole picture thing."

"Why?"

"Well, he'd gotten cozy with Al Smith. Smith has emerged as a rabid critic of the President's."

"He's working for the Russians too?"

"I don't believe so, no. I personally questioned Mr. DeWitt about the theft on a couple of occasions. I think he's not a fan of the President, I think he was supporting the Knox campaign, but I don't think he had anything to do with the Russians."

"Why not? He seems like a logical candidate. He's in the right place at the right time; that's opportunity. He's anti-Roosevelt; that's motive."

"Yes sir, but he's also the guy that more or less cracked the case for us. He fingered Henry Bowman. If not for DeWitt, we would have had a hard time finding out where the money went. He cooperated with us. In fact, he initiated the cooperation. He set up Bowman beautifully. We were able to photograph the exchange of the stolen checks and DeWitt's sworn statement is enough on its own to put Bowman away. On top of that, he's a dyed-in-the-wool capitalist. I can't imagine him doing anything to help the Russians."

"So, the Caesar photograph and funneling the Birthday Ball money to the Knox campaigns are the only angles the Reds were working?"

"Just the only two we know about."

"How about Knox?"

"We sent Timmons from counterespionage out to Chicago to brief the field office there and go with them to talk to Knox. According to his preliminary report, he thinks Knox is in the dark."

"He's in the dark about a lot of things," Hoover agreed. "I don't see a true-believing Protestant like Knox climbing in bed with the God-less Communists. An allegation like that would snuff out his campaign before it got out of the batter's box." Hoover paused and stared out his office window. "How do we get the word out without looking like we're playing politics?"

"Sir?"

"I want this story out there. I want people to know what Knox was up to even if Knox didn't know himself. And I want the public to know that the FBI is protecting America. How do we get the story out?"

Corey smiled. "You remember Miss Roswell?"

# FRIDAY, FEBRUARY 14, 1936

# CHAPTER 71

**KNOX CAMPAIGN LINKED TO REDS! ATHEIST PARTY SUPPORTS PREACHER CANDIDATE; STOLEN MONEY USED TO LAUNCH CAMPAIGN; TOP AIDE IN FEDERAL CUSTODY**

WASHINGTON, D.C., February 14 (AP)— Joan Roswell, Los Angeles *Standard*—

The presidential nomination campaign of Deacon Owen Knox stumbled out of the starting gate as accusations surfaced linking the Chicago radio preacher with Communist provocateurs.

Knox's personal secretary, Henry Bowman, is in federal custody following an arrest on charges of robbery, kidnapping and possession of stolen property. The charges stem from the January 31 theft of more than $20,000 from the President's Birthday Ball event held at Washington's Shoreham Hotel. The money, in the possession of motion picture star Ginger Rogers and the President's private secretary, Marguerite LeHand, was donated for the purpose of treating polio patients.

This reporter has learned that federal authorities have linked Bowman with

Miriam Adler, a British national working as a Soviet agent in the United States. Authorities are piecing together a bizarre puzzle of Russian efforts to influence the outcome of this fall's U.S. presidential election.

J. Edgar Hoover smiled when he read the headlines in the Friday morning editions. Even the *Herald* had run the story on page one. *That ought to keep the Reds on their heels for a couple of months. It won't do the Bureau and me any harm at the White House, either.*

Corey Wainwright arrived in FBI Director Hoover's office at 2 p.m. Friday, as he'd been ordered.

"Wainwright," Hoover began after the agent took his seat. "I've been thinking." The Director was pacing the floor in front of his elevated desk, his hands clasped behind his back, his head down, his words sounding in cadence with his steps.

"Yes sir?"

"You've done a good job on a couple of very high-profile cases, both of which, due to connections with the White House, have been hot potatoes. I like having a reliable man around who stays out of the limelight and who can work with that gaggle surrounding the President without getting sucked down into the political muck that seems to coat everything that comes out of the building."

Corey wasn't ready for what came next.

"I'm reassigning you." Hoover stopped talking and walking at the same time, turning to stare at his agent. "You're going to work out of headquarters and report to me."

"Sir?"

"You're going to be my special agent on political cases, cases that are too hot to handle through routine channels, cases that need a diplomat's touch and an agent's investigative skill. What do you say, Wainwright?" Hoover's dark eyes seemed to drill holes right into Corey's mind.

"I say, 'yes sir!'"

Hoover laughed and clapped his hands together. "Excellent! This will yield great benefits for the Bureau!"

Corey could think of at least one personal benefit as well.

The Tabard Inn, located at 1739 N Street near Dupont Circle, was the domain of a South Carolina woman named Marie Willoughby Rogers. She had opened the hotel, whose name was derived from Chaucer's *Canterbury Tales,* in 1922. The Tabard was situated in three nineteenth-century town houses that had been cobbled together as her finances allowed. It was famous for its fine dining.

On Friday night, Missy and Corey Wainwright had a lot to celebrate as they entered The Tabard. The red menace had been halted at the White House gates, the Birthday Ball money had been recovered, and Missy had successfully recruited a very eager young woman from the office of Cissy Patterson who would be joining her staff the following Monday. She had received a dozen roses and a thoughtful card from the actress Ginger Rogers, expressing her relief that the money had been found, and inviting Missy to visit her in Hollywood.

Corey could hardly wait to tell Missy about his new assignment with the FBI.

Plus, it was Valentine's Day.

"Uh oh," Missy said as they entered

"I don't know if we'll be able to get a table tonight," Corey said. "There's a line."

Nevertheless, the couple decided to try their luck. Ahead of them in line, they spotted Joan Roswell and Wallace DeWitt.

"Ah'm so sorry," Mrs. Rogers was saying to them in her broad Southern accent. "We're just full as a tick tonight. Ah couldn't squeeze you in with a shoe horn and a big ol' can of Crisco."

Wallace pulled a twenty-dollar bill from his wallet and spoke in the Georgia accent he had worked so hard to lose. "Would this hey-ulp?" he asked.

"Ah'm afraid not," Mrs. Rogers said, shaking her head. Then she looked over Wallace's shoulder. "Miss LeHand!" she cried. "Oh, what a pleasure to see you. Two for dinnuh? Come right this way!"

As Missy and Corey swept past the reporter and her high-rolling beau, the White House secretary smiled. Wallace and Joan had a lot to learn about Washington, a town where the coin of the realm was not coin per se, but power and influence. Missy had it in spades.

"Well dear," Joan said, shrugging. "Shall we try room service at the Willard?"

Wallace grinned back at her. "Sounds good to me."

# EPILOGUE

## Moscow

In late February, Ambassador Bullitt waited in an ornate ante room inside the Kremlin. He had returned to the Union of Soviet Socialist Republics following a two-month home leave in the United States and was paying a courtesy call on the Soviet People's Commissar for Foreign Affairs, Maxim Litvinov. His instructions from President Roosevelt were to make no mention of the election issue, to pretend that it had never happened.

"There are greater issues in play between us and the Russians," Roosevelt had said.

Bullitt looked up at the sound of approaching footsteps. A short, stocky man in a loosely cut, gray suit nodded his head and extended his hand.

"Mr. Ambassador, Comrade Litvinov awaits you in the Tea Room. Would you be pleased to follow me?"

Without waiting for a reply, the man turned and began walking back in the direction from which he had appeared. Bullitt followed, noting the reflection of the golden light of the chandeliers in the man's steel gray hair.

Along a wide corridor decorated with scenes of Soviet agricultural life on one side and heroic paintings of Lenin, Stalin, and the revolution on the other, Bullitt kept pace just behind his escort. After walking what had seemed like a hundred yards, the escort turned right, leading Bullitt through on open pair of heavy wooden doors trimmed in gold around bright red panels.

"Mr. Ambassador!" Litvinov said with a broad smile. "Welcome back to Moscow!" He shook hands with Bullitt and nodded to the escort who proceeded to the side of the room where an elegant silver samovar had been set up. "How was your visit to America?"

"It was wonderful, Comrade Commissar, although of course I missed my many Russian friends while I was away. I trust you and Comrade Stalin have been well since last I saw you."

"Yes, yes, quite so." The escort approached, a delicate porcelain tea cup and saucer in each hand. He offered one to Bullitt, the other to Litvinov. "Thank you, Vassily."

"Thank you, Comrade, for agreeing to see me. I am sure your calendar is filled with many important appointments and tasks. I bring you greetings from President Roosevelt, the Congress, and the people of the United States of America, who look forward to strengthening the bonds of friendship growing between our two great nations."

"On behalf of Comrade Stalin, Premier Molotov, and the peoples of the Union of Soviet Socialist Republics, I welcome you back to our great country." Litvinov turned away for a moment and snapped his fingers.

"Comrade?" the escort replied.

"Tell Mikhail we are ready."

"Yes, Comrade." The escort exited into a side room.

"Tell me, Mr. Ambassador," Litvinov resumed, "what are your plans now that you are back?"

"I need to reconnect with my staff, for one thing," Bullitt said with a chuckle. "We have an American saying: 'when the cat's away, the mice will play.'"

Litvinov laughed. "We have a similar saying in Russia. Ah, here." He reached out and took Bullitt's cup and saucer, handing them to his aide. "I thought we might take advantage of our meeting to have a picture made. Here, stand beside me." Litvinov maneuvered Bullitt into the correct pose with the skill of a Hollywood press agent. "Now let us shake hands and smile for the camera."

Bullitt followed his host's lead, turning, smiling and facing the photographer as the camera came up to eye level. Something registered in his mind. A bright flash and Bullitt was momentarily blinded.

Bullitt's eyes began to clear. He smiled at Litvinov and then looked back at the photographer, a skinny man with a wispy moustache. It couldn't be!

*Mikhail?*

# HISTORICAL BACKGROUND FOR THIS BOOK

Many people have no idea that Franklin Delano Roosevelt founded the National Foundation for Infantile Paralysis, better known as the March of Dimes. He used the prestige of his office and his experience as a polio survivor to raise awareness of the disease—and millions of dollars to help its victims and find a cure. When he was approached with a proposal for a nation-wide night of "birthday balls" to be held on his birthday in 1934, his reply was, "If my birthday will be of any help, take it." That January 30, more than six thousand balls were held and more than a million dollars were raised—$17 million in current dollars. The balls continued throughout his presidency, and often Hollywood stars would come to Washington as celebrity guests. Ginger Rogers was one of these, attending in 1936.

Our readers may be surprised to know that polio has not been conquered across the world. An international campaign spearheaded by the World Health Organization and Rotary International began in 1985, and the number of cases fell from 350,000 that year to just 17 cases in 2017. To learn more about Rotary's PolioPlus campaign, visit www.rotary.org.

This book contains a large cast of historical characters, beyond Missy, Grace, the Roosevelts, J. Edgar Hoover, and Miss Rogers: Governor Al Smith; publisher Cissy Patterson and her press lord kin; presidential advisor Harry Hopkins; and White House staffers Louis Howe, Steve Early, and Dr. Ross McIntire. The views expressed by Ambassador William C. Bullitt, who was indeed

Missy's long-distance boyfriend, are based on Bullitt's early recognition of the threat of Stalin and world-wide communism.

As in our book, the President's private "Hail, Caesar" birthday party was held at the White House. However, the notorious picture of Franklin Caesar and his admirers didn't leak out until decades after his death. The fun thing about fiction is that we are able to fudge dates and

facts, so we moved the year of this infamous party to 1936; it was actually held in 1934. In the picture above, Gracy Tully is standing at the far left, with Missy LeHand sitting at her feet. Eleanor Roosevelt is standing to the President's left, with his valet Irwin McDuffie behind him and his daughter Anna to his right. Louis Howe was, in fact, the planner of this event. He is the second person from the right side. Steve Early is looking into the camera at the far right.*

Some of the language in the book, including Al Smith's speech at the Liberty League dinner and FDR's radio address on the night of the Birthday Ball, is quoted verbatim. So are Louie Howe's words about using cameras to record the progress of polio patients at Warm Springs.

Our two main fictional characters are Corey Wainwright and Joan Roswell, both of whom were instrumental in the solving of the kidnapping in SHIRLEY TEMPLE IS MISSING. Likewise, Deacon Knox is a fictional character, though he was inspired by a historical one, the Catholic priest Father Charles Coughlin, who has been called "the father of hate radio." Coughlin, based out of a Detroit suburb, was a thorn in FDR's side for the first two terms of his presidency, until his popularity washed up on the shores of World War II and condemnation by his own Catholic church.

If your curiosity about Missy and her times is piqued by our mystery, we recommend the following books:

- *The Gatekeeper: Missy LeHand, FDR and the Untold Story of the Partnership that Defined a Presidency* by Kathryn Smith. New York: Touchstone, 2016.

- *Ginger: My Story* by Ginger Rogers. New York: HarperCollins Publishers, 1991.

- *March of Dimes* by David W. Rose. Charleston, S.C.: Arcadia, 2003.

- *Roads Not Taken: An Intellectual Biography of William C. Bullitt* by Alexander Etkind. Pittsburgh: University of Pittsburgh Press, 2017.

*Hail Caesar* photo: Collection of the FDR Presidential Library and Museum.

# ABOUT THE AUTHORS

Kelly Durham and Kathryn Smith attended D.W. Daniel High School near Clemson, South Carolina together, but didn't become friends until more than forty years later when Kathryn began editing some of Kelly's novels. This is their second collaboration.

Kelly lives in Clemson with his wife, Yvonne. They are the parents of Mary Kate, Addison, and Callie, and also provide for their dog, George Marshall. A graduate of Clemson University, Kelly served four years in the U.S. Army with assignments in Arizona and Germany before returning to Clemson and entering private business. Kelly is also the author of THE WAR WIDOW, BERLIN CALLING, WADE'S WAR, THE RELUCTANT COPILOT, THE MOVIE STAR AND ME, HOLLYWOOD STARLET, TEMPORARY ALLIANCE and UNFORESEEN COMPLICATIONS. Visit his website, www.kellydurham.com, or contact him at kelly@kellydurham.com.

Kathryn lives in Anderson, South Carolina with her husband, Leo. They are the parents of two grown children and the grandparents of four small children. A graduate of the University of Georgia, Kathryn worked as a daily newspaper reporter and editor before entering nonprofit management work in Anderson. She is the author of the only biography of Marguerite LeHand, THE GATEKEEPER: MISSY LEHAND, FDR, AND THE UNTOLD STORY OF THE PARTNERSHIP THAT DEFINED A PRESIDENCY (Touchstone, 2016) as well as A NECESSARY WAR, a collection of interviews with World War II veterans. Kathryn speaks widely on Missy LeHand, sometimes impersonating her in period costume. Visit her website, www.kathrynsmithwords.com, and the Missy LeHand page on Facebook.

# ABOUT THE COVER ARTIST

Jed Smith, a native of South Carolina and a high school mate of the authors, moved to Italy after a long and successful career as a senior creative leader in marketing. Today, Jed focuses his talents on personal expression and embraces writing, painting, and photography with equal passion. His blog, ItalyWise.com, which has developed a loyal following, chronicles his transition to becoming an American expat in Italy. Jed shares insights and advice about managing a multitude of logistics, as well as writing about navigating a host of mental and emotional challenges that come with making such a monumental life change.

An accomplished painter, Jed is a Signature Member of the prestigious National Watercolor Society.

## Don't Miss the Next
## Missy LeHand Mystery!

# *Eleanor Roosevelt Goes to Prison*

On a spring vacation in 1936 at the Little White House in Warm Springs, Georgia, the Roosevelts learn of a grave miscarriage of justice involving a black woman convicted of murdering her employer and condemned to death. But there are unanswered questions about the night of the murder. First Lady Eleanor Roosevelt goes to the state prison farm to make some inquiries, and soon Missy LeHand and Corey Wainwright are drawn into the case.

Meanwhile, Hollywood reporter Joan Roswell journeys to Atlanta to interview a first-time novelist named Margaret Mitchell, whose soon-to-be-published book *Gone with the Wind* is the talk of Tinsel Town. On the train, she spots up-and-coming actress Ida Lupino, who is headed to Warm Springs for polio therapy. Naturally, Joan smells a scoop, and heads to Warm Springs after her interview with Mitchell is completed.

You won't want to miss this third installment in the Missy LeHand Mystery series, to be published in 2019.

Kelly Durham and Kathryn Smith

28067252R00172

Made in the USA
Columbia, SC
05 October 2018